ON THE RECORD

ON THE RECORD

BY JOE LEE

DOGWOOD
PRESS

Cover art by Bill Wilson

Library of Congress Catalog-in-Publication Data

Lee, Joseph Thomas, 1965-
    On the record / Joseph Thomas Lee.
        p. cm.
    ISBN 1-9721611-0-4
    1. Mississippi—Fiction.   I. Title.

PS3612.E343 O6 2002
813'.6—dc21   2002073552

**DOGWOOD
PRESS**

DOGWOOD PRESS
1022 Wakefield Place • Brandon, MS 39047
601-919-3656
DogwoodPress@bellsouth.net

For Leslie

ACKNOWLEDGMENTS

My sincere thanks to Leslie Staehle Lee, Joseph and Marilyn Lee, Charlie and Vicky Staehle, John and Jan Lewis, Duke Denton, Bruce Coleman, Andy Smith and Cindy McCraw-Dircks— this novel wouldn't have been possible without your support and friendship. I'm also grateful to fellow writers Martin Hegwood and Larry Brown and Lemuria owner John Evans for their encouragement. Many thanks to my editor Kay Garrett, and a huge tip of the cap to my agent and marketing director Ralph Atkinson. All of you have helped make a dream come true.

PROLOGUE

Dec. 1999

Maureen Lewis glanced at her watch again before returning her gaze to the 2000 Accord across the showroom. It was dark green with a V-6 engine and had many of the bells and whistles she wanted, but replacing her elderly Civic wasn't something she would do at Capital City Motors.

"Ma'am, are you sure I can't get you some coffee?"

Maureen turned to the blond receptionist, forcing a smile to hide her irritation. The young woman was probably ten years her junior and a polite sort, but she'd made no move to check on dealership president Sonny Hollins in the thirty minutes Maureen had been here. It probably unnerved the receptionist that Maureen was still on her feet, but she didn't want to sink into one of the white club chairs and give the impression she could wait all afternoon.

"What I'd really like is for you to check on Mr. Hollins. I know he's busy, but this is important. It won't take but a minute."

"Yes, ma'am," she said, reaching for the phone. She covered her mouth in embarrassment. "I apologize. Maureen . . ."

"Lewis. Maureen Lewis, with the Attorney General's office."

The receptionist conferred with Hollins' secretary, then looked up. "He will be right up."

Maureen nodded. She resigned herself to waiting longer, since this was exactly what the receptionist said the first time. She could manage another half hour if necessary, although the last thing she wanted was to return to the office without having seen him. It wouldn't be the first time, and there was precious little she could do when he blew her off.

"Ms. Lewis. What can I do for you?"

Maureen looked up, surprised. She stood at her full height of five-two and adjusted the jacket of her navy suit. Hollins was approaching sixty, a handsome man who looked sharp in his blazer and khaki slacks. He was five-ten with a full head of salt and pepper hair, a strong jaw and a long, thin nose. His smile didn't hold much warmth, however, and his glare—on display now—held even less.

"Hello, Mr. Hollins. Is there somewhere we can talk?"

He glanced at her briefcase. "You said this wouldn't take a minute. Right here will be fine."

Maureen frowned. The receptionist was fifteen feet away, and the good old boy who'd asked three times if she wanted to test drive one of the 2000 models was within earshot. "Are you sure you'd rather not do this in a conference room, or your office?"

A chilly grin. "I have people in my office, Ms. Lewis, and they're waiting on me. Now what is it that's so important?"

"We've received quite a few complaints about last week's ad in *The Jackson Times*," she said self-consciously. What an awful forum in which to conduct this kind of business, and Hollins knew it. "A $5000 rebate was offered on several Accords and Preludes, and customers found out when they got here that the rebate had already been applied to the sticker price. In other words, there was no rebate."

Hollins glanced at the salesman in mock bewilderment, then looked down at Maureen. "Make a deal with you, then. We don't run the ad any more, and the whole thing is forgotten."

"No, sir. The sale is over, so we can't just pretend it didn't happen. Our office has reviewed this matter carefully and determined that a civil penalty of five hundred dollars is in order. I'd very much like to sit down somewhere and show you what . . ."

The salesman stepped forward before Hollins reacted. "Ms. Lewis, are you sure you don't want to take this Accord over here out for a spin? Got your name written all over it. Pretty lady like you in a hot car like this . . ."

Maureen's jaw tightened, but she ignored the man. Hollins' grin broadened, and he motioned the man back across the floor. He turned back to Maureen.

"You stay put for one second. I'll be right back."

He returned two minutes later brandishing a check. "Five hundred dollars, payable to the Attorney General's office of the state of Mississippi. And if you promise never to set foot on my lot again, I'll go back and get you another one."

A stifled giggle from the reception area. Maureen, angry enough to kick this man where it hurt, forced a smile as she met his eye. "Thank you, sir, and please watch the content of your advertising very carefully."

"Oh, you have my word, Ms. Lewis," Hollins said, his voice dripping with sarcasm. More giggles. "By the way, tell Frank Cash to give me a yell, will you?"

* * *

A strong cold front was coming through, and the temperature had plunged fifteen degrees in the forty-five minutes she was inside the dealership. She swore to herself as she shivered in the gusty wind. She called Cash's office from her car and was on hold for a short time before the Attorney General picked up.

"Hi, Maureen. What's up?"

"Just served Hollins with the papers. Paid in full."

"Did he?" Cash said, surprised. "Very good."

She exhaled. "Frank, that was the most humiliating thing I think I've ever been through." She described the scene, riding in the general direction of the office on State Street but in no hurry to return to work. "I know he's your friend, but I would appreciate it if you would say something to him."

A long silence. "I will, Maureen. That's totally uncalled for, and I'm sorry."

"I could handle it a little better if we could fine these people more than just chump change. It's not just him, Frank. Everybody but the poorest side of the road vendors can pretty much pull out a checkbook and tell us to buzz off, and I'm sick of it."

The Attorney General sighed. "You're right, but however antiquated our Consumer laws are in this day and age, that's what is on the books. All we can do is enforce them."

* * *

Late that afternoon Maureen's private line rang. It was her friend Janine May, the veteran columnist at *The Jackson Times*.

"Just confirming Happy Hour. Usual time and place?"

"Not today, Janine," she said, describing the scene with Hollins. "Learned a long time ago not to drink after a bad day. Let me have a rain check."

"Certainly. Just don't let clowns like him get under your skin. Hell, Maureen, write a new Consumer bill yourself. All our esteemed Legislature can do is say no."

Fifteen months later

Maureen hurried up the marble steps of the Mississippi State Capitol, wrinkling her nose at the damp, musty smell which always permeated the building this time of year. It was an overcast, late-February day, with a cold mist that generated enough moisture to require an umbrella.

The Capitol had been remodeled in recent years. The stained glass in the Rotunda and the silver frames encompassing the pictures of previous lawmakers kept the stately old place steeped in tradition. The historic reminders of the state's past were preferable to the impersonal surroundings of an office complex, but the millions of tiny steps were a drag—especially when one had a cold. Maureen paused on the second floor landing to catch her breath, then resumed her trek to the balcony. Janine was waving and arriving from the other direction. Hardly anyone else was in attendance.

"Morning, hon!" Janine was a tall, chipper brunette in her mid-forties, grayer and heavier than the ten year old stock photo which ran alongside her column. She towered over Maureen, who was also more slender. "Thermos full of decaf. Can I pour you a cup?"

"Please. I hope we're up soon. I'll catch pneumonia if we sit here all day."

"We should be. I heard the big education bills are after lunch."

Maureen gazed over the House floor. Her pulse quickened as she took in the large electronic scoreboard which recorded the votes. The wording of her Consumer Protection Act had been diluted several times by special interest groups after she submitted it to a pair of interested Representatives from Hinds County. On many occasions she had felt enough political heat to wash her hands of the whole thing—Attorney General Frank Cash in particular struck her as surprisingly lukewarm about its chances. Yet here it was, having passed all the subcommittees and now on the floor for a full vote by the House. If it survived, the Senate was next.

"You still feel good about this?"

Janine smiled. "In a Democrat-controlled House? You'll take sixty percent, I bet. The Senate is where it's gonna be tough. Craig still working on the car lobby?"

A headache kicked in at the mention of Craig Grantham. Grantham was Cash's Chief of Staff, an energetic sort with the gumption it took to promise anything to anyone at any time. He also maintained an impressive facade when forced to renege on those promises later. Some of the biggest campaign contributors of all were Jackson car dealers, and word was that the Consumer Protection Act wouldn't stand a chance in the Senate without Grantham's efforts.

The car dealers were often guilty of deceptive advertising, however, and the maximum civil penalty of $500 allowed by the original bill did nothing to stop them. Maureen was asking for penalties of up to $50,000 in the most extreme cases, but she feared Grantham was quietly telling the car dealers to ignore the bitchy redhead from Consumer Protection if the bill became law.

The redhead gazed at Janine. "I'm gonna spill my guts one of these afternoons at Happy Hour. Tell you what Craig Grantham really does around that office. Might make you quit journalism altogether."

Janine's eyes lit up. "On the record?"

Maureen's first smile of the day. "Maybe."

*   *   *

Minutes later the elderly Speaker of the House banged his gavel and addressed the floor. The first bill was a slam-dunk, a clean air project sponsored by a Representative from North Mississippi. Then the Speaker drawled that it was his intention to call the vote on the Consumer Protection Act. Maureen did well not to spill her coffee.

The Representatives cast their votes, plugging their cards into the electronically-linked slots, and the score was tallied quickly. Her heart now thudding, Maureen sat on the edge of the wooden seat and gripped the armrests. When the dust had settled, 75 of the 122 House members had voted in favor of the Consumer Protection Act.

"Piece of cake." Janine gave Maureen a high-five as the final numbers on the big screen displayed her victory. "Now I need a quote. On the record."

Maureen grinned, exhaling. "I'm delighted that our Representatives feel that the Consumer Protection Act is as important a piece of legislation as we do at the Attorney General's Office. I hope the members of the Senate will see fit to pass it as well. I just can't emphasize how much more leverage our office will have in defending our state's consumers against fraudulent advertising and business practices if this bill becomes law."

"I love working with people who talk in sound bites," Janine said, closing her notepad with a snap. "I'll see if I can snag Frank and Craig."

"Craig will take all the credit if it passes the Senate, but he won't say much today. Doubt Frank will, either. This was a formality, far as they were concerned. If you will, mention that the original bill was passed in 1972. I'm not sure how many folks know that, and Frank sure isn't making an issue of it. The differences in penalties are just staggering."

Janine nodded, scribbling. "The Senate vote is tomorrow, right?"

"Sure is. Probably won't sleep a wink."

* * *

The rain was gone the next morning, and Maureen armed herself with pepper spray and walked the streets of Belhaven in the chilly sunrise. The hilly, old neighborhood was lined with beautiful pines and magnolias and boasted a number of historic homes, although crime now infested the area close to downtown. Her apartment complex was constructed in the heart of the historic district and had twenty-four hour security, something neighbors said was unheard of even ten years ago.

A hot shower followed the walk. She lingered, hoping the steam would unclog her sinuses. The phone rang as she toweled off. She answered without checking the Caller I.D. unit, her gut telling her this was work-related.

"Get up here!" Janine said. "They're about to start! I've got plenty of coffee."

Ten minutes later she scurried up the Capitol steps. The balcony was completely empty this morning, and Maureen heard a loud "No!" from the floor as she hustled to join Janine. The Senate voted by roll-call, and she glanced at the scoreboard.

"I've missed half the damn vote! Why didn't Grantham call me?"

"He may not have known it would be this early."

"He practically sleeps with them! He knew damn well when it would be."

Heart pounding and her stomach in knots, she set aside the coffee and sat completely still. With two votes left they trailed 25-23. After an unexplained delay, a deep-voiced black senator from Cleveland voted for the bill.

One vote left. She had to have it or the bill failed, and her office would have no choice but to continue with the wrist-slaps provided by the horribly outdated legislation from a generation ago. She said a silent prayer, preferring to lose in a landslide than in a vote this close.

"Senator Wells," boomed the Lieutenant Governor from the podium. Maureen flinched. Wells was a Republican from Hinds County, one of the names Craig dropped repeatedly while discussing how difficult it was to grease some of these men. She didn't know for sure since she had missed half the vote, but it appeared most were voting along party lines. But maybe Wells . . .

"Yes."

A murmur from the Senate floor, which Maureen barely heard over her own gasp. Wells had voted for the bill! She glanced at Janine, whose jaw dropped open. Both looked down at the Lieutenant Governor, a Democrat from Meridian. That was the extent of what she knew about his politics, other than the fact that he and Governor Bobby Greene didn't exchange Christmas cards.

"Members of the Senate, we have a tie. Therefore, with the power vested in me by the Constitution of the State of Mississippi, I cast my vote the break the tie . . ."

Maureen gripped Janine's hand—

". . . and vote in favor of the Consumer Protection Act."

The Lieutenant Governor abruptly banged his gavel, nodding at the young man who updated the scoreboard. Another murmur permeated the Senate floor, and a moment later the ticker read 26-25.

"Oh, my God!" Maureen said, tears welling in her eyes.

"Oh, Maureen!" Janine said, squealing. She threw her arms around her friend, then grabbed her pad and pen. "And I get the first quote!"

"Oh, dear. Janine, I don't know what to say. I'm so happy. I'm amazed—thankful—you know the drill. My God, I don't believe this." She wiped her eyes and gathered herself. "Uh, I'm hopeful that Governor Greene will see fit to sign this piece of important consumer legislation that our lawmakers obviously feel merits a great deal of importance. Can you put that into a couple of coherent sentences?"

"Certainly." She grinned. "Can you believe it came down to the Lieutenant Governor? I can't wait to talk to him."

"I may send him a bottle of champagne."

TWO

The Mississippi Attorney General's Office was located in two separate buildings. Frank Cash and his inner circle occupied offices on the fifth floor of the Carroll Gartin Building, which also housed the Mississippi Supreme Court and was located across the street from the Capitol. The Public Integrity, Medicaid Fraud, Human Services and Consumer Protection Divisions worked out of 802 North State Street. The brick structure with the drab, gray interior was only five blocks away but perceived in some quarters as a step-child rather than an equal partner.

Maureen was in her office before eight, putting on makeup at her desk and still trying to catch her breath. The room featured an ego wall of diplomas and professional citations as well as house plants and a pair of Ansel Adams wall hangings. An enlarged photograph of the Mississippi Gulf Coast adorned the wall behind the conference table. The room had a certain smell, as did all the offices in this building. It was a strange but not unpleasant combination of light paint fumes and disinfectant, as the musty carpet emitted a noticeable odor when the weather was damp.

"Understand congratulations are in order," Jeff Garland said, entering the room. He was a veteran investigator, one of the employees she had inherited after the promotion to Consumer Director seven years ago. He was about forty, tall and medium-built with black, horn-rimmed glasses which gave him the look of a computer geek.

"It isn't a done deal yet," Maureen said, closing the door for the daily staff meeting. Two of the other three investigators had entered behind Jeff: Sherry Forster, a black woman Maureen brought with her from Public Integrity, and Paul Bush, the young law student. Ashleigh Dunn, five years behind Maureen and the only other attorney of the group, was in the final stages of a pregnancy and keeping banker's hours. Ashleigh's father was a former state Senator, and he was an influential lobbyist and a major Frank Cash campaign contributor. "Remember, Greene has ten days to sign or veto. If he does nothing, it becomes law."

"It's money in the bank, Maureen," Sherry said. "Everybody says so. The Senate was the big hurdle."

"Let's hope. The timing is terrific," she said, permitting a grin. "There were two more calls about the Capital City Service Department on my voice-mail. That's at least ten the last few days."

"I've answered that many," Paul said with a smirk. "So has Ashleigh. She'd tell you if she were here."

Maureen ignored him, turning to Jeff. "You were telling me about a neighbor who had trouble with them."

"Horror story. It'll sound better coming from him."

"Write down his name and address. I'll see him this morning." She got to her feet. "Busy day, gang. Lunch meeting in Clinton and a couple of other stops, so I'll be out most of the morning. Page if you need anything. Sherry, when Ashleigh gets here, there's a store I want you two to visit in Ridgeland. Couple of calls about fancy designer dresses that sound like fakes. Guys, you're on phones until I get back. Every call is important now. And not a word to anyone about the bill until it's law."

THREE

"**M**r. Randle? Maureen Lewis," she said an hour later as a man about her age opened the door of a home in an affluent Madison subdivision. He was a pediatrician and clad in green hospital scrubs.

"Steve. Come in," he said, offering his hand. The house was spotless except for the great room, which was awash in kid toys. *The Jackson Times* was spread across a scuffed coffee table, a steaming cup of coffee to the side. "Didn't know who to talk to about this, and my wife suggested Jeff. Coffee?"

"No, thanks," Maureen said, retrieving a legal pad from her briefcase. "So. You had a bad experience with Capital City Motors."

"My Accord is nine years old and has 132,000 miles on it. I was due for an oil change and had a small leak. I'm talking about a handful of drops over the last few months in my garage, not puddles. And the horn was out. Wife was on me about that— afraid I wouldn't pass the state inspection. Anyway, the mechanic said six hundred bucks. The leak was apparently serious—the wrong-sized plug had been used on the last oil change, and oil had gotten up in the belts and messed up a bunch of stuff. Pretty extensive repair. I got a little panicky and agreed to it."

A grin. "My Civic isn't as old, but it has one-sixty. Know how you feel."

Randle sipped his coffee. "Wife picks me up after work and says, 'Call 'em back, tell 'em to fix your horn and change the oil, and get a second opinion on the leak.' So I called from the car and didn't get anyone . . ."

"What time of day was this?"

"Six-thirty in the evening. No answer, so I called again first thing next morning. Got their service advisor—this woman— and she said, 'I think everything's done, but I'm not sure. The mechanic stayed late and worked on it.' That made me feel a little funny, so I told her I was coming to get it, and I specifically said not to repair the leak if he hadn't already started. All I wanted was the oil change and a new horn."

Maureen wrote. Randle's warmth had disappeared when she looked up. "The mechanic was working on it when I got there, which was twenty minutes later. First thing I noticed was a big pile of parts in an oily box. He gave me this big grin and said, 'That was one hell of a leak, but it's fixed now.'"

A sardonic smile spread across Maureen's face.

"The leak was fixed. He said the timing belt and water pump were messed up, so both had been replaced. Then he started talking about the sealant around the hoses. They didn't have to be replaced that day, but I was looking at $3000 down the road. By then I was getting mad. I asked about the oil change. It was done, but he hadn't even started on the horn! I recounted the conversation with the woman, and he claimed she said the leak was priority, not the horn. So I told him to stop right there and tell me what I owed."

"I can't wait to hear this."

"Eleven hundred dollars! I started yelling, and the service advisor came running over. I asked how the bill got so high when no one had talked to me. She said she'd called at five-thirty the day before and left a message. I told her I didn't get a message—my pager never went off—and she finally admitted she'd called the clinic. Even though I specifically said the pager was the first option. That made me furious."

"That way she could add five hundred dollars to your bill without your approval."

"Exactly what I said. Didn't faze her a bit. She said, 'Mr. Randle, you told this mechanic to do whatever it took to fix your car.' I never said that, but by then I knew I wasn't going to get anywhere arguing with her."

Maureen wrote quickly. Randle let her catch up before continuing.

"I'm not sure the car is worth eleven hundred dollars at this point, which I said half a dozen times to those people. But here's what really bothers me: I put two hundred thousand miles on my first Honda, and I was told as recently as six months ago I would put another hundred on this one."

"Who was servicing it?"

"I get the oil changed somewhere else, but Capital City has always handled the major service. Thing is, everybody in the garage is new since I was in there last, and suddenly the car is falling apart. They might be telling the truth about the plug. But shouldn't there have been more oil in my garage if that much got all the way up through the car?"

"I'd think so, what little I know. You didn't bring the parts home, did you?"

Randle led her to the garage, which smelled of freshly cut firewood. He presented her with the box. Half a dozen parts were resting in a puddle of oil.

"There's a mechanic we use for things like this. Would you mind if I run these parts out there? I can't make any promises, but I want him to see this."

"Please do. Is there a chance I'll get some of it back?"

"Maybe. If we get that far, I can get your input on what you think is fair."

"Get whatever they'll give you. Just make sure you tell them I'll never get near the place again, and that I'll tell everybody I know about this."

* * *

Hinds Junior College was in Raymond, a small town a few minutes south of Jackson. She picked her way through the tree-lined campus, finding the burly mechanic in the garage surrounded by students. He waved her into the fray, inspecting the parts with a cabled flashlight as she explained Randle's plight. He had a sad smile on his face when he looked up.

"Here's what this boils down to: Assuming this man has taken care of his car, most of the parts are probably original. And with that many miles, it's not uncommon for a bunch of things to crap out at once. I can't tell what really needed replacing since there's oil all over everything. Very clever. I have one question, though. What about you folks?" he said, turning to his students. "What's fishy about this?"

A long-haired man of perhaps twenty spoke, asking why the timing belt had been replaced. The mechanic nodded firmly, handing the box to Maureen.

"Exactly what I want to know. I'll sign anything you want stating that there was no need to replace the timing belt. Not with 20,000 miles on it. Recommended replacement is every ninety."

"What about the oil?"

"Doesn't matter." He grinned. "And remind those folks, Maureen, that oil drips down into the pan, not up. I want a good explanation for how so much oil got up near the hood. Make them give you a straight answer when they try to dance."

* * *

Capital City Motors was a family-owned Honda dealership which had relocated recently to north Jackson after many years in the downtown area. Maureen avoided the hovering salesmen and toted the box of parts to the garage. She approached the service counter and glanced around. Several mechanics were looking her up and down, and they weren't subtle about it.

"May I help you?" a woman said, her nameplate identifying her as Katrina. She was a tall blond and probably her age, although the lines on her face and circles around her eyes indicated hard living. Her voice was rough from cigarettes.

"Who's your service manager, please?"

"That would be Gordon Smith."

"Is he here?"

"I'm Gordon Smith." A very tall man with brown hair and a neatly-trimmed beard stepped into view. He was perhaps forty and towered over Maureen. "What can I do for you?"

"Mr. Smith, I'm Maureen Lewis with the Attorney General's Office. Do you have a moment to talk?"

Smith frowned. "What brings you here?"

"Is there a place we can talk?"

"Right here."

Not that again. She hesitated, glancing around. The blond was now staring, her eyes hard. The uniformed mechanics were trying to eavesdrop as they did their work. Everybody suddenly seemed tense, which she found interesting.

"We've had a number of complaints about your department recently. People are saying they've felt pressured into service that perhaps wasn't necessary."

Smith glanced at Katrina, who remained in place but said nothing. "Our mechanics are the best in the city, ma'am. ASE certified. We would never knowingly charge a customer more than the repair is worth. I will tell you that customers complain about the labor charges, but you get what you pay for. Do you have anything specific?"

"A woman in Byram told me yesterday that her CRX was going dead at intersections. She brought the car to you three times, and after charging over a thousand dollars in repairs, you told her it was bad gasoline, even though she's gassed up at the same place for years. The car is still going dead."

Smith said nothing. Maureen recounted her visit to Steve Randle's home. A noticeably young mechanic walked through on his way to the garage, blond and cleaner than most of his colleagues. He purchased a soft drink from the vending machine and lingered before departing.

"We have the signature of our own mechanic stating that there was no need for the timing belt on Mr. Randle's car to be removed. It was installed only twenty thousand miles ago."

"It was covered with oil, Ms. Lewis."

"After your mechanic put it in an oily box."

Smith's jaw tightened. "I don't believe that."

"And is it a practice of yours to leave a revised estimate on a customer's voice mail, then do the work without confirmation from the customer?"

Smith looked at Katrina sharply. Maureen followed his eyes. So she was the service advisor. "The Civic with the oil leak," she said casually, opening a four-drawer filing cabinet. "We talked to him at four-thirty that afternoon."

Maureen turned to her. "You didn't talk to him, ma'am. You avoided his pager and left a message at his clinic after it had closed for the day. That was at five-thirty, not four-thirty. And you close at five-thirty, do you not?" she said, raising her voice when Katrina tried to cut in. "Mr. Randle tried to call here that night at six-thirty. He says no one answered, yet you told him the mechanic stayed late and worked on his car."

Katrina glared down at Maureen, hatred in her eyes. "The phone rings in here. It doesn't ring in the garage."

"That still doesn't explain why you authorized five hundred dollars of extra service when the customer didn't agree to it."

"He told the mechanic to do whatever it took to fix his car!"

"That's not what he told me," Maureen said slowly. She let

her gaze linger on Katrina before turning to Smith. "I'd like to talk to the mechanic, please."

Smith sighed and strode through the garage. Maureen followed. "Billy!" he said sharply. A pot-bellied man of perhaps fifty approached a moment later. He was covered with grease and smelled of cigarettes. Dirt was caked under his fingernails.

"Billy worked on the car." Smith turned to him. "The Civic the other day, with the big oil leak."

The mechanic's Adam's Apple bobbed. He shot a glance at Smith, then Maureen.

"Whatcha wanna know?"

"When you worked on that car, how late that night did you stay?"

The mechanic blanched. He looked at the floor, then at Maureen. "Uh, seven-thirty or eight, I think. I ain't real sure."

Maureen grinned. She held the man's gaze until he became uncomfortable.

"I know it was past seven!"

"Mr. Randle firmly stated that he'd put off having the leak repaired because only a few drops of oil were on the floor of his garage," she said slowly, taking care to make sure her words were clearly understood. "If that's the case, how'd so much oil get way up inside the car and damage the belts and water pump?"

The mechanic licked his lips. His voice was high and pinched when he spoke, and his words emerged in a rush. "You see, ma'am, he been taking his car to one of them off-brand places! They put a plug in there that didn't fit! Happens all the time, because these young kids who work at these places don't know their butt from a . . ."

"I understand, sir." Mechanics all over the garage had stopped to watch. Katrina was staring from her perch. "No one disputes that the plug was the wrong size. But there were only a few drops of oil in his garage, and they accumulated over a long period of time—I'm talking about the better part of a year."

26

"But you don't understand that . . ."

"And oil drops down into the pan, does it not?"

The mechanic looked to Smith for help, flustered. "Of course it does. Everybody knows that!"

"So how did all that oil get way up inside the engine? There must have been gobs of it to ruin all those parts."

"I don't know! It just did!"

She couldn't help a grin. It broadened as she turned to Smith. "It just did. I don't consider that a satisfactory explanation. You'll have to do better than that, Mr. Smith."

"Billy, get back to work," Smith said angrily. "I don't have time for this. Until you can bring me substantiated proof. . ."

"You will make time for this, sir!" Maureen said loudly, glaring up at him. "We are getting complaints about your department every single day! People are telling us they felt pressured into service they didn't think they needed, and pressured to buy new parts which didn't take care of the problem they had. And in this case, since Mr. Randle was charged five hundred dollars for repairs he didn't agree to, and perhaps a lot more in repairs he may not have needed, I'm inclined to agree!"

"Get back to work!" Smith said, circling the room with his eyes. "Follow me," he said to Maureen. He strode into the service office and glowered at Katrina. "Where's Irv?"

"He's leaving for a meeting . . ."

Smith disappeared down a hall. A minute later he returned with a heavy man in a suit. The man forced a smile.

"Ms. Lewis, I'm Irv White. Follow me."

Her heart beat faster as she strode down a carpeted hallway, well away from the garage. White was clearly an executive, and she wondered if they were on their way to see Sonny Hollins. But they entered what was obviously White's office—pictures of him with his family and grandchildren were displayed prominently, along with several plaques on the paneled walls. He sat behind his desk and gestured at a wingback chair across from him.

"How's ol' Frank Cash doin'?"

"Just fine," she said, her antenna going up. Awfully quick to play the Frank card.

"Sonny and Frank been playin' golf together for years. He's a fine man. Anyway, Gordon said we've got a disagreement about some service done last week."

"We do, Mr. White, but I'm more concerned about the number of complaints we've received since first of the year. It isn't just one."

White frowned. "What kind of complaints?"

"They vary, but like I told Mr. Smith, everyone who has complained felt pressured into service they didn't need, or paid for incorrect diagnoses and had to pay more to get the problem taken care of."

White smiled again. "I don't know about that, Ms. Lewis. Our mechanics are top-notch . . ."

"I know. ASE certified and all that. But let's talk about the Civic Mr. Smith and I were discussing." She recounted Randle's story, then produced the affidavit with the signature from the mechanic in Raymond. By then White's warmth was gone.

"All right." He opened a catalog. "Timing belt for a ninety-one Civic is ninety-nine bucks. Call it a hundred. Fair enough?"

"What about labor?"

Another glance at the catalog. "Suggested labor on the timing belt is half an hour. Now you're at one-fifty."

Maureen frowned. "Half an hour? Mr. White, I just put a new timing belt in my own Civic. Cost me nearly three hundred dollars."

Now White's jaw was tight. "I don't know where you took your car, but . . ."

"I also have a serious problem with the fact that your service advisor left a revised estimate on this customer's voice mail, then did the work without getting his approval. The difference was five hundred dollars!"

"Look, Ms. Lewis, I don't know what you think you're going to get out of us . . ."

"One-fifty is far short of what's fair."

White's glare sharpened. "Two hundred. Take it or leave it."

"We'll take it." She sighed, getting to her feet. "You have his address in your files. When can he expect a check?"

"Payroll goes out Friday. Will there be anything else?"

She lingered in the doorway. White was still at his desk. "Bear in mind, sir, that each time a complaint is lodged against this dealership, we keep it on file. And we're awfully concerned with how many calls are coming in. I might add that the total lack of concern for this customer shown by everyone here—including yourself—is really disturbing. He made it quite clear he'll never set foot in this place again. If I'm in your shoes, perhaps I call and offer some sort of apology."

White looked up. Sweat was on his brow. "Will there be anything else, Ms. Lewis?"

"No, sir. I'll see myself out."

"I'll tell Mr. Hollins you came by. I'm sure he'll be glad to hear it."

FOUR

Maureen gave the Clinton Chamber of Commerce her standard half-hour speech, combining the usual consumer awareness tips with a handful of subtle plugs for the Attorney General. Lunch was the usual thank-you, and today's meal was a home cooked plate of fried chicken, English peas, creamed potatoes and cornbread. She enjoyed every bite and washed it down with sweet tea, quietly deciding on a can of Slim-Fast for supper. Keeping the pounds off was a hell of a lot harder at thirty-four than twenty-four, even with regular exercise.

Half a dozen messages were on her voice mail when she returned to work. There was another complaint about the Capital City service department and several calls about an increase on the monthly bill from Metro Cablevision. There was a call from best friend Erica Bennett, who was checking on the weekend trip to Bay St. Louis. The final call was also of a personal nature. It had come a couple of hours ago.

"Ms. Lewis, my name is Tom Chapman. I work in public relations at Capital City Motors." He paused, and she wondered if this had to do with the encounter this morning. "I realize you have no idea who I am, but I'd like to meet you. I've seen you on television and read your quotes in the paper for several years, and you seem like an interesting lady." He chuckled, a hint of nervousness in his voice. "I'm not a stalker or anything. I'd like to meet for coffee. If you're married—or not comfortable with the idea—I understand."

He left a phone number, indicating that he would try again in several days if he hadn't heard back from her. She stared at the receiver before hanging up.

FIVE

Bay St. Louis was a small town on the Mississippi Gulf Coast with just under eight thousand residents. It was a predominantly Catholic area with strong ties to New Orleans, and many locals, including Maureen's mother June, spoke with an accent reminiscent of the Crescent City. The Bay was still a charming place where everyone knew each other, but all agreed that the gaming industry had changed the area forever.

The Lewis clan had been in Bay St. Louis for generations.

Maureen's father Graham had been president of Coast Bank for twenty-five years. One of the best and brightest of his time, he had taken the operation from a lone Bay St. Louis location to over a dozen along the coast. Relations with his son were non-existent, however. Jack, six years older than Maureen, wanted no part of the banking business and moved several states away when an argument about his choice of career turned violent. Things worsened over the years, and Jack hadn't darkened their doors in over a decade. It was a shadow which would likely hang over visits home the rest of her life.

"Welcome!" Graham said cheerfully. Rain was falling, and he hustled toward them with a giant Bay/Waveland Yacht Club umbrella. He was six-two with the olive eyes Maureen had and thick brown hair. A mild heart attack had slowed him five years ago, but he still played golf daily. June, a short, petite woman who was aging gracefully, appeared and spread plastic silverware and napkins across the picnic table on the screened-in porch. The air was heavier here, and the scent of salt was always in the air.

"Hello, girls. Graham demanded we eat an hour ago."

"We're prepared, Mother," Maureen said, giving June a quick hug and gesturing at a sack of po-boys. "Knew Dad would die if he didn't eat before six."

Maureen dug in. Erica, who wasn't as hungry, chatted with June and Graham as she ate. Erica clerked for a Supreme Court justice in Jackson and had moved to the capital city about the time Maureen did. She was also from Bay St. Louis, a tall, pretty woman with long, brown hair and eyes. She and Maureen graduated together from Our Ladies Academy before their undergraduate work and Law School at Ole Miss.

"Come up for air every couple of minutes, okay, Mo?" Graham said, addressing Maureen by her childhood name. Erica used it as well, but everyone in the Jackson area knew her as Maureen. "Don't want to have to call the paramedics. So how's Big Frank?"

She rolled her eyes. "Slick as ever."

"What's ahead for him, you think?"

"He denies it in the press, but he wants Washington real bad. Something in the Justice Department is a good bet. Rumor has it the Attorney General's health is failing."

"You think they'd pick Frank, Mo?" June said.

Graham turned to his wife. "You bet they would. And as loyal as Mo has been over the years, she'd be right in the middle of the group he'd take with him."

"Let's not get carried away, Dad."

The phone rang. Graham disappeared into the house. June spoke when he was out of earshot, leaning forward.

"You won't believe what your father wants to do, Mo. Wants us to go to Nashville and surprise Jack. Make up and start over."

"With no warning?" Erica said.

June sighed. "I'll go if he insists . . ."

Maureen frowned. "Mother, don't. That's not the way to . . ."

"Hush! We'll talk about this later. Here comes your father."

Graham reclaimed his seat and beamed. "Mo, you're not going to believe who that was! Ben Barnes' son!"

Maureen's jaw tightened. She let her sandwich fall. It landed with a plop in the gravy below.

"Dad, did I not tell you . . ."

"I didn't set that up, Mo, I swear!"

"He just called out of the blue? Or did some fortune teller let him know I would be here?"

June looked up sheepishly. "I ran into him at the grocery store the other day. He asked about you, and he seemed, well, so lonely . . ."

"That's great, Mother! You invite him for supper, too?"

"No, dear! We just thought you might call him while you're down. We've always thought the two of you would make such a nice couple."

"Quit trying to find me a husband, damn it! Both of you!"

Conversation ended for several minutes. Maureen broke the ice, still angry at her parents and wanting to turn the tables.

"Dad, Mom says you're thinking about dropping in on Jack. You sure a letter wouldn't be a better idea?"

Graham frowned, still stung. He glared at his daughter, then his wife.

"Graham, Mo would certainly want to know."

He sighed, then gazed across the table. The Lewis and Bennett families had been close for many years, and discussion of Jack in front of Erica was routine. "Do you realize how long its been since your brother and I have spoken to each other, let alone the last time we had a meaningful conversation? I've never even met that wife of his."

"You think he's going to welcome you with open arms?"

"I don't want my son to go to his grave with regrets about his relationship with his father."

"Dad, I don't think he's entirely to blame for . . ."

"And I don't want to go to mine like this, either."

Maureen sighed, pushing her food away.

"Mo, I think your father realizes a lot of things he didn't a few years back," June said, touching her husband's shoulder. "He's going to try a lot harder to see Jack's side of things."

Maureen sighed. "That's good, Dad, but wouldn't a letter be a little easier on both of you?"

"What if he doesn't write back?"

"Then you've tried. Put everything you want to say in a letter, and make it encouraging. And if he blows it off, he blows it off. That's all you can do."

"Give it a shot, Graham," Erica said, a supportive smile on her face. "Were I in his shoes, I'd be a lot more open to a letter than an unannounced visit."

"I'll think about it."

*   *   *

Maureen and Erica were stretched out that night on twin beds in her old bedroom. Shag carpet was still on the floor, and childhood photographs lined the walls. The yellowed poster of Paul McCartney was still there.

"You rebounded nicely after biting their heads off."

Maureen glared at her friend. "I don't care what he does with Jack. I'm sick of the whole thing. But he's got a lot of nerve to try to set me up after Richard."

"That was five years ago, Mo."

"Erica, I'm talking about the whole charade of finding me the right husband, just like he tried to find Jack the right career. And you see where it got him."

Erica fidgeted. "I've wanted to ask you this for a long time: Are you uncomfortable around Keith?"

Maureen closed her eyes. Keith was Erica's fiancé, a successful Jackson businessman who introduced himself at church two years ago. He was divorced and a decade older, easy to be around. Even his kids, whom he saw each weekend, were well-behaved. Being around Keith was not a problem, but his presence was a reminder that her own love life was dead as a doornail while her best friend was being courted by Mr. Right.

"Of course not. I like Keith a lot—I really do. One of us was bound to find a nice guy sooner or later. It's just depressing being a third wheel."

"You're always welcome, with or without him."

"I know, and I appreciate it. I wish he had a twin."

Erica grinned. "You gonna call that guy at the car dealership?"

"He said he would call back if he didn't hear from me."

"You've gotta be a little curious. And, Mo, if your father's potential rejection of him is a factor, ignore it. I know you're tired of hearing it, but this is your life, not his."

Maureen met her friend's eyes. As usual, she had scored a direct hit.

"At least talk to him. He might be a real nice guy."

SIX

Craig Grantham rang Maureen's private line after the staff meeting the following Monday, informing her that Governor Greene had called an afternoon press conference—sounded like the Consumer Protection Act was one of the things he wanted to sign. She thanked him and hung up.

"Line one, Maureen," her secretary said from her desk in the foyer a minute later.

"Hi, this is Tom Chapman," a male voice said, approximately her age. "I left a message for you the other day."

"Hi," she said, startled. "I haven't had a chance to call you back." She fidgeted. "So you want to have coffee, huh? Got a resume I can look at?"

He laughed. "Just wanted to meet you. I'm not a vagrant or anything."

Maureen smiled. "You work at Capital City?"

"I'm in public relations. From here originally. Got through at Mississippi State seven years ago. I'm twenty-nine."

"Interesting. Got five years on you. And I'm a Rebel."

"Hoddy toddy! So what do you say?" he said confidently.

"One day this week, I suppose. That's about as specific as I can get. And it may have to be on short notice."

"They're real flexible here. Lemme give you my direct line."

The secretary transferred another call as she was getting off the phone.

"Ms. Lewis?" a young male voice said timidly. "You were at the garage the other day, right? At Capital City Motors?"

"Who's this?"

"Uh, you ain't tapin' or nothin', are you?"

"No."

"My name is Ronnie Landrum. I'm a mechanic."

Maureen snapped her fingers, catching Jeff's attention. He

35

pulled the door shut.

"How can I help you?"

"I, uh, wanted to talk to you about something—something real serious. I called in sick today so I could call you from home, and I just done got up the nerve now, my wife badgering me and all."

"What would this be in regard to, sir?"

"You're sure you ain't taping, ma'am? I can't afford to lose my job."

"Mr. Landrum, I'm not taping a thing. Now tell me why you called. Nobody at the dealership will know we're talking."

He took a deep breath. "When you was here the other day talking to Gordon and Katrina, I walked through and heard everything."

She frowned. "Blond hair, and a mustache? I think I remember that. You're a youngster, aren't you?"

"Yes, ma'am. Anyway, you was right, about Billy doing a bunch of work on that man's Civic he didn't need to."

"Really?" Maureen said slowly. A woman in the background implored him to tell everything he knew.

"I am!" he said. "I'm sorry, Ms. Lewis. That's my wife. She's having to hold my hand to get me through this, I'm so nervous. Anyway, she's right—what Billy done is just the tip of the iceberg."

Maureen stood, walking around to the front of her desk. "How so?"

"You sure I won't lose my job?"

"You have my word. Now tell me what's going on."

"I've worked there since October. Far as I can tell, they hadn't been making as much in service as they thought they should. So right after Thanksgiving, Gordon had this meeting and said we were gonna have this profit sharing program. Since then he's been on all of us in the garage to do as much work on every vehicle that comes through there as we can. And if we hit the new budget each month, everybody—all us mechanics, too—get a piece of the action."

"You're saying extra money goes into your paycheck?"

"Yes, ma'am," he said, suddenly close to tears. "I didn't know what to do. My wife and I are both Christians, and we knew it was wrong, but we were afraid if I spoke up I'd get fired. When I found out who you were and why you'd come over, I told her our day was coming. She begged me to tell you."

"Does Mr. White know about this? Irv White?"

"It was his idea, what Gordon said."

Her eyes widened. "What about Katrina?"

"Ms. Lewis, she's the worst. I don't mean to speak bad of nobody, but that woman runs around there even worse than Gordon, trying to get us to do work that don't need to be done. Good Lord, you should have seen her the morning Billy repaired that man's Civic."

"You saw this happen, Mr. Landrum?"

"I work right next to him. That morning, Katrina comes running over there and wants to know how far Billy was on that oil leak. He said he ain't even started it, and . . ."

"Wait a minute. She told me he stayed late and worked on it the night before."

Landrum snorted. "Ms. Lewis, I know for a fact Billy left at five-thirty that day, 'cause I walked out with him. Sometimes we stay if we're real backed up, but not that day."

"So what did Katrina say to Billy?"

"When she found out he hadn't done anything to the leak, she told him the customer had just called and was on his way. She looked at him like she was gonna rip his heart out, said he darn well better have it fixed before he showed up. If the man asked why the leak was fixed instead of his horn, tell him he misunderstood."

"In other words, lie."

"Yes, ma'am." He paused. "I ain't ever seen Billy work so

fast. Heck, I ain't ever seen nobody work that fast."

Maureen sat heavily on the edge of her desk. "Mr. Landrum, I do need to tape this."

"Oh, now, Ms. Lewis, I can't afford to get fired. We got our hands full trying to pay bills and feed our little one."

"You will not get fired, sir. You have my word. But this is a big deal. Customers are getting cheated every day, aren't they?"

He heaved a sigh. "Yes, ma'am. I know it's wrong—I wasn't raised that way. I guess I'll come in and talk, if you can promise they won't know it was me. When you want to do this?"

"Today, if possible."

"All right. We'll be in this afternoon. We'll leave our little boy with his grandma."

Maureen walked into Sherry's office and closed the door. "Need you to stay a little late today. No more than an hour."

"What's up?"

She explained. Sherry whistled. "They'll be here at five-thirty. Make sure we have fresh batteries for the tape recorder."

SEVEN

It was windy and cold on the Capitol steps that afternoon. Maureen shivered as she stood alongside Cash and Grantham and glanced at the bare trees. A podium littered with microphone flags was set up for Governor Bobby Greene, a brawny man of sixty with carefully-styled white hair. A young man in a suit nodded a moment later, and Greene approached the podium. The gathering was probably fifty, a third of which was media.

"Good afternoon. Glad you all could make it today, especially you in the media. Like to announce what I'd say is a pretty doggone historic bit of legislation, especially given the dog-fight in the House."

This was the teacher pay raise bill.

"But I am delighted that our elected officials have come together to recognize the fact that our educators come first in this state, and always will."

A smattering of applause and a soft snort from Grantham. Maureen smiled to herself. Greene vetoed the same bill two years ago and was crucified for it. Now he was grinning from ear to ear as he endorsed it. Politics.

"That's right—an across the board five percent pay increase for all our teachers, all over the state at all levels of public education, will go into effect with the beginning of the new school year this fall. I know it's not as much as all of us would like . . ."

"Please," Grantham said quietly, drawing a discreet smirk from Cash.

". . . but I think you'd agree that it's an awfully good start, and it'll be law as soon as I can put my Bobby Greene Hancock on it. Hand that legislation here. And give me a pen that works."

"Oh, now he's for teacher pay hikes?" a female voice said softly, suddenly in her ear. Maureen recognized the cigarette breath immediately.

"Hi, Janine. What a chameleon."

"Also, this is an interesting bill," Greene continued. "I'm putting my signature on what Attorney General Cash and his staff call the Consumer Protection Act. Quite a few folks have badgered me about signing this thing since it went through the Legislature, and A.G. Cash seems to feel quite strongly about it. The Attorney General has been kind enough to join us, and at this time I would like to invite Mr. Cash to the dais and let him tell us a bit more about what the Consumer Protection Act will do for our citizens."

More applause. Cash was in his late-forties. He was tall, slender and handsome with brown hair and eyes, dapper in a navy pinstripe suit. His made for television smile was already in place.

"Thank you, Governor Greene. It's a pleasure to be here and witness your signature on what my staff and I feel is an outstanding piece of legislation: The Consumer Protection Act. This bill will allow our office much greater latitude than we've ever had in cracking down on criminals who've taken advantage of our state's consumers. Folks who are determined to cheat the people of our state through fraudulent business practices best think twice—this bill makes it possible for our office to charge these con artists with felonies in many cases, not just slaps on the wrist."

"Off the record—was he really for this?" Janine said softly. Maureen, equally discreet, turned and wrinkled her nose.

"I'd like to thank my Chief of Staff, Craig Grantham," Cash said without missing a beat. "Without his help and support, this bill wouldn't be in front of the governor. And certainly Maureen Lewis, Director of Consumer Protection, who deserves a tremendous amount of credit for drafting the bill and seeing it through the House. Her staff will be in the trenches enforcing the new law."

More applause, and Maureen allowed herself a smile. "Nice going," Grantham said, nudging her.

"You, too," she said, managing a half-hearted smile. She turned to Janine and rolled her eyes. Janine smiled down at her pad.

Cash cleared his throat and continued. "Let me assure all of you on this historic day that our office will continue to do whatever is necessary to protect the citizens of this state from ripoff artists, con men and deceptive advertising practices. We're extremely grateful to the Mississippi Legislature for helping this dream become a reality, and as I turn the floor back over to you, Governor Greene, let me add that the people of our great state are deeply appreciative of you for putting your signature on it, sir."

Cash even stuck out his hand, which Greene shook while managing a smile. That was news, and flashbulbs popped. The men were bitter political enemies and regularly traded barbs in the press.

"Happy hour tonight? Or dinner?" Janine said as the gathering broke up.

"Love to, but it may be late. I'll page you. Got something big to tell you about—off the record."

* * *

Ronnie Landrum and his wife didn't arrive until six. The couple was dressed in denim from head to toe and barely looked old enough to vote.

"This won't take long," Maureen said, placing the tape recorder in the center of the conference table. "And I assure both of you that your name, Mr. Landrum, will not come up. Management will never know you talked unless you tell them yourself."

A nervous laugh. "You don't have to worry about that, ma'am. Are you gonna play this for the Attorney General?"

"If he wants to hear it." Landrum's eyebrows widened, and Maureen smiled reassuringly. "Like I said, your name will not get back to Mr. Hollins."

Landrum confirmed that the plan was designed by Irv White and approved by Sonny Hollins, although Gordon and Katrina oversaw the garage and monitored the amount of service done on each car. He admitted that his last six paychecks were two to three times what they were when he started. He also recounted a discussion he overheard between Gordon and Katrina—both were receiving monthly bonuses if a quota was met.

"And you have a pretty good idea the other mechanics are also getting this much?"

"Oh, yes, Ms. Lewis. The men on both sides of me—Billy is one of 'em—said the same thing. Gordon comes around every once in a while, puts his arm around me and tells me what a good job I'm doing. And says if we keep doing such a good job, everybody's gonna win big."

"Has management ever acknowledged that what they're doing is wrong?"

Landrum shook his head. "No, ma'am."

"Have they indicated how long this new system would be in effect?"

"No, ma'am. Gordon ain't said, but he's acted like it'll go on indefinitely."

"Has there ever been any kind of threat—even something real subtle—that you or someone else would get in trouble if anyone found out?"

Landrum glanced at his wife. She patted his hand and smiled at him.

"Only from Katrina. Billy told me that after you left the other day, she told a couple of the guys that there would be you-know-what to pay if anybody told. I'd be more scared of her than I would anybody else, you wanna know the truth. Ain't never seen a woman so mean."

"Do you have any contact with Sonny Hollins?"

Landrum smirked. "Mr. Hollins don't associate with none of us in the garage. That's fine with me, though. He's pretty intimidating."

* * *

Half an hour later Maureen nosed into the Irish pub at the corner of Jefferson and Fortification. She'd changed into a rugby shirt and jeans and joined Janine at a small table well away from the bar. The clientele at this hour was mostly professional, although college kids took over at night.

"Well, it's about time," Janine said cheerfully. A pitcher of beer and a huge plate of chips and salsa were in front of her. She took a final drag from her cigarette and put it out, mindful of the fact that Maureen didn't smoke.

"Sorry for the delay," Maureen said, pouring herself a beer. She took Janine through the story, beginning with Steve Randle's problems. Janine was into her second beer by the end.

"That Hollins character is on the ads, right? Is he management?"

"He's the big dog. The department head I talked to dropped Frank's name. Reminded me that he and Hollins are golfing buddies."

"Great. And Frank wasn't excited about your bill."

"On the record, all for it. Makes him look like a hero. Off the record—in the elevator—pretty lukewarm." She smirked. "He e-mailed this afternoon, compared it to a brand-new hot rod."

"Don't leave skid marks on the toes of anybody important."

"That's how I took it. But this is an outright con job in the garage."

"The one good thing my worthless ex did years ago was teach me a little about cars. Enough to know when I'm really being had."

"Consider yourself fortunate. Anyway, we'll look at their records. That's the first step. The bill gives me subpoena power. Didn't have that before."

"Keep me posted. And have some of this," Janine said, shoving the chips toward her.

Maureen made a face. "I don't want to fill up on this garbage. If you want dinner, let's go have a nice meal."

"And give up my perch where I can gaze at all these cute young college boys?" Janine said, grinning. "They'd die if they knew that fat, gray-haired old woman in the corner was lusting after them."

"Speaking of which, I got an interesting call. Some guy named Tom Chapman, said he'd seen me on TV and read my quotes in the paper. Wants to have coffee. Never gotten a call like that before." She laughed to herself. "He's in public relations at Capital City Motors."

Janine threw back her head and laughed, catching the attention of many of the bar's patrons. "The plot thickens."

"This was before the mechanic talked. Erica wants me to meet him, by the way. Said if my father's potential rejection of him was a factor, not to think a thing about it. This is my life, after all," she said, sarcasm in her tone.

Janine met her eyes. "I know you disagree, but I'm convinced that at least part of why you fell for Richard was rebellion against your father."

Maureen closed her eyes and sighed.

"I know—I'm in no position to talk. I'll probably never get over the fact that after two kids and fifteen years of marriage, the love of my life was cheating. You see how aggressively I pursue men. But Erica's right, Maureen. Don't assume your father didn't learn a pretty valuable lesson, even if he never says a word about it, and don't turn down coffee because you're afraid your father won't like him if they somehow meet."

"I get the message," Maureen said wearily, sipping her beer. "What I'm more concerned about is whether he's a psycho. I'd like this a lot more if someone could vouch for him."

EIGHT

Maureen arrived early Monday morning and spent an hour wording the subpoena for Capital City Motors. It demanded copies of their service records, beginning with the previous week and going back through last August. If Ronnie Landrum was telling the truth, this window would paint a clear picture of when the new program had gone into effect.

"Is Mr. Hollins in, please?" Maureen said at eight-thirty, giving the receptionist on the showroom floor a professional smile.

She was in a dark suit, having dressed carefully for the occasion. Several salesmen who jumped to their feet at her arrival were backing away.

"He should be here any minute." She glanced out the window, and Maureen followed her eyes. "That's him now."

Hollins entered the showroom, a younger man with him. He gave Maureen a quizzical smile as he passed through. He didn't remember her.

"Mr. Hollins, this lady wanted to see you."

Hollins stopped and extended his hand, looking Maureen over. "Sonny Hollins. How can I help you this morning?"

"Good morning, Mr. Hollins, I'm Maureen Lewis with the Attorney General's Office. Do you have a moment to talk?"

The smile faded immediately. "Go on back. I'll be right there," he said to the younger man. "I knew I recognized you. I've left two messages for Frank Cash about that stunt you pulled the other day."

"Yes, sir. I won't be but a minute." She started to extend the legal-sized envelope in his direction, certain he wouldn't ask her to his office. He spun and departed, however. She glanced at the receptionist, who frowned. It wasn't the young lady who had giggled when Hollins embarrassed her a year ago.

"Give him just a moment, ma'am. I'll ring his office after he gets his coffee."

Five minutes later the receptionist spoke with Hollins.

"Have a seat. He'll be right up."

Thirty minutes later Maureen smiled to herself and got to her feet. She handed the envelope to the receptionist.

"Looks like he's gotten busy."

"I can ring him again."

"Just make sure this gets in his hands."

* * *

The morning raced by, as Maureen handed out mundane

assignments with new enthusiasm and reminded her staff how much more firepower they now had at their disposal. She remained at her desk, carefully scanning ads in the area newspapers. The car dealers were notorious for misleading print ads, and in the past she had been limited to empty threats. Not any more, however.

Her private line rang just before noon. Only her parents, Erica, Janine and Cash's inner circle had the number.

"Maureen, we have a problem," Cash said abruptly. "Two angry messages from Sonny Hollins last Friday, and a really heated one about an hour ago. You mind telling me what the hell you're doing to him?"

Adrenaline shot through her. "I sent him a subpoena, Frank," she said slowly. "Standard operating procedure."

"What I understand, you marched right into their service department, accused two people of lying, embarrassed a mechanic, then tried to show up Irv White!"

Her mouth fell open. "Frank, that is absolutely not true! My phone is ringing off the hook with people who've been ripped off by their service department, and I went over there to find some things out. I was referred to Irv White . . ."

"And today you had the audacity—without speaking to me, of course—to confront Sonny Hollins, a man I've known many years, and serve him a subpoena? He said that thing you left looked like an indictment!"

"Frank, that was no different from . . ."

"Sonny Hollins is different! He carries a lot of weight here! I haven't decided how I'm going to handle this yet, but for the time being, you back off Capital City Motors. Understand?"

Silence.

"Maureen? Did you hear what I said?"

"Yes, sir," she said quietly.

Click.

* * *

Smith Park was situated between the Capitol and the Governor's Mansion. It was the site of the occasional acceptance speech and concert, with picnic tables, a marble fountain and walking trails for those who worked downtown. Despite the dead grass and bare trees this time of year, the park was a pleasant diversion from the crowded eateries and an escape from the office. Maureen met Erica there half an hour later, unpacking steaming carry-out plates from the grocery several blocks away. Starving, she dug right into a piece of jalapeno cornbread.

"What has you so worked up?" Erica said. "You were high as a kite after the bill passed."

"I subpoenaed records from Capital City the other day," Maureen said, her mouth full. "Sonny Hollins complained to Frank, and Frank just blistered my ass and told me to back off. That's the first business I've even contacted, and he's already putting the brakes on."

Erica grinned. "And you go after one of the biggest fish of all, of course."

"Oh, so we use kid gloves on Frank's cronies and save the heavy artillery for side-of-the-road vendors?" A sigh. "I just wish he'd said it was going to be like this in the beginning. Shouldn't have even bothered writing the damn thing."

"Let Frank cool off. I can't believe he would shut you down completely. Did you call that guy yet?"

"I was all geared up, then Frank called. Now I want to call Janine and drink beer."

Erica laughed. "Chin up. He'll still be there tomorrow."

"Level with me: You really think meeting him is a good idea?"

"Mo, if he worked at the bus station or somewhere, I'd say no. But from what you've described, chances are he's not a criminal. Consider it a blind date. If you can't stand him, you never

47

have to see him again."

"And if he's a jerk and won't leave me alone, I can pull rank and have Frank tell Hollins."

"Now you're thinking."

NINE

Her heart pounded as she opened her planner the next morning and found Tom Chapman's cell phone listing. Regardless of her relationship with her father, butterflies plagued her whenever faced with a task of this sort. She was seconds away from placing the call when the secretary buzzed.

"Maureen, Craig's here."

She sighed. "Send him in."

Grantham entered a moment later. He was a short, good-looking guy in his late-thirties, always quick with a big, patronizing smile and transparent praise. She knew exactly why he was here and had a good idea of what he would say.

"Hi, Maureen," he said, taking one of the padded chairs across her desk. "Nice job on the bill. We've gotten some good press."

She forced a smile but said nothing.

"I know Frank sent you an e-mail the other day, but he's concerned that he didn't make clear how careful we need to be." A pause, as he smiled his loathsome smile. Grantham played his role to the hilt and didn't care if one saw right through the song and dance. "Maybe I need to spell out Sonny Hollins' importance a little better. Frank and I are probably at fault for not doing that."

"They go way back, Craig. That's no secret."

"Of course they do. And Sonny could have played either part in "Grumpy Old Men," he said, chuckling. "But he's someone we need to keep happy. President of the car dealers association. Tremendously influential in the Senate."

Maureen waited him out. Showing exasperation would only make this worse.

"I know Frank didn't give you an opportunity to tell your side of the story. If you can give me the condensed version, that would be helpful."

She studied him. Sounded like Frank was getting ready to see Hollins.

"A mechanic overheard the conversation I had with Gordon Smith, their service manager. The mechanic called the next day and said that there was a full-blown scam going on."

"What do you mean by full-blown scam?"

"Unnecessary repair work. Incorrect diagnoses. A whole bunch of things."

"Can you prove this?"

"The mechanic came in. We got a sworn statement from him. And a tape."

"So you sent a subpoena?" he said, raising an eyebrow.

"The subpoena simply asks for the records. The mechanic says this has been going on since last November. I asked for records going back through last August. This is standard operating procedure, Craig."

"Fair enough." Grantham smiled. "Is that tape handy? Like to let Frank hear it."

"It's in the car, and I've gotta leave for an appointment," she said, kicking herself. She knew she'd never see the original again if she turned it over to him. But if she had even a few minutes, she could rush home and copy it. "Can I get it to you later in the day?"

"Bring it by the office on your way back. Fair enough?"

"Consider it done."

TEN

"Tom Chapman. May I help you?"

"Hi, it's Maureen Lewis," she said from her car half an hour later, fighting to keep the nervousness from her voice. "Still up for coffee?"

"Sure! What day?"

"It's a little hard to plan right now. How about this morning?"

"Yeah, I can do that, uh, Maureen. Can I call you Maureen?"

She blushed. "Anything but 'Ms. Lewis.'"

"Will do. Late as it's getting, want to make it lunch?"

"I suppose so. How about Hal and Mal's at eleven-thirty?"

"Great. I'm six-two, medium build, dark hair. I'll be in a white dress shirt and khaki's."

"Got it. I'm five-two, auburn hair . . ."

"I know what you look like. I'll see you there."

* * *

She nosed her car into the crumbling parking lot an hour later. Someone wearing sunglasses and matching his description was standing on the wooden landing, gazing at the traffic on State Street with his arms folded. It had to be him. She walked carefully, praying she wouldn't trip in her heels. She took her time up the stairs, breathing an internal sigh of relief when she reached the top. The delicious smell of sauteed onions filled the air.

"Hi. Tom Chapman," the man said, sticking out his hand. Dressed and built just like he said, with a nice smile. The voice was pleasant, too.

"Maureen Lewis," she said, hoping her palm wasn't clammy.

"Nice to meet you. Let's get in line before it gets backed up." He turned to her a moment later. The designer shades were off now, revealing handsome brown eyes. "Glad you could come. Busy over there?"

"Always," Maureen said, removing her own sunglasses. They had beaten the lunch crowd, and she requested a corner booth in the back when the hostess asked if they had a seating preference. She hid behind the menu, nervous around this total stranger. A dark-haired waitress in jeans brought sweet tea and recommended the special, which was red beans and rice. Both opted for it, Tom adding a bowl of gumbo.

"I dress well for a vagrant, don't I?"

She forced a smile, still not comfortable yet. "What do you do at the dealership?"

"Make training videos, write press releases. The radio and television spots are made through an ad agency. My father has an agency in Columbus. That's the direction I'd like to go. I've sold radio and TV ads before."

"You're from Columbus?"

"I'm from here. Parents moved there when Dad opened the agency. What about you?"

"The Coast. Bay St. Louis."

He smiled again. "Went there for spring break once. How long you been with the A.G.'s Office? Been seeing you on TV for a couple of years, at least."

"Moved up here nine years ago. Been in Consumer the last seven."

He finished his gumbo and pushed the bowl away. "I hope this is okay. I don't have pictures of you all over my apartment or anything. There's no Maureen Lewis shrine."

She giggled. "That's good to know."

"For a while I thought you were with Emergency Management or something like that, because you were on TV every time I turned around after that tornado hit Meridian last fall. And the ice storm in the Delta."

"It's not as glamorous as people think. We spend a lot of time chasing shadows and working petty little cases."

"You're in management?"

A nod. "I have three investigators, and there's a staff attorney."

"Give them the petty little assignments?"

She smiled. "Not all of them. But none of us kill ourselves in state government. Took me a while to learn that. I suppose I'm a better manager than I used to be, because the troops are responding pretty well right now. Don't know how closely you keep up with the news, but the governor just signed our bill. The Consumer Protection Act."

He was nodding. "I saw Greene and Cash on the news the other day. Think I read something from you in the paper."

"That's a pretty big deal," she said evenly, careful to stay clear of pointing the conversation toward the car dealership. "My handiwork, actually. What we do is stop con artists and fraudulent business practices. The penalties are a lot more severe than they were, so everybody's got a little more zip in their step."

"Congratulations."

"Thanks. Is it fun making training videos?"

"I don't know if I'd call it fun. It's easy. My father thinks it's good experience." He wiped his mouth. "I suppose being a sales manager at a television station would interest me down the road. What about you? Want to be Attorney General?"

"Heavens, no. I'm no politician."

He smiled. "Hobbies?"

"Movies, I guess. Music. The Saints."

"Me, too, every year. Lose or lose. What kind of music do you like?"

"The old stuff. Crosby, Stills and Nash, Dan Fogelberg." She checked her watch and got to her feet. There was no hurry, but she had reached her comfort limit. "Gotta get back to work. Thanks for lunch. It was nice meeting you."

"You, too. I'll call again sometime, if that's okay."

She nodded and smiled, then departed.

* * *

Her private line rang the moment she walked in.

"It's me," Frank said, calling from his car. "Sonny has agreed to let you see the records."

A grin spread across Maureen's face. She waited him out, passing on a variety of sarcastic responses she longed to use.

"So you should have them in a couple of days."

"Good."

"And you'll stay in close touch with me on what you find, if anything."

"Yes, sir."

ELEVEN

Jeff handed Maureen a VHS cassette of the new Walker Brothers ad the next morning. Walker Brothers was a Jackson family business with a dozen locations around the state. They saturated all forms of media with their campaigns, running several specials a month on washers and dryers, air-conditioners, televisions and stereo equipment.

"AT WALKER BROTHERS, WE'RE OVERLOADED WITH WIDE-SCREEN PROJECTION SCREEN TV'S! WE'VE GOT TO MOVE 'EM, SO FOR A LIMITED TIME ONLY, WE'RE SELLING THEM TO YOU, OUR LOYAL CUSTOMERS, FOR LESS THAN WHAT IT COSTS TO MAKE THEM! YOU HEARD RIGHT . . .WIDE-SCREEN THIRTY-FIVE INCH PROJECTION TELEVISION SCREENS, FOR LESS THAN WHAT IT COSTS TO MAKE THEM!"

Disclaimers were carefully positioned to identify which models were available during the sale, but Maureen didn't even watch the entire ad. She smiled at Jeff.

"Less than it costs to make them? Pretty creative. You saw this at home?"

"It was all over the news last night. I knew you'd want a copy, so I called Channel Two."

"Thanks. Nice work."

She left Frank a voice-mail. He returned her call late that afternoon.

"And the ad specifically says that they're selling the big-screens for less than it costs to make them? That's pretty outrageous."

"Yes, sir. There's absolutely no way . . ."

"I have no doubt. Your call, Maureen. Do what you think is fair."

This was the last thing she expected after the episode with Sonny Hollins. "I want the ads pulled. I'm thinking ten thousand dollars, Frank, since this is a first-time offense. They try this again and we hit them harder."

"You have my blessing."

She stared at the receiver before responding. "Good. I'll call now and pay them a visit in the morning."

* * *

The oldest Walker brother was the general manager. He was angry, but he backed down when Maureen mentioned that her actions had the backing of the Attorney General. His lawyer urged him to agree to the suggested civil penalty, rather than fight in court and bring the negative publicity a lawsuit would generate. She arrived at the office before noon and stepped around a mountain of boxes in the foyer.

"The Capital City records," the secretary said. "Took those men ten minutes to get everything here."

She glanced around the otherwise empty office. She'd given

assignments yesterday afternoon in lieu of a morning meeting.

"Page everybody, tell 'em to get here as soon as they can wrap up what they're doing. Hope nobody has any weekend plans."

* * *

Maureen and her staff spent the next three days on the Capital City paperwork, searching for abusive billing patterns. They took short breaks for lunch and supper, which Maureen paid for. By Saturday night she was grouchy.

"So what determinations can we make at this point?" she said, leaning back and rubbing her eyes.

"That Sonny Hollins is an asshole," Paul said.

"Seriously."

"The overcharging went into effect in December," Jeff said, adjusting his glasses. "The across the board five hundred dollar increases had to be Christmas bonuses. Indicative of the fact they were all going to get rich real soon."

Maureen nodded. "What can we tell about the service itself? Any idea how much money is being made from it?"

"We'd probably have to go back farther to get enough repeat customers to really know, but strictly in terms of makes and models? Eye-popping numbers," Ashleigh said. Maureen was surprised she was still here; eight months pregnant and unmotivated under normal conditions, Ashleigh nonetheless had been here the whole time and seemed as enthused as anyone. "Take the Preludes, the ninety-nines, specifically. Twelve had the 30,000 mile routine maintenance done before December, and eight have had it since. Best I can tell, customers are paying two- to three hundred percent more than they were."

"But that ain't nothing compared to what we're finding on the older cars," Paul said.

Maureen glanced at Sherry.

"I've found at least two dozen older Civics and Accords–including Mr. Randle's–which had massive amounts of work done that clearly cost hundreds less five, six months ago."

"Any insurance cases?"

"Almost none. If the car gets totaled, they deal with the insurance company. Can't make any money that way."

Maureen got to her feet and stretched. "Okay, gang. We're done. Nice work, all of you. Two comp days. Fair enough?"

Appreciative murmurs from around the table. Ashleigh lingered in the doorway as the others departed. She was a tall, strikingly pretty girl, with long, black hair and blue eyes. Maureen didn't like her attitude and had butted heads with her in the past, but she seemed to have taken a genuine interest in this case and proved helpful.

"You can use those days any time, Ash. Take a long weekend if you want, or tack 'em on to your leave."

"I'll let you know." She zipped her jogging suit and slung her purse over her shoulder. "Pretty crummy what they're doing over there. You gonna stick it to them?"

Maureen glanced up and smiled. "I'll talk to Frank Monday. We'll send a message. Have a good weekend."

TWELVE

Cash's office was on the fifth floor of the Gartin building. The Supreme Court, where Erica clerked, was on the third floor, and it was not uncommon to share an elevator ride with a member of the Court. The building was modern and maintained with more care than its counterpart on North State, and Cash occasionally gave press conferences on its front steps.

Maureen confirmed an appointment with her boss and stepped off the elevator early Monday afternoon. She was shown into his office immediately. It was spacious and impressive, with an oak desk, leather sofa, a mahogany coffee table and matching chairs. There were shelves with law books, journals and artifacts from his years in politics and the legal profession. Plaques and citations lined the walls, and pictures of his wife Joyce and their teenaged daughter were on his desk. He had a fantastic view of the Capitol.

"Hello, Maureen," he said, rising from behind the desk and offering his hand. The jacket was off, the tie loosened. "How are things at 802?"

"Busy. But nothing we can't handle," she said easily, making herself comfortable across from him. It was a perfunctory question and didn't merit more than a generic response. The fact that he was making small talk was a good sign. He cut directly to the chase when hostile, as was the case a week ago.

"Glad to hear it. I really appreciate all the hard work you put into the bill."

"Thank you."

"So what brings you here? Capital City?"

Maureen opened her briefcase and removed a manila folder. "This won't make you happy, but I hope you'll read it thoroughly before making a decision."

Cash grunted, removing the three typed sheets. She knew he'd discovered the dollar figure when his eyes widened. He started to speak, then stopped. He read the first page and was halfway through the second when his phone rang.

"I was about to call you. Come down here in ten minutes. Thanks."

He returned to Maureen's memo, heaving a sigh as he finished. She waited him out, watching as he leaned back in his chair and put his hands behind his head. He stared up at the ceiling.

"A hundred thousand bucks? Damn, Maureen. Why not ask a million?"

She kept her mouth shut. Eventually he lowered his gaze

to hers.

"I've known you for years," he said slowly. "You're a fair, decent person, and you do a terrific job. And I've never, ever known you to go out of your way to hurt someone, and I don't believe you're trying to do that now."

"No, sir."

"But, Maureen," he said, rising from behind the desk. He came around and sat next to her. "Sonny Hollins sees this, you know what he says? 'This means war.'"

A tight nod.

"I can't have that in this office. He's a major player in this town. Maybe you don't realize the clout he has. Not just with me, but in the House. Especially the Senate. Craig had to bend every which way to get him on board when he was shopping your bill in the Senate. Because when Sonny finally said he'd support it—rather reluctantly—that brought on more than just a bunch of lobbyists. It brought Senators who likely wouldn't have been with you. Without Sonny, we might not have this Consumer Protection Act. And I don't think I have to tell you there's an election eight months away. We'd all like to be here another four years."

Acid burned in her gut.

"You're convinced beyond the shadow of a doubt that Sonny has this serious a problem down there?"

"Yes, sir."

"And you realize you're asking a hundred grand, even though the maximum in the bill is fifty?"

She sighed. "Based on the extreme nature of this offense, and the fact that it's open-ended, I think it's justified. He's on pace to make more than a million dollars in unnecessary repair work this year. A million, Frank."

"He'll fight this tooth and nail."

"I don't think so, sir. He doesn't want a lawsuit. You've said that yourself about the car dealers."

A long, contemplative silence from the Attorney General. Then he got to his feet. Startled, so did Maureen.

"Let me get back to you," he said, suddenly gracing her with his media smile. "I certainly appreciate your hard work. I'm not sure there's another soul in the office who puts this much effort into a project."

"Thank you," she said. It was a nice compliment, but rang hollow. "So I'll wait to hear back from you, I guess."

"Give me a few days. And keep up the good work, Maureen."

THIRTEEN

The following night Cash and Joyce journeyed to Lake Caroline in Madison County, where Sonny Hollins maintained a luxurious home on several acres of land. Joyce and Hollins' spouse knew each other well from years of socializing and chatted in the kitchen as dinner was prepared. Hollins led Frank to his game room, which featured a projection-screen television, club chairs, a full bar and a pool table. A spectacular view of the lake was visible during daylight hours. He closed the door and made drinks.

"So what's on your mind, Frankie?"

"Maureen Lewis seems to think the folks in your garage aren't playing by the rules."

Hollins racked the balls and broke them, sinking two and coming close to making a third. He allowed a satisfied smile.

"You care to guess the kind of money she wants?"

"Make me laugh."

"A hundred thousand dollars." A pause. "She has a tape. It ain't pretty, Sonny."

Hollins pocketed two more balls, his soft touch giving way

to aggression as he missed an easy shot. He was flushed when he looked up.

"I get my hands on the son of a bitch who talked, he won't know the meaning of torture when I'm through with him."

Cash missed a shot, then gazed back. "That tape never sees the light of day, and I shut Maureen Lewis down—if I can count on some more help. Soon."

"How much?"

"Fifty."

A grunt. "And you'll keep that bitch off our asses?"

"Never let you down before."

Hollins ran the table, blasting the eight ball into the far corner pocket. "All right. But I'm serious, Frank: There'll be real trouble if she turns up the heat."

FOURTEEN

Maureen discovered messages from Tom and Janine when she arrived at work the next morning. Both asked her to the Mal's St. Paddy's Parade & Festival, which was Saturday. She was mulling this over when Frank's secretary rang her private line.

"He's going out of town in half an hour. Wanted to know if you could get over here for just a minute."

Ten minutes later she stepped off the elevator in Cash's office, checking her face in a hand-held mirror. This likely had to do with Capital City, and she wished she'd had some warning. She felt more confident when dressed up, but she would have to make do in the white button-down, olive slacks and plaid blazer she'd thrown on this morning.

"Good morning!" Frank said brightly, in the foyer as she

arrived. He showed her into his office and closed the door. "You remember Nathan McMichael."

"Hello, Ms. Lewis," McMichael said in his drawl, rising and offering his hand.

"Mr. McMichael," she said, barely managing a handshake and ignoring Grantham altogether. McMichael was the Executive Director of the Motor Vehicle Administration. It was his job to regulate the state's car dealerships, although he reportedly spent the lion's share of his time playing golf and drinking with the local dealers. His appearance was an immediate indication that Cash wouldn't be sinking his teeth into Hollins.

Cash returned behind his desk, gesturing for Grantham and Maureen to take the seats across from him. McMichael made himself comfortable on the sofa. He crossed his legs, a self-important smile on his face.

"Maureen, we've arrived at a decision," Cash said quickly. "We realize you won't be crazy about it, but we think this is best for all concerned."

McMichael smirked, a gesture intentionally lacking in subtlety. He clearly knew about the proposed penalty, and he had the nerve to thumb his nose at her. Her jaw tightened.

"This is a little broader than Capital City," Grantham said, offering his smile. "Ultimately, Nathan is to regulate the car dealers. That's what his office was designed to do. And as busy as you and your staff are going to be with the myriad of projects you'll take on over the next few months, you'll still have plenty to do."

Maureen could barely sit still. She flicked a glance at the grinning McMichael, ready to punch him, then turned to Grantham. "You can't be serious. You're not putting this guy in charge of the car dealers, are you?"

Cash's smile faded. He gazed at Maureen, then settled on Grantham. "Why don't you and Nathan go down to your office. I'll buzz you on my way out."

Grantham nodded at McMichael, who was sulking after Maureen's comment. The men left the room, leaving the Attorney General alone with her. He remained behind his desk.

"I have the utmost respect for what you do in this office, Maureen, but . . ."

"This is Craig's idea, isn't it?" she said quickly.

Cash's eyes narrowed. "It's my decision. And I strongly suggest you take a good look at the bigger picture, rather than getting so wrapped up in seeing things done your way."

Maureen looked away, biting her tongue. Cash got to his feet. The meeting was over.

"Frank, with all due respect, sir, it really concerns me that you're bringing McMichael into this. I fully assumed you wanted to talk about Capital City . . ."

"Nathan will handle that. Nathan will handle all dealings with the car dealers, effective immediately. You are to pass along any complaints you receive about Capital City and anyone else to him. Craig and I will be staying in close touch with him." He put on his jacket and picked up his briefcase, gesturing at the door. "What I need from you is to concentrate on the other aspects of Consumer. And Craig's right—there are plenty of them."

* * *

Furious, she squealed out of the Gartin parking lot. She stalked through 802 and sat at her desk, lowering her face into her hands.

"Maureen?" Sherry said, knocking on the open door.

"What?"

"Channel Thirteen ran a Capital City ad this morning that didn't sound right. I'm going out there to get a copy now. Said something about selling cars for less than it costs to make them."

Maureen's head snapped up.

"They're gonna be in some hot water, aren't they?"

* * *

An hour later Maureen slid the cassette into the VCR, her adrenaline flowing.

"CAPITAL CITY MOTORS HAS A PROBLEM! WE'RE OVERSTOCKED WITH 2000 ACCORDS, AND WE'VE GOT TO MOVE 'EM! SO RIGHT NOW WE'LL SELL YOU A BRAND-NEW 2000 ACCORD FOR LESS THAN IT COSTS US TO MAKE THEM! YOU HEARD RIGHT . . . A 2000 ACCORD FOR LESS THAN IT COSTS TO MAKE THEM!"

She was so angry she could hardly stand still. She rewound the tape and watched a second time. Disclaimers were carefully positioned to identify which models were on sale, but the pitch was repeated three times and plastered on the screen twice. She ejected the tape and turned to Sherry, trying to hold her tongue.

"Thank you. I'll let Frank know."

FIFTEEN

Erica owned a house in a Madison subdivision twenty minutes from North Jackson, not far from Jeff's friend Mr. Randle. Maureen joined her for supper that night and once again took in the surroundings. The contemporary furniture, Monet prints and imitation Oriental rug were all well within her means, as was the mortgage payment. She just couldn't imagine buying a house without a husband to share it with, but that clearly wasn't a problem for Erica.

"Can I help with anything?" she said, plopping down on a stool in the kitchen. It was loaded with gadgets, and Erica was making bread to complement the lasagna already in the oven.

"Just make yourself comfortable. More wine?"

"Not unless I want to spend the night."

"So what's this about getting out of Consumer? Or do you just need to vent?"

She sighed. "How am I supposed to face my investigators? What do I tell the consumers?"

"Send them to McMichael, just like Frank said. And tell your staff the same thing. This is politics, Mo, nothing more. You know that."

"I just wish they'd taken Consumer this seriously before I went to the trouble of writing the damned bill. Know what Frank said? That I should look at the big picture, rather than focus so much on the way I want things done."

Erica faced her. "Any truth to that? You are a control freak, you know."

"It isn't fair," she said quietly, pouting. "Of course it's neat to see my name in the paper when we've socked someone who was up to no good. But what about Jeff's neighbor? What about that old woman in Byram who's raising her grandkids? She's out a thousand dollars she doesn't have because those bastards purposely won't fix her car!"

"I didn't say it was fair."

"What angers me the most is that TV ad. That one's for me— I just know it. 'Screw you, Ms. Lewis,'" she said, spitting the words.

"Maybe so. But let's go back to why we went to Law School in the first place. You remember?"

Maureen nodded, her eyes closed.

"If we could help one person at a time, we'd make a big difference. And with this bill, you've made a lot of difference. Okay, the car dealers may be out of reach. But the people you wanted to help the most—the elderly, the poor, the uneducated— they're the ones using the check-cashing services and the cheap furniture stores with the spiked interest rates. And you can still jump on those businesses with both feet. It's obvious Frank'll let you do that."

Maureen was silent.

"And the Consumer Act is yours. Not Craig's, even though he got it through the Senate, and not Frank's, even though he'll blather all day when it suits him politically. Nobody can ever take it away from you."

"Wish you'd been in Frank's office to say all that," Maureen said. She frowned, noting that Erica was setting the kitchen table for two. "Keith gonna be late?"

"He and a buddy are bowling. Told him we needed a little time together."

"Thank you. You guys going to the parade?"

"If the weather holds up."

"Want some company? Tom called—I'll see if he wants to go. You guys can judge whether or not he's on the level."

Erica grinned. "You're on."

SIXTEEN

The heavy rain in Saturday's forecast arrived on schedule, drenching the rowdy crowd. Loaded with purple beads and full of green beer, Maureen, Tom, Erica and Keith scrambled back toward Hal & Mal's, which served as the starting point of the parade. They piled into Keith's Explorer and opted for billiards at a reservoir club, followed by spicy crawfish and more beer. Nothing from Tom indicated what was coming.

"Dancing?" he said at the end of the meal, draining his glass of beer.

"We're gonna call it a night," Erica said, long since having given Maureen a subtle thumbs-up when Tom's back was turned.

"We're old folks. Maybe another time, though."

They dropped Maureen and Tom at Gartin, where Maureen had suggested he leave his car. It was the only one in the lot.

"Late movie?" he said, shielding his eyes from the rain, which was falling again.

"I'll fall asleep." She hesitated. "Come over for a minute, if you want."

He drove her to the apartment complex, entering after she punched numbers on the keypad and opened the security gate. She entered the combination on the foyer door, opened her apartment and flipped on a desk lamp, rousing her elderly tomcat. He grunted and trotted away.

She turned to face him, shaking the rain out of her hair. "Anything to drink?"

Tom kissed her. She stared at him. He did it again a moment later, drawing her closer. Shock and excitement powered through her veins. Suddenly his tongue was in her mouth. A moment later she pulled back, flushed.

"Water would be fine," he said casually.

She stumbled into the kitchen and retrieved a glass, nearly dropping it. An ice cube tumbled to the Berber carpet as she presented it to him, her hands shaking. He smiled and made himself comfortable on the love seat. She ducked back into the kitchen and fanned herself, then joined him.

"TV? Music?"

She reached for the remote and knocked it onto the floor. She leaned over to pick it up, now beet-red. He pinched her behind, causing her to chirp in surprise. She jerked, nearly knocking the water from the glass coffee table.

"Stop it!"

She stared straight ahead, looking for the Weather Channel. The local forecast appeared a moment later. Rain blanketed the state, with more to come.

"Nice place you have here. Love the shot of the beach. Use

the fireplace much?"

"Never have, actually."

"I probably wouldn't, either. Enjoy the parade?"

She turned to him, trying to hide how flustered she was. "It was fun. You don't have any trouble finding a party, do you?"

"When I'm in the mood. What about you, Wild Thing?"

"I know sarcasm when I hear it," she said. "Is the word "square" stamped across my forehead?"

"Not at all. The image I have of you is in a suit, I suppose. Enjoyed meeting your friends, by the way."

Goodness, he changed gears quickly. Was it the beer? "Erica and I go way back."

"She and the guy serious?"

"They're engaged. He's divorced, has kids."

"Is she?"

"An old maid. Like me," she said, a half-smile on her face.

"I'm surprised."

She blushed. "You know where flattery will get you."

"I'm serious," he said, sitting closer. He took her hand and played with her fingers. "You're a good catch. You're either too caught up in your career, or you've been hurt."

"We've all been hurt, I guess," she said carefully. "What about you, Mr. Mysterious? Tell me a little about yourself before you start probing my past."

"I'm divorced."

This took her by surprise. "Really? I had no idea."

"Three years ago. That's about how long we lasted. Got serious too fast and married right out of school. I fit her needs when we met. I didn't six months later. Hung on as long as I could, then gave her the divorce. What about you? I guess you'd have said if you had a serious boyfriend."

She reached for the water. "I don't date that much. You're right about the career."

"Hard to meet a decent man, isn't it? I almost didn't call

because I wasn't sure you'd even talk to me."

She considered her response. "There's no way to know what anybody's about these days. And nobody wants to lower their standards." She didn't dare touch on the problems with her father. "I've met a couple of nice men at church—that's where Erica met Keith—and once in a while a mutual friend comes up with someone. That's how I met my last boyfriend," she said, omitting the fact that Richard was her only serious romance. The actual dates she had been on since their disastrous breakup could be counted on one hand.

Lightning flashed close by. A huge clap of thunder startled both of them. Then the power went off. Tom threw back his head and laughed.

"I was just about to tell you how attracted I am to you. Maybe that's not a good sign."

Maureen swallowed involuntarily, feeling sweat on her forehead. This reminded her of her first date in high school. They sat in silence for the next minute, Maureen staring straight ahead. She jumped as he touched her hand.

"I'm very attracted to you," he said softly.

He pulled her closer, ever so gently. His hand cupped the small of her back as he leaned in and kissed her. He kissed her cheek before shifting her. Now she was in his arms, his hands around her waist. He kissed the top of her head, then her ear.

"Stop," she said softly.

He backed away. She got to her feet and shook her head. She felt along the coffee table and found the glass, then edged into the kitchen. She gulped down more water before returning. Now Tom was on his feet.

"Maybe I need to go."

What to do, what to do. She cursed herself for being so inexperienced. He was probably embarrassed, not likely to ever call again.

"No," she said, just audibly enough for him to hear. "Don't."

"You sure?"

"I'm sorry. I'm shy," she said, arriving at a comfortable description of her fear and excitement.

"Not the lady I watch on TV," he said, a smile in his voice.

"That's easy. I'm talking to a reporter. Not a . . ."

"Not a psycho who has a Maureen Lewis shrine in his living room," he said, laughing. Another kiss on the neck. This time she ran her hands through his hair and pressed herself against him.

"Tom?"

"Yes?"

A long moment. "I'm very attracted to you, too."

SEVENTEEN

She managed smiles and polite conversation the next morning before turning down his offer of breakfast. She told him to give her a call. She dashed for the bathroom as soon as he left, getting sick. Nerves, she was sure, and the beer from last night. She felt well enough later in the day to call Erica and reveal the news. Erica was astounded. Yes, he had used a condom. Had one in his wallet. No, she hadn't asked if he'd put it there with her in mind. She didn't want to know.

Back to reality Monday morning. There was a complaint from a consumer who was angry at what he considered dirty pool from Hamilton Ford, a truck dealership in North Jackson. Maureen didn't even let the man finish his story about the rebate in the newspaper ad—she cut him off and gave him McMichael's name and credentials. When he called again five minutes later, angrier still because he was forced to talk to a recording, it was all she could do not to send him directly to Cash.

"How was the parade?" Janine said, calling just before lunch.

Maureen's first smile of the morning. "Interesting. Have to fill you in."

"You can do that tonight at the baseball game. Ole Miss and State—the Mayor's Trophy Cup. How does a couple of beers and a hot dog sound, plus the chance to yell at those stooges from Starkville?"

"Terrific," she said, laughing.

*   *   *

Smith-Wills Stadium was packed, but Janine directed Maureen to a pair of corporate seats behind home plate with a great view. The annual game between the state's largest schools brought more people to the park in one night than the local independent team did in a week, and electricity was in the air. The smell of cheap beer and hot dogs lingered. Maureen's mouth watered, and she waved at a leather-lunged vendor who was hawking peanuts.

"Business or pleasure first?"

"Pleasure. You look too happy to talk business."

Janine laughed. "That's coming. An old flame of mine—a college boyfriend, before the ex—called out of the blue. He's moving to Jackson next month!"

"Great!"

"I tried not to show how excited I was—saved that 'til after I hung up and danced on the ceiling," Janine said, smiling broadly. "He's with a bank. Last time I talked to him—fifteen years ago—I'd just started with the paper. We're having lunch when he gets here."

"What's his name?"

"Grant. Divorced, also has kids. I'll keep you posted." Janine dug into her hot dog. "So did the guy come to the parade?"

Maureen nodded.

"Have a good time?"

Maureen nodded again, nothing on her face.

"Well?"

"He's great in bed," she said, lowering her voice.

Janine spilled beer down the front of her shirt. She squeezed Maureen's hand, grinning from ear to ear. "Did I hear you right?"

Maureen blushed. She looked around before speaking. "I don't know what came over me. The way he looked at me, the way he touched me—holy smokes."

Janine lowered her voice. "I'm gonna get all hot and bothered, you keep talking like that."

Maureen giggled, breaking open another peanut. "He spent the night, and I did well not to freak out the next morning when I realized he was in my bed."

Janine squeezed her shoulder. "Good for you. All you needed was a little encouragement from Aunt Janine."

"Seems like a decent guy. I'd like to think I wouldn't jump in bed with someone who wasn't. It's not like I have a lengthy history with men," she said self-consciously. She took a big bite of hot dog and changed gears, describing the meeting with Cash, Grantham and McMichael. Janine's smile disappeared.

"You're right about McMichael—he's worthless. His idea of riding herd over the car dealers is guzzling martinis with them." Janine applauded as Ole Miss loaded the bases. "This is what I wanted to tell you: I'm doing a story for Friday about campaign contributions. Did you know Cash has ten times as much money in his war chest as Brandon Buckhalter already?"

"I've heard he's concerned, but I can't believe to that extent. Buckhalter is a nobody, outside Vicksburg legal circles."

"And speaking of car dealers, there was a $50,000 contribution from Sonny Hollins, dated this past Friday."

Maureen stared. She barely reacted as the Ole Miss batter smashed a pitch over the wall for a grand slam home run. She spoke when the applause began to die down.

"Hollins jumped Frank the minute I brought the subpoena! Frank sent Craig, and Craig's eyes popped open when I said I had a tape of the mechanic. Now I wish I hadn't said anything."

"You made a copy, I hope."

"You bet your booty I did." She leaned closer. "Janine, I was proposing a one hundred thousand dollar penalty for what's going on in Hollins' garage. Now it's out the window, and there's suddenly a fifty thousand dollar donation from Hollins in Frank's campaign account?"

Janine whistled to herself.

"And some guy called this morning, pissed off at the new Hamilton Ford ad in the paper. I sent him to McMichael like Frank told me to. Guy called back this afternoon, furious. Said he's gotten the recording all day and wants to know what I'm going to do about it."

Ole Miss was continuing to score, but Janine wasn't paying attention now. Her brown eyes, usually so warm, were all business.

"Hon', if you ever get ready to go on the record with this—if it doesn't cost you your job—let me know."

EIGHTEEN

As much as she tried to concentrate on the small projects, Maureen found herself paying attention to the car-related complaints. There were more calls about Hamilton Ford. Capital City service complaints continued to stream in, and consumers were angry and frustrated that there was no way to speak with Nathan McMichael.

A grueling workout with Erica the night after the baseball game did little to make her feel better. A glass of wine and the harmonies of Crosby, Stills & Nash also failed to ease her mind. She retrieved the cassette of the Capital City mechanic from her briefcase, muted the music and plopped into the recliner. She was seconds into the tape when the intercom buzzer startled her.

"Yes?"

"It's me," Tom said. "You in the middle of anything?"

"Don't you know how to use the phone?"

"Just thought I'd stop in."

"How'd you get in, anyway? You memorize the code?"

A pause. "Look, if this isn't a good time . . ."

She depressed the buzzer. A moment later he appeared at her door. He was still dressed from work.

"Come in, I guess." She was in a tank top and plaid shorts, with no bra, no makeup and glasses instead of contact lenses. She gestured at herself. "This is what you get for showing up with no notice."

He grinned. He stepped closer, leaning in for a kiss. She stood firm.

"Hold your horses, young man. If you thought you'd just show up and get a little action on your way home for the day, you're badly mistaken."

He stepped back, a trace of the smile still on his face. Did he find this funny?

"Seriously, try some flowers or a nice meal. I refuse to be someone's entry in their little black book."

Now the smile was gone. He started out.

"Tom!" she said, following him into the foyer. "Forgive me. I've had a rotten day."

He turned around. "I wasn't thinking that far ahead, honest. How 'bout some yogurt?"

She glanced at herself again.

"Go fix yourself up. Sounds like you need to get out for a while."

* * *

An hour later they returned to the apartment. Their small talk, though mindless at times, made her feel better. Even his gloating about Mississippi State's remarkable comeback to beat Ole Miss didn't bother her.

"I started to call you. Didn't know if you were a baseball fan."

"At least you considered using the phone," she said with a wink. "Come in and cheer me up some more."

She led him directly to the bedroom. Minutes later she clung to him. They were both gasping for breath.

"You can take your bad mood out on me any time," he said in a burst of quiet.

She laughed but remained silent. He spoke five minutes later, still holding her.

"So what's going on in that pretty little head of yours? I can hear the wheels turning."

She got to her feet and disappeared into the bathroom. She returned a moment later in a robe. "Glass of wine?"

"Sure. How 'bout some music?"

"CD's are in the cabinet next to the TV."

He was in his boxers when she appeared with the wine. The tape! It was still in the deck and carefully labeled. She inched toward him, then yanked his shorts up. He yelped, jumping backward. She discreetly removed the cassette and slid it behind the components.

"What the hell got into you?" he said in disbelief.

"I generally don't have men running around here in their boxers. I'm in a Van Morrison mood. Can you handle that?"

"Sure, as soon as I get my shorts out of my stomach."

She giggled, sipped her wine and was quiet, allowing him to slide an arm around her.

"You still haven't answered me, gorgeous. What's happening under all that red hair?"

Maureen was replaying the conversation with Janine at the ballpark. "Nothing, really. Just a long day."

"I'm a good listener."

She leaned up and kissed his cheek, then rested her head on his shoulder. "You're a good lover, too."

"I'm serious. Try me."

"Tom, it's nothing. Some things I just need to leave at the office. Still learning how to do that."

He kissed the top of her head and was still. She breathed an internal sigh of relief and closed her eyes.

NINETEEN

At that moment Ashleigh Dunn's husband Warren Mullins looked over the grocery list from a sofa in their upscale North Jackson home. Warren had spent the last hour working at the computer while Ashleigh was stretched out in front of the projection-screen television, nibbling from a bag of potato chips. She was in sweats, her bloated stomach a hideous sight. An afghan covered her feet.

"And that's all the cravings you can think of?" Mullins said, a tall, fit, blond man in his early forties. He was a stockbroker and proud of the fact that he'd swept the daughter of one of the state's most influential people off her feet.

"My feet are craving to be rubbed." She batted her eyes at him. "Ben & Jerry's is three for five bucks, according to the circular."

"Your blood sugar, remember, Ash? One more week, then you can have all you want."

The hint of a frown. "My sugar is fine. Don't be gone long."

Ashleigh muted the television as her husband drove away and

dialed Grantham. He was still at his desk.

"Hi. Thought he'd never leave." A pause. "Thought Maureen was gonna lose her shit today."

"How so?"

Ashleigh laughed. "Call after call about the service thing, and they call back all pissed off when they get Nathan's machine. Her door was closed, but I could hear her telling herself to take deep breaths and relax."

"She can handle it."

"When are you gonna talk to her?"

"Don't worry about it."

Ashleigh frowned. "Look, Craig, don't play hard to get."

"Ashleigh, you will be Director of Consumer Protection when you come back from maternity leave, and Maureen will be safely tucked away where you'll have no contact with her and where she'll have no influence. This had Frank's blessing weeks ago," he said, annoyed. "Why do we have to go over it each time we talk?"

"So our esteemed Attorney General won't forget. He has a lot on his mind."

"What's that supposed to mean?"

"Nothing. I trust you'll get everything taken care of."

"For the last time, it won't be a problem."

Her grin broadened. "You gonna make it watching that little video of us, since you can't have the real thing until the doc says so?"

Grantham took his time. "I wish I had video of you with your legs spread, begging for my tongue."

Ashleigh giggled. "And you'll still have me with all the baby fat? I won't be your slim, trim sex toy for a while."

"More to love."

She laughed. "A whole lot more. Anyway, just take care of Maureen. She's been on her private line a lot the last few days. I don't want her fucking this up for everybody."

"Got it."

"Good. Sweet dreams." She smiled. "Make that wet dreams. About me."

TWENTY

A scam perpetrated by Metro Cablevision tied Maureen up the rest of the week, as did a pair of out of town luncheons. Flowers from Tom arrived Friday, with an invitation for a "nice meal on the town" over the weekend.

"Well, what have we here?" Ashleigh said, grinning as she inspected the spring arrangement. She was in a jogging suit, saying goodbye to the staff in a leisurely fashion. Maureen forced a smile, ready for her to be on her way. "Tom, huh? When do we get to meet him?"

"He just earned another date with the flowers."

Ashleigh snorted. "I can count the number of times on one hand I've gotten flowers from Warren, but I guess that's what old married couples do."

"You haven't been married two years, Ash."

A wink. "Just seems like a hundred, Maureen. Let me give you a hug. I don't know how you stay so slim."

"Hardly."

"You look great. And I'm the size of Rhode Island. When I'm moving around again we'll play that set of tennis we've never gotten around to."

Another forced smile. "Any time. Give my best to Warren."

* * *

The candlelight dinner at the Italian restaurant in Ridgeland seemed like something from a movie. He was a gentleman all night, opening doors and holding chairs for her. They drank a bottle of wine with the meal and opened another at her apartment. Concerned about his capacity to drive and yearning for his touch, she asked him to stay.

He awakened first the next morning. Reluctant to rouse her, he padded into the living room, fed the cat and ran the channels. He nosed around the stereo cabinet and found a pair of headphones above the cassette deck. A lone tape was visible. He eyed the label.

CAPITAL CITY MOTORS (RONNIE LANDRUM)
3/13/01—ORIGINAL

His adrenaline flowed. Hollins would want to know what this was about. He donned the headphones and muted the speakers, positioning himself where he would see her stir in time to stop the tape. Then he listened.

TWENTY ONE

The office was more efficient with Ashleigh on leave, and Maureen tried to concentrate on only what she could control. An electric company was busted in mid-April, leading to a substantial civil penalty and attention from the press. Tornado damage in Forest a week later resulted in price gouging by con artists who appeared as quickly as termites, and her staff was all over them. Nearly everyone settled rather than taking their chances in court, and money poured into the Attorney General's Office.

"You're doing an amazing job," Cash said, smiling across his desk. It was Monday, May first. She had been summoned as soon as she arrived at work. "Folks at the Better Business Bureau think we should elect you queen."

"I've heard from half a dozen civic and community leaders in Forest who think you walk on water," Grantham said, his smile in place.

Maureen nodded. She prepared for bad news, perhaps that there wouldn't be enough in the budget for a raise. No big deal; she drew a nice salary, and she had her eye on the U.S. Attorney's Office in the future.

"This is probably going to come as a surprise," Cash said. He stepped from behind the desk, sitting on its front. Now they were cozy, almost intimate. "There's a position I'd like to offer you this morning: Director of Consumer Litigation."

"Maureen, this is something we've created especially for you," Grantham said. "You'll be in charge of all criminal and civil cases coming out of Consumer, and with your work ethic and knowledge of the department—as well as your love of the court-room—we think it would fit you like a glove."

"We know you want to be in court more," Cash said. "We've known that from the day you started. This would get you there, away from a desk full of paperwork and a calendar of speeches. I'll also move you over here. High time we got you out of 802."

Maureen stared, moving from Cash to Grantham. More money, more time in court, and an office in Gartin? This sound-ed too good to be true.

"Who would I report to?"

"Craig and me," Cash said. "But you'd be your own boss."

"And I'd choose the cases we'd handle."

It was a statement, not a question. Cash hesitated briefly, then shook his head. "Craig will do that. I'll sign off on them."

A frown spread across her face. "You just said I'd be my own boss."

Grantham jumped in again. "Maureen, we're convinced that in a short period of time you'd grow into a comfort zone which . . ."

"I'm not real sure about this," she said, addressing the Attorney General. "From what you're describing, I'm probably better off where I am."

Grantham glanced at Cash, then turned to Maureen. Now the smile was gone. "That's not going to be an option."

Maureen's eyes flashed. She zeroed in on Grantham, trying to read him. Cash eased a bit closer. "Ashleigh Dunn will become Consumer Protection Director effective July first," he said.

Maureen's jaw dropped open. She stared at her boss, then Grantham. Both gazed back, nothing to read on their faces.

"Did I hear right? Ashleigh? What the hell is going on here?"

"We are promoting Ashleigh, just as we promoted you seven years ago. We've gone to great lengths to establish a position which would benefit you as well as this office," Grantham said. His voice now carried a warning. "We strongly recommend you take a hard look at it."

"And if I don't?"

Cash sighed, tenting his fingers. "We'd hate to lose you. And we know you're a lot more qualified than Human Services . . ."

"I'm not working in Human Services!"

". . . but that's the only other position we have open which would pay you anything close to what you're making now. I'd like an answer by the end of the week."

Maureen heaved a harsh sigh. She got to her feet and strode from the room, leaving the door open. Cash closed it. He placed his hands on Grantham's shoulders.

"This better not come back to bite us. Do you understand me?"

"It won't, Frank. You have my word."

TWENTY TWO

The motel across the street from the Capitol had served as home away from home to the state's legislators for years. Many had regular rooms when in session. Hamilton Dunn, the former Senator from Jackson, kept a room while in office. Dunn consummated several affairs there, the last with a leggy paralegal who was dating a law student named Craig Grantham. Grantham, then twenty-four, became enraged upon learning that he had been dumped in favor of the Senator.

He anonymously clued in Eleanor Dunn, a socialite and vindictive sort who immediately launched messy divorce proceedings against her husband. He attempted to get back at the Senator further by pursuing their daughter Ashleigh, then an undergraduate at Mississippi College. Their on-again, off-again fling continued after thirteen years, despite the fact that both were married and Ashleigh had just given birth to a child.

Grantham arrived at noon and paid cash for his room. He was sprawled across the bed reading the *Wall Street Journal* when Ashleigh arrived a few minutes later. She was in an orange polka dot sundress and more full-figured than before, although a strict diet and a daily regimen of walking and swimming was melting the excess pounds quickly. Her infant son was with a sitter.

"No champagne? Not even a glass of wine?" she said with a smirk, kissing his cheek as she kicked off her shoes. "You're pretty sure of yourself, aren't you?"

His eyes twinkled as he took her into his arms. "What first? Business or pleasure?"

Ashleigh's evil smile. She backed a step away. "Pleasure is contingent on business, and it better be what I want to hear."

"Frank and I talked to her this morning. It's your show effective July first."

"How'd she handle it?"

"She was upset. We think she'll look for something else and hit the road pretty quick."

"And she's out of 802?"

"Will be when you come back."

Ashleigh's smile broadened. "Very good." She touched her tongue to his ear. He closed his eyes. She touched his genitals, feeling his erection. "I haven't let him touch me. You're first. I'm pure as the driven snow."

Grantham threw back his head and laughed, then helped her undress. Their lovemaking, which was aggressive and at times bordered on violent, ceased after simultaneous climaxes. She heaved a contented sigh.

"Let's go away somewhere. Virgin Islands, maybe. Lay out on the beach all day, drink and fuck all night. That sound like fun, Craig Grantham?"

"What about that little boy of yours?"

"That's what my darling husband is for. His idea, his problem."

"Sounds like a plan."

Ashleigh sulked. "You've been saying that for five years, ass-hole. We've never gone anywhere."

"Prosecutor's conference is in two weeks. We always have fun on the Coast."

"Sneaking around is getting old."

"Please. You live for it."

A pause. "I've forgotten the mechanic who turned in Sonny to Maureen. What's his name?"

Grantham's brow furrowed. "I didn't tell you his name. And I'm not going to."

"I think Sonny should know."

"Consumer is yours. Maureen is out of the picture. Enough is enough."

"Not for me."

"You want the mechanic fired?" Grantham said, sitting up. "You know that's what'll happen."

"I don't want him fired. I just want to talk to him."

"The answer is no."

She rolled onto her side and pouted, facing away from him. "Maybe I'll sell you out, Mr. Big Shot. Maybe I'll just rock your world. You won't know which way is up after I get through with you."

Grantham stood and put on his boxers. A smirk was on his face. "You're so cute when you don't get your way. Those baby-blues of yours practically catch fire. And you get real loud—but you're all talk. Always have been."

"Push me too far and see where it gets you," she said, getting to her feet. She dressed quietly, continuing to pout. He spoke after knotting his tie.

"Let the smoke clear, Ash. Then you can savage Maureen all you want, if it's that important to you."

TWENTY THREE

Maureen lasted an hour behind her desk before complaining to her secretary of migraine symptoms. She took the rest of the day off, barely making it home before bursting into tears. She called her father first, interrupting a meeting. Erica visited at lunch, arriving at the exact moment Ashleigh entered Crosby's room.

"God, Mo, I'm sorry. I'm shocked. I really am."

Maureen fought back tears of anger. "You should have seen them, trying to sell me this laughable demotion of a position where I'd be no more than a glorified pawn."

Erica took her time. "Is there any chance—any at all—that this might be a good opportunity?"

"No," Maureen said in a whisper. "Not with Craig determining my assignments. It would be even worse than it is now. I just want to know why they didn't give this to Ashleigh and leave me alone. As lazy as she is—and as much as she sucks up to them—that would actually make sense."

* * *

"I've thought about it all day, and I still don't have a clue," she said to Janine that night over beer and pizza, emphasizing that the discussion was strictly off the record. She was under enough control to vent without crying. "I can see sending the car dealers to McMichael to protect campaign dollars, no matter how much I despise it. But why take me completely out of the equation? Why not just give her this new position and leave me where I am?"

"I was gonna ask the same thing. What did Frank say?"

"I wasn't thinking fast enough to ask. And until Erica reminded me, I'd forgotten her daddy is the big car lobbyist."

"Politics."

"It sucks," she said, spitting the words. "This can't be something they just thought of. I'd love to snoop around her office, see if I can find some sort of paper trail. I have a key."

Janine glanced around before continuing. "A guy in our newsroom got fired a few years ago. I don't remember why. But word got around that the head computer geek pulled up all his e-mails and discovered what he did and who he conspired with. They had everything he had sent and received going back ninety days. I'm not recommending you break into her computer, but it's an option."

The hint of a smile formed on Maureen's face. "The department head works in Gartin. His name is Jerry Eckland. He's big buddies with Craig and Frank. But his assistant works in 802. He's a pretty nice guy."

"How well do you know him?"

"Not very. But I may have to trust him."

TWENTY FOUR

Aaron Penn's office was in the 802 basement, an area used for storage and repair of the office computers. He was a short, well-dressed black man in his mid-thirties who wore tortoise-shell eyeglasses. He smiled in surprise when Maureen knocked on the open door the next morning. The office was chilly—the air-conditioning ran full-blast at all times to keep the equipment cool.

"Long time, no see," he said, coming out from behind the desk. She shook his outstretched hand. "To what do I owe this pleasure?"

"Need your help. Can I close the door?"

Penn nodded. He returned behind the desk, muting the radio. "What's up?"

"Not here. Can you have lunch?"

"I'm leaving for Gartin in a few minutes. I'll be there all day."

"I need ten minutes. Call me on your way out and I'll meet you in the cafeteria," she said, scribbling her private line on the back of a business card.

Curiosity spread across Penn's face, but she strode away.

* * *

He rang twenty minutes later. She parked a block from Gartin and walked discreetly along President Street before disappearing into the parking garage. Almost no one was in the cafeteria at this hour. She ordered black coffee and settled in a booth at the back of the cafeteria, thirty feet from the nearest patron. She contemplated what she was considering. Aaron was easy to get along with and knowledgeable about computers. There was no reason not to trust him, although she had no idea of his relationship with Eckland. If he got word of this, it would go right to Craig and Frank, and she was likely out of a job.

Penn joined her five minutes later with his own coffee. "Before I forget, congratulations on the Consumer bill. First chance I've had to tell you."

A brief smile. "Thanks."

"So what's the cloak and dagger stuff about?"

"If you don't want to do this—or can't—that's fine. But you have to swear every bit of this conversation stays here."

He eyed her. "Okay."

"Frank and Craig just offered me a new position," she said, having already determined what he needed to know. "It sounded like a promotion, but after they described it I told Frank I wanted to stay in Consumer. Craig said that wasn't an option." A pause. "Ashleigh Dunn replaces me July first."

Penn leaned forward. "The Senator's daughter? She just had a baby. She's also despised by half the people in the office. How the heck is she gonna run Consumer?"

"I'm not gonna go into specifics, but some pretty ugly things have happened lately. Maybe it's all a coincidence, but I want to find out what kind of input she had. I'm wondering if some folks are getting too dirty for their own good. And if someone is after me. I know that's vague, but there's no reason to suddenly pull me out of the department when it's flying higher than it ever has."

"What do you want from me?"

She met his eyes. "I want into her computer. I wouldn't ask if it weren't absolutely necessary, Aaron. And I'll pay you very handsomely for it."

"Before I ask how handsomely, let me explain something: If Ashleigh follows the office directives and backs up her network files every night like she's supposed to, you can get on her computer and pull them up on the C: drive. You don't need her password to access her files on the network. It's a little security flaw not everybody knows about. Won't cost you a dime."

"I realize that, Aaron. I'm talking about her e-mails, which I can't get. I want everything she has sent and received as far back as you can go."

Penn frowned. "You sure you want to go that route?"

"Like I said, it's something I think I have to do. Would you rather not?"

"How handsome are we talking about?"

"Five hundred dollars."

A slow nod. "I can live with that. If for some reason I can't get in, you don't owe me and we never had this conversation."

"And if you bring me a folder of printed e-mails, I write you a check on the spot. How far can you go back?"

"One hundred twenty days."

"Wow," she said, flipping calendar pages in her head. "How long will it take?"

"Depends on how many there are. It'll likely be on a weekend, when I can get my sister-in-law to help with the twins."

Maureen glanced around the cafeteria. A Supreme Court justice and two others were seating themselves several booths away. Last thing she needed was them overhearing this conversation. "As quick as you can, Aaron. Call when you're ready and I'll meet you."

TWENTY FIVE

"Oh, Mo," Erica said, groaning. "For God's sake, please don't go through with this."

"I think it's riskier not to," Maureen said cradling the phone as she stretched out on her sofa. Depressed, she'd turned down dinner with Tom and ordered pizza. She ate too much and still felt bloated two hours later. "More I think about it, more I think I'm being set up."

"But you're talking about committing a very serious crime!"

"Maybe so, but I'm doing it."

"You're making a huge mistake, not to mention going against everything you've ever been taught about honesty and decency . . ."

"Erica . . ."

"You haven't even run this by your father, have you?"

She groaned. "He'll say the same thing you are—that I wasn't raised this way, and my clean-as-a-whistle reputation goes right down the chute if I'm caught. But something's going on, Erica. I just know it."

"And there's no way to talk you out of this, is there?"

"I'll be careful. That's the best answer I can give you."

A long moment passed. "How's Tom?"

"Wants me to meet his folks. Don't know if I'm ready for that or not."

"Hmm. Pressure?"

"Not really. I just don't know what I want yet. I know I'm not ready to tackle Dad, and I'm sure if I meet his folks, he'll want to meet mine."

"Don't get ahead of yourself. Just bask in the glory that a handsome, younger man likes you." A pause. "And for God's sake, please think about this other stuff before you go through with it. I don't want to start visiting you in prison."

*　*　*

She met Tom at the Ridgeland mall the following night and bought lingerie to wear in front of him. They were seconds from departing when his face fell.

"Tom Chapman, is that you?" An attractive older woman with dark hair approached and gave him a quick hug. She wore a black pants suit and carried herself in a way that rang an odd bell with Maureen. "How in the world are you?"

Tom managed a smile. "I'm fine, Mrs. Dunn."

Maureen froze. The body language was the same, and Ashleigh was indeed all over the face. "I'm glad to hear that. I trust your folks are well."

"They are."

"And your brother and sister?"

"Everybody's great."

"Wonderful!" She turned to Maureen and offered her hand before Tom could introduce them. "You sure do look familiar. I'm Eleanor Dunn."

"Maureen Lewis. Nice to meet you."

"From the Attorney General's Office, of course! Ashleigh has talked about you so often you seem like family. Your Consumer Protection Act is a wonderful service to the people of this state."

Maureen forced a smile, a stress headache already coming on. The totally fake charm and sincerity, so visible in her daughter, were even more pronounced in this obnoxious woman.

"Thank you. How are mother and baby?"

"Oh, you know my Ash—killing herself trying to get her figure back. She loves that little boy, though. Me, too. Never thought I'd want to be a grandparent, but I'm having the time of my life playing with the little guy."

"Tell her I said hello."

"I sure will. It is so nice to meet you," she said, shaking Maureen's hand again before turning to Tom. "So what are you doing now? Last I talked to your folks, you were selling TV ads."

"I'm at Capital City Motors. Public relations."

"Oh, Sonny Hollins is such a dear! You tell that man I said hello."

Tom forced another smile and reached for his keys. "I'll do it. Nice seeing you again."

Maureen waited until the woman was out of sight before sizing Tom up. He had met Sherry, Jeff and Paul several days ago, and all spoke well of him. But Paul saw him with Hollins and two other men at a downtown restaurant today. They were having a great big laugh over lunch.

"The nerve of her to mention the Consumer Act with Ashleigh about to take over. How well do you know her?"

"Hardly at all."

"She made it sound like you guys are real tight. You know Ashleigh, too?"

"We go back a long way, but I don't know her very well. I didn't realize she was the one you work with."

Maureen watched as Eleanor disappeared from sight. "That's just great. All I need are Ashleigh and her mother gossiping about me."

"Let 'em talk. It's not worth ruining our evening."

TWENTY SIX

Maureen discovered a voice mail from the Attorney General when she arrived at work the next morning. Cash wanted her in his office as soon as possible, and the fact that it was left at almost the exact moment she and Tom were confronted with Eleanor Dunn made her paranoid.

"Thanks for getting over here right away," Cash said, closing the door. "Before anything else is said, I want you to know how much we've valued your contribution to this office over the years, Maureen, whatever you decide."

They want me to resign, she thought to herself. She forced a smile and sat down across from the Attorney General. She ignored Grantham, who was next to her with his legs crossed.

"I'd very much like to stay, Frank, and I have no desire to work in Human Services. If you guys are definite about

Ashleigh running Consumer, I'll certainly take this new position."

Grantham smiled. Frank nodded vigorously. "I'm glad to hear that. I know you have your doubts, but we assure you that you'll be in court often and will take on as many high-profile cases as we can give you."

"Believe me, you won't be shuffling papers," Grantham said. "We may get to a point where we decide you need an assistant. You'll have full authority to bring someone in you feel comfortable with."

Maureen continued to ignore him. "Ashleigh starts July first?"

"Correct," Cash said. "I talked to her mother a few days ago. She'll probably come in the last week of June. We'll make every effort to see that there's as little awkwardness as possible during the transition," he said, directing a look at Grantham. "What would help is for you to make notes on your open cases. Do that at your convenience, and get them to Craig."

"No problem," she said, lying. Ashleigh could ask for them herself.

"Craig and I went over salary this morning. We'll move you from sixty-two to seventy, effective the day you start."

Her eyes widened in spite of herself. "Thank you."

"Thank you, Maureen," Cash said, getting to his feet. Grantham did likewise. "I know you don't agree with the way this is being handled, but I'm hoping down the road you'll look back and see that this move was worth it for you. We certainly hope it will be."

"Me, too, sir."

＊　＊　＊

Tom was at his desk that morning when Hollins buzzed over the intercom, asking him to his office. He groaned, rubbing his temples. He had tossed and turned most of the night.

"Yes, sir?"

"Come in, Tom. Sit down," Hollins said, a smile on his face. Plaques and citations adorned the walls, and an expensive set of golf clubs was in the corner. A small refrigerator was behind the desk. "Two things: I've booked a series of speaking engagements and need a presentation video, eight or ten minutes long. General info about the dealership, roots in the community. What'd I'd really like is for you to go out and get some satisfied customers on tape, make that a big part of it. Need it in two weeks. Spend as much money as you need to. Within reason, of course."

Tom was nodding. "Yes, sir. Get right on it."

"And what do you have for me on Maureen Lewis?"

A pause. "I had lunch with her that day. Seems pretty hard to get to know."

"Oh, Tom," Hollins said, his smile becoming chilly. "You've sent her flowers. And last night you were with her at the mall, looking at lingerie. Sounds like you're getting to know her quite well."

Tom looked away.

"So tell me what you've found."

The words hung in the air. "Mr. Hollins, I'm interested in her. A lot. I've realized I'm not comfortable with the idea of . . ."

Hollins rapped the desk, startling him. "I don't care what you're comfortable with! You're sleeping with her, young man! God only knows what she's shared with you about this place!"

"She hasn't said a word. I don't talk about the dealership, and she doesn't talk about . . ."

"Don't lie to me! I told you what I wanted. Are you going to do it or not?"

Tom faced him, his jaw tight. "No, sir, I'm not."

"You're making a big mistake. I'll give you one last chance to change your mind."

Tom said nothing. Hollins slammed his palm against his desk, then paged over the intercom. Irv White appeared seconds later.

"Tom is no longer employed here," Hollins said tersely. "He's about to clean out his office. Stand over his shoulder and don't take your eyes off him until he's completely off our property."

"Yes, sir. This way, Mr. Chapman."

TWENTY SEVEN

It was mid-evening before Tom caught his parents. He had a long talk with his father about his future, then solicited input on how to talk to Maureen.

"Hi. I know how late it is. Can we talk?"

"Now?" Maureen said, glancing at the clock radio. It was midnight. She had been asleep two hours.

He exhaled. "Please? It's important."

She let him in twenty minutes later. She gestured at the couch, taking him in as he fidgeted.

"Lost my job today," he said, looking at the floor.

"What?"

He looked up. "I have a confession to make. I'd seen you on TV before, but the idea to meet you came from Hollins. It was a mandate, actually."

She stared. "Hollins wanted you to ask me out? Why? Information?"

"Yes. And I haven't said a word. I swear I haven't." She started to speak, but he held up a hand. "I do know what's going on in the garage. I listened to your tape."

Her eyes narrowed.

"The morning after the parade, you were still asleep and I was going to listen to music. It was behind the headphones."

"You bastard!" she said, furious. She was on her feet instantly. "Get out! Don't ever call me again!"

"Maureen, please let me explain. I lost my job over this."

She turned away, trying to hold her temper.

"I knew I wanted to see you again after we had lunch that first day, so I lied to Hollins. Said you were aloof, probably seeing someone. Your name didn't come up again until today. He asked what I'd found out, and I said I hadn't seen you any more. He didn't buy it. He knew we were at the mall last night. Knew we looked at lingerie."

"Oh, for God's sake! Eleanor Dunn told him?"

"Or Ashleigh. I don't know. I wasn't completely truthful when you asked how well I knew her."

"I see. One more thing you weren't completely truthful about."

He closed his eyes and looked away. A long moment passed before he continued.

"Ashleigh and I graduated high school together. She's mean as a snake, and if she has an axe to grind, she'll stop at nothing to get you. My best friend got involved with her our junior year, and you should have seen the stuff she did to him."

"What the hell does that have to do with anything?"

"It's a pattern. She did the same thing in Law School. Slept with professors to pass courses, framed a girl for cheating and got her kicked out because the girl went out with a guy she liked." He met her eyes. "People don't change, Maureen. She's dangerous, and her mother's the same way. If you think she's after you, you're probably right."

"I wish you'd told me this in the beginning . . ."

"I swear I had no idea that was the Ashleigh you worked with until last night!"

". . . and I'm really upset about the tape. That's quite an invasion of privacy. You snoop around on my computer, too?"

He sighed. "Of course not. I apologize about the tape. I was just curious, but that's no excuse. If I wanted to exploit our involvement for personal gain, I would have gone right to Hollins."

She nodded slightly. "Your family knows her family?"

"They're all from here, including Sonny and his wife. Mom and Dad weren't in their circle, but he said Eleanor probably sees him socially. The way Eleanor gossips, it wouldn't be beyond her to tell him." He paused. "I sure didn't think I'd lose my job over it."

"Hollins must consider me a real threat."

"I'm sure he does."

"Did you know what was going on before you heard the tape?"

"No. I was insulated from the garage. We shot some video in there, but that's all." He got to his feet. "Look, I know you're upset, but I hope . . ."

"Give me some space. That's what I need right now."

TWENTY EIGHT

Lunch with Erica two days later, this time at her apartment. "What would I do? I'd have given Keith another chance, I think."

"But he lied to me!"

"Mo, he wouldn't have kept calling if he weren't interested, and he must like you to stand up to Hollins. What a horrible situation to put an employee into."

Maureen rolled her eyes.

"I know this is about trust, and I don't blame you for being upset. But give yourself a few days to cool off, then see him again. If he doesn't strike you as sincere, get rid of him."

* * *

A card arrived the next day. He called the following night.

"Okay, apology accepted. The card was nice."

"Would dinner Saturday night be totally out of the question? Just dinner?"

They ate Mexican, gobbling fajitas and enjoying a Margarita. She relaxed and enjoyed his company, finally revealing the demotion to him.

"But she's a lawyer, too," he said. "If they're trying to promote her, wouldn't that be right up her alley?"

"That's the burning question. Still makes no sense to me."

"There has to be something behind this, something that has nothing to do with logic or common sense or what's good for the office."

"Politics, Tom. I'm sure that's what it is."

"Maybe. But these people are all tight and go back a long way. You're an outsider, and you stepped on some serious toes when you went after Hollins. Maybe it had some repercussions."

Her eyes narrowed. "What are you saying? If you know something, you'd best speak right up . . ."

He spread his arms innocently. "I have no idea, Maureen. But something you're not seeing yet is driving this. I'm talking about everything, not just the new position."

She started to tell him about Aaron's project but decided against it. He drained his Margarita and suggested a round of miniature golf. High school kids were everywhere, but they ran into a high school classmate of his named Sara. Her husband was instantly familiar, a blond man with glasses in his mid-thirties. He was introduced as Mike Morgan, the morning weather anchor on the ABC affiliate.

"Guess who we ran into the other night?" Tom said, addressing Sara. "Eleanor Dunn. Maureen works with Ashleigh at the

Attorney General's Office."

"I'm sorry to hear that. Not exactly one of my favorite people." She turned to her husband. "What were you saying yesterday about what that reporter told you? Something some Legislator said?"

Morgan turned to Maureen and Tom. "Our weekend anchor, Carolyn Davis, was at Cash's press conference yesterday. A drug bust in Madison County, I think."

"He was there at dawn, overseeing everything with the cameras rolling. What a guy," Maureen said, not trying to hide her sarcasm. "Please continue."

"Carolyn said a Senator she knows was in the back, having a big laugh with several other men. She asked what was so funny. The Senator—off the record—was talking about some high-up who works for the Attorney General, part of the entourage he takes when he travels. The guy has been stepping out on his wife for years, apparently pretty brazen about it. Only person who doesn't know is her."

"Did Carolyn find out who it was?"

"I don't know. But she's anchoring tonight," Morgan said, glancing at Sara. "We could ride out there if you want. She might have a minute to talk."

Maureen didn't hesitate. "Let's go."

* * *

The newsroom was busy, with a producer, several news photographers and talent readying themselves for the late newscast. It was a loud, boisterous atmosphere, with phones ringing and instructions and barbs being shouted across the room. Carolyn Davis was at her desk, putting on makeup. Morgan led them through the maze of desks and computer terminals and waved.

"What're you doing up here on your day off?" she said, a short black woman of perhaps thirty, already dressed for the show.

"This lady has a question for you," he said, introducing Maureen. Carolyn recognized her and stuck out her hand. Maureen shook it, keeping her voice down.

"You talked to a legislator yesterday who said one of Cash's people is having an affair?"

Carolyn hesitated. She shot Morgan a nasty look.

"I don't want the Senator's name. But a friend of mine may be getting burned, and I'd like to know who's stepping out."

"His Chief of Staff," she said, lowering her voice. "But you didn't hear that from me."

Maureen's eyes widened. "What'd the Senator say?"

She hesitated again.

"Carolyn, things are brewing that would shock the general public. Tell me everything he said, and you have my word you're first on my call list if there's a story."

She glanced around, then lowered her voice to a whisper. Maureen leaned forward. "The Legislators stay at the motel across from the Capitol—I'm sure you know that. Frank's chief has his own room. Been using it with this chick for years."

Maureen's heart pounded. "Who is she?"

"He wouldn't say."

"Okay," she said, exhaling. "Thanks, Carolyn."

"You just remember who to call when you have a scoop."

TWENTY NINE

Her pager beeped as the couples parted company. She called from the car, not recognizing the phone number. A male voice answered.

"It's Maureen. Somebody paged me?"

"It's Aaron. Where are you?"

"South Jackson. You ready to go in?"

"I'm a block from 802. I was gonna get started, but somebody was in your office."

"In my office? When?"

"Just now! I could see the lights from the street."

"Shit! Did you tell the security officer?"

"I didn't see one."

"Go back, Aaron, and call the police if the rent-a-cop isn't there! I'll be there in ten minutes and park in the back. Wait for me."

"What was that about?" Tom said, concern on his face.

Maureen hesitated. She didn't like the idea of sharing this with him. But she didn't know Aaron well and was trusting him.

"I'm working with that guy on a project. He thinks somebody just broke into my office."

*　　*　　*

Penn was having a heated discussion with a uniformed security guard when they arrived. A storm system was approaching, and lightning flashed in the distance. Winds whipped the bushes and trees, sending small piles of dead leaves across the parking lot.

"He says he didn't see anything, Maureen." Skepticism was in his voice.

"Like I've told you five times now, I was on the north side of the building," the guard said defensively. He was an older, squat man and shot a mean look at Penn before gesturing across the lot, which opened onto North Street. "I can't be everywhere at once."

Maureen, Tom and Penn talked to him for another minute, getting nothing in the way of help. They entered the office and disabled the alarm. The Consumer suite was locked, as was her office when they reached it. Maureen flipped on the lights and went to her desk, searching each drawer.

"Everything's like it's supposed to be."

"What's in here?" Penn said, gazing at the four-drawer file cabinet.

"Case files," Maureen said, striding across the room. She opened the top drawer. "Oh, my. Somebody was definitely in here."

"How do you know?"

"This drawer is usually stuffed full. Now everything fits easily." The files were alphabetized, and she was most of the way to the back when she stopped. "I knew it—the Capital City file is gone." She looked at Tom. "My copy of the subpoena was in a clear plastic folder with blue binding. With all the manila, it's the first thing you see in this drawer."

Penn stepped closer. "What's going on here? You think she took it?"

Maureen glanced toward the street. "We may know once we get her e-mails." Tom's eyes widened, but she ignored him. "Ready?"

"For the last time, are you sure you want to do this? Did you check her C: drive like I asked you to?"

She snorted. "You know what's there, Aaron? Bogus time sheets—she doesn't do half the stuff she says she does—and three years of Junior League newsletters. Not a damned thing about any cases she's ever worked."

He hesitated. She stepped toward him. Lightning flashed close before thunder rattled the building.

"Whoever was in the file cabinet works here. They're not coming back tonight. Now please get started before the damned power goes off."

*　*　*

Penn retreated into Ashleigh's office and shut the door. Maureen quietly explained her hunch and his involvement to Tom, then stared into space. Had Nathan McMichael been here?

If so, was Craig in on this? And who the hell was Craig having an affair with?

An hour passed, a heavy thunderstorm rattling the building. The lights flickered several times but stayed on. The LaserJet printer at the secretary's desk finally whirred into life. Maureen's heart leaped. Penn entered the room, wincing as his eyes adjusted to the overhead light. He was using a flashlight in Ashleigh's office.

"Probably four hundred. You want 'em all?"

"Every last one. Sent and received."

The door closed a moment later. Tom removed the first sheet from the printer.

"Don't," Maureen said. "We'll read later. Watch the front. I don't want any surprises."

* * *

Penn took a bathroom break an hour later and said they were over halfway through. It was after two when the last page was printed. She hadn't dared to read any of them.

"Everything's shut down just like it was booted up," he said. "Absolutely sure of it."

"Shouldn't you have worn gloves?" Tom said.

Penn cocked an eyebrow at him. "I work on these computers. My fingerprints are on all of them. Trust me."

Maureen put the pages in a pair of expandable folders, then presented him with a check. "Hope you're not locked out of the house."

"No sweat. She knows about the money."

The security officer was in a yellow rain slicker when they departed. He was keeping dry near the building entrance and made a big point of looking Penn up and down. He reached for his cell phone when they were out of sight.

THIRTY

Maureen was up before seven. She made coffee, fed the cat and settled into the recliner. She opened the first folder, her adrenaline flowing, and faced the first message. It was dated January 21.

Craig -
When is this gonna get done?
Ashleigh

When is what going to get done, Maureen thought to herself. The second message, also dated January 21, went to Hillary Bankston, a former colleague from Medicaid Fraud. She was a gossipy woman who played tennis with Ashleigh and ran in her social circle.

Hi, Hill -
Lunch next Monday would be terrific—my turn to treat. I'll be here another three, four weeks, less if I don't feel like it. Saw Craig's wife at Gartin the other day...boy, is she putting on the pounds. I heard she's frigid and they haven't slept together in over a year!!! She gets much bigger and we'll call her Frigidaire!!! After the baby's born, we'll get back on our happy hour schedule again and play some tennis.
Ashleigh

Maureen reread the message, frowning. It had been established that Craig was cheating, but with whom? How the hell did Ashleigh know intimate details about his marriage? Did she know who he was sleeping with? And God, poor Evelyn Grantham. She was a gentle soul who had given up a teaching position to support her spouse's climb up the political ladder.

These days she kept house and played the role of supportive wife, and Maureen gnashed her teeth at the thought of Craig destroying her while fulfilling his macho fantasies in a motel room.

The next messages were simply gossip, although one dated February 2 caught her attention. It was sent to Lisa Vick, a lawyer in Criminal Appeals and another tennis buddy.

Hey Lisa -

How's tricks? You think you've got a slave driver for a boss? Try working for Maureen. What a bitch! Thinks she's God's gift to state government. I'm sick and tired of seeing that stupid twit every time I turn on the TV. By the way, notice that she's never, ever with a guy? What's her friend's name—the clerk for the Supreme Court Justice? You see them together a lot. You don't suppose . . .well, I won't go there. I'll be on leave soon so I won't have to deal with her for a while. Stay in touch . . .

Ashleigh

The notes dropped off for a few days. Maureen closed her eyes, trying to recollect how often Ashleigh was at the doctor by then. Seemed like she missed a lot of hours about this time. A flurry of transmissions went out February 11, however. She vented about a particular assignment to several people, and the word "cunt" was used in the note to Hillary. A bland smile spread across Maureen's face. That was the day she sent Ashleigh and Paul to stop an unlicensed vendor who was selling merchandise from an eighteen-wheeler at a busy North Jackson intersection. Ashleigh claimed to have a headache, then suggested the assignment was beneath her. Maureen remembered her response—she told Ashleigh she had a drawer full of resumes from people who would kill for the assignment and to get moving.

The last note that day was to Craig.

Mr. Grantham:

    I'm ready to rip the ugly red hair right out of you-know-who's head. The nerve of her to send me to a goddamned broken-down truck with that kid Paul today! Fucking bitch actually implied she'd get somebody else in here if I didn't do what she said. I'm tired of waiting around on this, Craig. Either shit or get off the pot.

Ashleigh

Maureen's eyes widened. Did Ashleigh have enough clout to strong-arm her right out of the department? And how did she get away with talking to Craig like that? Was Craig paying attention? In any case, it wasn't appropriate.

The next e-mail, also to Craig, was dated Monday, February 14.

Craig -

    What the fuck were you doing calling the house this morning? You don't EVER pull that! Thank God Warren was in the shower! What were you thinking? Were you in the sauce a little early, or too late last night? Where was Mrs. Grantham—in a coma? Think before you drink, damn it!

Ashleigh

Maureen paced through her living room. Why would Craig ever need to call Ashleigh at home early in the morning? Tom was still asleep, and she poured more coffee and read on. The next message was sent two hours later, also to Grantham.

Happy Valentine's Day, Dearest.

    Sorry about being such a bitch in that last note—it just scared me. I have something for you, too . . .

Ashleigh

This was getting strange. A Valentine gift? Of course she didn't want Warren to know about that. She couldn't be involved with Craig, could she? Maureen scratched her head, having gone through about half the sent e-mails. The Consumer Bill was days away from being voted on by then, which meant Ashleigh was in the office perhaps another month before taking leave. The next message was dated Monday, February 21. It was also to Grantham.

Hi, Darling -

The earrings are beautiful. But I'm sorry—I hurt too much. How many times do I have to tell you I feel like hell right now? Besides, I don't know why you have any desire to touch me as big as I am (I'm flattered, though). Anyway, the baby'll be born in a month, and the doc wants me to wait another month. Then my once-gorgeous body will be yours for the taking (you have to honor your promise to have me with all the extra pounds—I'll hold you to it). In the meantime, watch that video of us. I know it isn't the real thing, but it's the best I can do right now.

Love ya, Ashleigh

"Oh, my God!"

"Maureen? You okay?" Tom appeared a moment later, his hair askew. Concern was on his face. He glanced around, his eyes coming to rest on the pile of e-mails on the love seat.

"Oh, Jesus," Maureen said, scanning the note again. "Go throw some water on your face, then read this."

His eyes widened as he took in the information. "Grantham and Ashleigh! Son of a bitch!"

"Yeah," Maureen said. The pile of pages she'd read was between them. "Surprise, surprise. I wonder if I'm the last to know."

She read on. There were references to the motel in her notes to Craig, but nothing which exploded from the page like the Valentine e-mail. Then a flurry of complaints about all the attention bestowed upon Maureen when the Consumer Bill became law. She threw back her head and laughed.

"Good grief, what a jealous bitch!"

"I'm on the one where she's cutting up Grantham's wife. That's some nerve, isn't it? You think that Hillary woman knows about them?"

"The whole office may know, Tom."

Her eyes grew to the size of saucers when she read the next note. It was dated Monday, March 6.

Frank -

One of the mechanics at Sonny's place spilled his guts! Do you know anything about this? The stupid bastard came in and told Maureen everything! I looked all over her desk and in her file cabinet, but I can't find his name. She's talking some serious shit—getting ready to subpoena Sonny and "flex the department's muscles." Warn him!!!

Ashleigh

She handed the page to Tom. "My worst nightmare."

His jaw fell. "Cash is in on it! That's why he pulled you off Sonny so fast!"

"I don't believe this. I absolutely don't believe what I'm seeing."

She read on. A rare note to the investigators that same day— Ashleigh warned Sherry, Jeff and Paul that Maureen was serious about the hours they would work if push came to shove with Capital City Motors. Maureen snickered at the cover. Sure enough, there was another note to Cash later that week.

Frank -

Maureen's hell-bent on making an example out of Sonny!

*Don't take her lightly—she'll be on him like white on rice, not
to mention every other car dealer around!*
Ashleigh

The remaining messages were gossip, including another sav-
aging of Evelyn Grantham—the diatribes against Evelyn made a
modicum of sense now that Maureen knew Ashleigh was
involved with Craig. The last message which caught Maureen's
eye was dated Friday, March 17, a week before Ashleigh departed for maternity leave. Maureen read it a second time, eyes wide
in disbelief.

Craig -
*Okay, I'll hang out all weekend with Maureen and these
other morons and eyeball everything they're doing. But I'll tell
you something: You're gonna make this up to me. For
starters, I want a firm date on when you're deep-sixing that
red-headed dyke. No more bullshit, Craig. Don't you start
hiding behind Frank Cash now.*
Ashleigh

A flurry of e-mails went out to her pals the following week,
notifying them that the impending C-Section was days away.
Promises of lunch, tennis and drinks were made for later. One
final note was sent to Grantham. It was dated Friday, March 24.

Hello, Kind Sir . . .
*I like the salary increase a lot. I'll like it even more when
you give me a definite start date. I'm disappointed you won't
let Maureen work for me, but I can't have everything, I guess.
The one thing I want—and I insist on it—is the name of that
mechanic, Craig.*
Love, Ashleigh

"Ashleigh and Craig are sleeping together, and she was pushing him to get rid of me," Maureen said rhetorically, rubbing her temples. "I don't think she was going to Frank to get me fired, although she went right to him when she realized I was after Hollins. And she already knew the mechanic had talked."

"And she wants his name. Ugh."

"That scares me." She reached for the second folder. "Let's have a go at these."

The first sheet was dated January 17. She snorted and handed it to Tom. "You asked how well we got along. This sums it up perfectly."

Ashleigh . . .

This is the third or fourth time I've had to ask you to go through me when you need time off. I don't care if you're out two hours or three days—I'm your supervisor, and you let me know, not Sherry, Jeff, my secretary or anyone else. This is standard operating procedure. I realize you're uncomfortable and making many trips to the doctor. I'm flexible about your hours and assignments, but not this. You have my home number, my pager and my cell, and you are to go through me when you're going to be away. I will speak to Frank about this if it happens again.

Maureen

"One more reason to hate you," Tom said, laughing. "There's probably a dartboard in her bedroom with a picture of you in the middle."

"That's about control. She was pulling that long before she was pregnant."

Ashleigh received a third as many e-mails as she sent during the previous four months, and few were of consequence. Maureen smirked as Hillary Bankston and Lisa Vick took shots at her.

Ashleigh . . .

 Let Maureen enjoy her fifteen minutes of fame. Everybody over here is having a big laugh at her high-stepping right now. Far as her sexual preferences, I have no idea, but her friend is actually serious with a banker—I've seen 'em together. Anyway, hang in there with the pregnancy. Let me know when you get the green light to drink again.

Lisa

"You mentioned Hillary—she's another of my big boosters," Maureen said, handing another sheet to Tom.

Hey, Ash . . .

 Have to find a new tennis buddy with you out or I'll blow up like Craig's wife. I may talk to that Jennifer chick from our league, the one so chummy with McNulty. She'll kick my ass, but I could use the exercise. Don't pay any attention to Maureen. Suggest she see a shrink for her insecurities and some sex to loosen her up. Leave a vibrator on her desk—sex alone is better than no sex at all.

Ciao, Hillary

"Damn. These women don't hold back, do they?"

"Hillary's ex is a chest cutter—they were married about ten years before he ran off with one of his nurses. She has a crummy little job a monkey could hold down, and I've heard stories about her personal life—she takes anti-depressants and spends her nights at reservoir clubs getting bombed and hitting on guys half her age. She knows Ashleigh is connected, and she sucks up because she thinks it will get her somewhere. Pretty pathetic, if you ask me."

"How do you know all that?"

Maureen laughed. "This is state government, Tom. Lots of folks with cushy jobs and time on their hands, and that means lots of gossip. If I wanted to, I could drink with those women at happy hour and find out everything about their personal lives, including every last detail about who's sleeping with who. But I'd rather scrub my toilet, and they know it. So I'm not surprised about the hostility." She sifted through the remaining pages, then returned them to the expandable folders. "Nothing at all from Frank or Craig, which doesn't surprise me. I just can't believe Ashleigh is stupid enough to send stuff this incriminating to them."

"She isn't stupid. She may overestimate what she can get away with, but she knows what this would do."

"Then could she have something on them?"

"I wonder. What worries me is her wanting the name of the mechanic. That's the kind of crap she pulled in Law School. It wasn't enough to simply ruin some girl's reputation by spreading a rumor that she had the clap. Ashleigh spent half a semester framing her and didn't stop until she was kicked out of school."

Maureen gazed at him.

"I'm not trying to scare you. But people don't change. And when she gets someone in her sights, look out below."

THIRTY ONE

Janine also lived in Belhaven, her house two miles away on Howard Street. The woodsy streets were lined with beautiful old homes, and hired security made regular loops through the neighborhood each night. It was her first choice if she were ever inclined to buy within the city limits, despite the fact that any purchase would be a fixer-upper and was on risky Yazoo clay. Foundation problems were almost a certainty in this area.

She was introduced to Grant, a tall man around 50 who was aging well. He was refinishing Janine's deck and moved to an indoor project to give the ladies privacy.

"The original handyman," she said as she poured iced tea. Maureen was stretched out, taking a rare opportunity to expose her fair skin to the sun. Birds chirped in the dogwoods and pines at the edge of the property. Kids played baseball in a nearby yard, using trees as bases.

"Look at you. Since when did you become a brunette? You've even gotten some sun!"

Janine grinned. "The gray I could take care of overnight. The thirty pounds will take some time."

"This sounds serious."

"Just might be. The girls are thrilled. They can't wait to meet him," she said. Janine's daughters were both at Ole Miss, the older of whom was in Graduate School. "And when do I meet your guy?"

"This week, I promise. Pick a day and we'll have lunch."

"Great." She sipped her tea. "You now have my undivided attention, unless he falls off a ladder."

"We're still off the record."

Janine nodded. Maureen took her through the events of last night, finishing with the e-mails.

"I need a cigarette. Please forgive me." She lit up, blowing the smoke away from Maureen. "I didn't really think you'd break into her computer!"

"She may just be sleeping her way to the top. Tom went to high school with her, though, and he thinks she might be out to get me." A glance at the baseball game. "Part of me wants to find a new job and just forget the whole thing."

Janine grinned. "A big part of you wants to know what's going on."

"And so do you, Ms. Reporter."

"All kidding aside, have you thought about running it by

your father?"

Maureen rolled her eyes. "Like I told Erica, I'll get an eternal guilt trip when I tell him about the e-mails. When he finally quits lecturing, he'll say to turn in the whole bunch. I'll get nowhere trying to explain that middle management in state government is a lot different from running your own bank."

"Especially when the reputation of a big-time politician is at stake." Janine took a final puff and stubbed her cigarette. "That makes me sick about Evelyn Grantham."

"You know her?"

"We've met. A woman who taught with her is a street over. I wonder if I should talk to her. Cheating is one of my issues, as you know."

"Please be discreet, Janine."

"Of course, hon'. So let's recap. Dunn's daughter—who's sleeping with Grantham—got him to move you out of Consumer and put her in charge, effective in July. That's politics, Maureen, but Tom might be right about the daughter. Had to be her in your office last night. And if she's demanding the mechanic's name, she clearly wants trouble. My guess is she'd try to get him fired and hang it on you."

"I don't know what I've ever done to her. Believe it or not, I tried very hard to get along with her."

"There are some nasty women running around out there. Some will stop at nothing to get back at someone—doesn't even matter why after a while. If you're a target, I wouldn't dwell on the reason. I'd just cover my backside."

"Should I talk to Frank?"

"I'm not sure I would, unless you wore a wire. Then you'd really need your ducks in a row. Would the District Attorney prosecute if he's dirty?"

"He's also a Democrat, Janine. You know that. I'd start with the U.S. Attorney's Office, if it got that far. Jimmy Haynes isn't a political ally of Frank's, and he's fair, based on everything I've ever heard about him. But what do I do right now?"

"Put locks on your file cabinet. Let Frank know somebody was in your office when they weren't supposed to be."

"What about Tom West? He's our chief of security."

"How do you know who to trust?"

Maureen sighed. "I'm thinking the same thing."

"Whatever you do, talk to the mechanic before Ashleigh does."

THIRTY TWO

"God, you look hot in that swimsuit," Grantham said at that moment, rubbing suntan oil on Ashleigh's shoulders. They were twenty minutes up the Natchez Trace, having brought wine and cheese after sex at Grantham's house. A speck of reservoir was in the distance, and the faint motor of a jet ski could be heard. They were tanning on a pair of beach towels, Grantham's Explorer shielding them from the road. An expanse of pine trees was on the other side.

"Yeah, I'm hot alright—hot and heavy. Still can't get rid of this tummy."

"Hardly, my dear," he said, pouring them a second glass of White Zinfandel. "You wouldn't get near a two-piece if you thought there was an ounce of fat on you."

Evelyn was with her parents for the weekend. Grantham was drinking beer and watching baseball when his pager went off last night. It was Ashleigh, who wanted into Maureen's office. Grantham objected at first, but he jumped to his feet when she revealed that her husband was at a conference two states away.

Ashleigh clinked his glass. "So when is the lovely and talented Mrs. Grantham due?" A snort. "What a horrible choice of words, big as she's gotten. Does she walk around asking if she looks fat, or is it just understood at the Grantham household that she's become a little butterball?"

Grantham's smile was smug. "As long as she cooks, cleans, runs errands and irons my shirts, I couldn't care less. She's a slave, not a sex toy like you are."

Ashleigh grinned. She ran her tongue across her lips and touched his genitals. Grantham felt an erection bloom. The truth was that he and Evelyn had sex just often enough for her to assume everything was fine. He lied to Ashleigh, of course, explaining that Evelyn had become unable to climax about two years ago, and the resulting stress had completely shut down their sex life and resulted in Evelyn's weight gain. In reality, Evelyn sat around an empty house all day, since Grantham didn't want her working and discouraged her involvement in outside activities.

Control and power had always turned Ashleigh on, and Grantham had no problem lying and cheating to maintain her interest. But keeping her in the dark about the events of the weekend might be risky—fallout from a disaster couldn't be explained away with simple denials, and Ashleigh would want his head on a plate if she didn't get what had been promised. He sipped his wine, looking at her over his sunglasses.

"Jerry Eckland called this morning."

"He want to go gambling?"

"No. He got a call from Tom West, who heard from the security guard at 802 last night. Aaron Penn, Maureen and some other guy were up there right after we were. They were in Maureen's office."

Ashleigh ripped off her shades, spilling the wine. "Did somebody see us, Craig?"

"I don't know. Jerry's gonna frisk Aaron first thing in the morning." A pause. "You're making this a lot more complicated than it has to be, Ash."

"Fuck you, Craig. You spend all morning getting your jollies, then wait until we're out here to casually mention we may have fucked up. And since I've spent the last four hours accommodating your every sexual whim, I'd like the name of the mechanic. Right this second."

Grantham sighed. Cash knew of the affair and had warned him to keep Ashleigh at a distance, and he'd kicked himself for blurting that he had the tape. She had spent the last month pleading, cajoling and threatening, and she moved in for the kill today—she did things for him a ten dollar whore might have turned down, all with an eye clearly on the prize. He should have seen it coming.

"Landrum. That's all I remember. I've only listened to it once."

"I want the tape."

"No tape. Ever."

A pause. "First name or last?"

"Last, I think. You can find that out." He leveled a finger at her. "But I'm warning you, Ashleigh—this better not come back to bite us."

THIRTY THREE

Warren Mullins was in his suit and out the door before seven the next morning. Ashleigh, still in her robe, batted her eyes and kissed him goodbye, promising that getting frisky was only days away. She changed the baby and warmed a bottle, hoping his crying would cease for the moment. She dialed Capital City Motors and asked for the service department.

"Gordon Smith," a weary voice said. "How can I help you

this morning?"

"Hi, Mr. Smith," she said loudly, pouring on as much debutante as she could muster. "Just wanted to let you folks know how happy I am with my CRX."

"Thank you, ma'am. We're glad to hear that."

"The mechanic—I think his name is Landy or Landrum . . ."

"Ronnie Landrum, perhaps?"

"Yes, Ronnie Landrum. So helpful—made me feel like I was dealing with a family member. Will you please tell him what a good job he did on the engine? Purrs like a kitten now."

"Yes, ma'am. And your name?"

"Peggy Roberson, from Morton. I'm five-three, blond hair, and—well, let's just say I'm dieting. Anyway, I brought it by about a month ago."

"Thank you, Ms. Roberson. And you come see us again, you hear?"

* * *

The infant fought sleep for half an hour before fading. Ashleigh looked at her notes and dialed Capital City again, this time using her natural voice.

"Ronnie Landrum, please, in the garage."

A minute passed before he picked up. "This is Ronnie."

Ashleigh frowned. He didn't sound eighteen. "Mr. Landrum? This is Sherry Forster with the Attorney General's Office. How are you this morning?"

"Uh, fine. What can I do for you?"

"I believe you talked to Maureen Lewis a few weeks ago."

"Yes, ma'am."

"I'm taking her place. Ms. Lewis is being promoted, and she'll work in a different department. I'm trying to get caught up on some of the cases she worked on. This one's a doozy. I understand there's some serious overcharging going on over there."

He hesitated. "Uh, that's right, ma'am. Who is this, now?"

"Sherry Forster, with the Attorney General's Office. So tell me where things stood the last time you and Ms. Lewis talked."

"She took my statement. Said she'd be back in touch. I ain't heard from her." He laughed to himself. "See her on TV all the time."

Ashleigh raised her middle finger. "When she took your statement, Mr. Landrum, you told her that you and the other mechanics were all getting a piece of the pie if a certain budget was met, did you not?"

"Uh, yes, ma'am. Listen, I don't got but a minute, and I ain't real sure 'bout talking right here in the . . ."

"We're just about done. What I need to know is this: Are you and everyone else still receiving this extra money each pay-check?"

"No, ma'am. It stopped right quick after I talked to Ms. Lewis," he said, lowering his voice. "Gordon—my boss—called a meeting of all the mechanics and said someone had turned us in. He was so mad I thought he was gonna start throwing things. All I could do not to pee in my pants."

Ashleigh grinned, pumping a fist. "I understand, sir. So nobody's getting extra, then?"

"No one in the garage. Be honest with you, I've thought about leaving 'cause morale is so poor now. Everybody's temper is short. Katrina bites off someone's head 'bout every day."

"I understand. But is the extra work—the unnecessary work—still being done?"

"Oh, yeah. That's why the mechanics are griping. They expect to see some of the return, and Gordon keeps promising it'll come back if someone pipes up."

"Okay, then. That's all I need, sir. Thanks for your help, and I'll be back in touch. You'll be the first to know how this shakes out. And please keep this conversation to yourself, of course."

"You don't have to worry about that, ma'am."

She checked on the baby. He was asleep. She made her way to her husband's computer.

5/13/01
Mr. Gordon Smith
c/o Capital City Motors
1836 Capital Drive
Jackson, MS 39211

Dear Mr. Smith,

As you may know, my department has finished its investigation into Capital City Motors. I am leaving Consumer Protection, although I'll maintain a residence here and will continue to need repair work done on my car. I'd like to see if a deal can be reached. In exchange for free repair work for as long as I own my car (with a promise that I'll buy a new one from your dealership), I'll give you the name of the mechanic who talked to us. His name is Ronnie Landrum. He told us everything, Mr. Smith. Ashleigh Dunn will be taking over my duties in Consumer Protection in July, and she'll be in touch with you and will no doubt want the kind of harmonic relations that the Attorney General and Mr. Hollins have had for years. You have my word that I will never go to the press with the information I have. Please contact me at your convenience.

> *Sincerely,*
> *Maureen Lewis,*
> *Director of Consumer Protection*

Ashleigh read the letter and smiled. She inserted a sheet of Maureen's stationery into the LaserJet printer. She carefully signed Maureen's name when the sheet issued forth, emulating

Maureen's block print as best she could. She put the letter to the attention of Gordon Smith, then walked out to the mailbox. The elderly gentleman across the street was retrieving his newspaper.

"Well, hello, young lady. How's Hamilton doing? And that baby?"

"Just fine, kind sir. Dad's great, and the little guy is just peachy."

"Glad to hear that. When are you going back to work?"

"Soon, I hope. Lots to do at the office."

THIRTY FOUR

Aaron Penn had been behind his desk five minutes when a knock on the open door startled him.

"Morning," Jerry Eckland said. Eckland was a beefy, brown-haired man with a thick mustache. Grantham was with him. "Understand you were here a little late Saturday night. Mind telling me what that was about?"

Penn's eyes flashed. "How'd you know about that?"

Grantham flashed his smile, easing the door closed. Eckland stepped forward, taking the seat across from Penn.

"That's not important, Aaron. What is important is why you were here from ten Saturday night until two Sunday morning. With Maureen Lewis."

Penn exhaled silently, fighting to keep his body language under control.

"What we'd like to know, Aaron, is why you guys were here at those hours rather then regular business hours," Grantham said. "By the way, who was the guy with her? Tall, dark hair, I think."

Penn shook his head. "Never seen him before."

Eckland eased forward, a smile spreading across his face. Coffee was on his breath. "We like you, Aaron, always have. And we don't want any trouble out of you. But Craig and I both find it real curious why a computer guy like you would need to be in Maureen Lewis's office on Saturday night."

"A project she wanted some help with. She didn't explain."

"I don't believe you. I'm going to ask one more time: What were you and Maureen Lewis doing up here Saturday night?"

Penn returned Eckland's gaze, saying nothing.

"You got something to hide, Aaron?" Grantham said, stepping closer.

"No, I don't. Do you?" Penn said, glaring at him. Grantham reddened. His smile disappeared. He shifted his gaze to Eckland, who was angry.

"Answer the goddamned question, Aaron!"

"And if I don't?"

Eckland leaned across the table. His face was a foot from Penn. "You're making a big mistake, that's what. And if you think playing the race card is gonna save your behind, you can forget it."

Penn's jaw tightened. He leaned across the table until he was nose to nose with Eckland. "I don't play the race card, Jerry. Now get the hell out of my office. You don't talk to me like that."

Eckland's eyes widened. He got to his feet, fists clenched. Grantham stepped forward. His eyes were hard.

"Let's just say, Aaron, that unless we get a straight answer out of you—right this minute— your job security is at ground zero. You follow me?"

Penn got to his feet slowly, his heart pounding. "You've gotten as straight an answer as you're going to get."

Grantham sized him up. "Fine. You're fired. Turn in your badge and keys. You have the option of writing a resignation letter."

Shock, then panic suddenly appeared on Penn's face. "What

the hell is going on here? I want to talk to Frank!"

"You'll have that chance," Eckland said. "Now clean out your goddamned desk. Let's go!"

* * *

Maureen arrived at work seconds later. She discovered a message from Grantham advising her that Cash wanted to see her right away. She muttered obscenities as she hustled to Gartin, now certain to be late for an appointment with an executive at Metro Cablevision. Gone as well was an opportunity to check on Aaron Penn. She would have to do that later in the day.

Cash's receptionist was on the phone, chatting away in hushed tones. It clearly wasn't office-related. She flipped through a magazine, growing angrier by the minute. She stood and caught the woman's eye.

"Is Frank here? I was told to come right over."

The receptionist terminated her conversation. "No, Maureen, he won't be in until this afternoon. He's at a press conference with the Sheriff and some other folks, about that juvenile detention facility."

Her eyes narrowed. "Is Craig here?"

"Haven't seen him."

She strode for the elevator in a huff. She called the cable executive from her car, apologizing for the delay and promising to be at his office in minutes.

* * *

It was late morning before she was behind her desk. On her voice-mail were requests for speaking engagements as well as complaints about merchandise sold at a sports memorabilia show over the weekend. Everything, she determined, would be delegated. Jeff Garland was always asking about handling some of the luncheons. He would get his chance.

"Line one, Maureen," the secretary said. "Aaron Penn."

"Hi," she said, lowering her voice. "I meant to come see you this morning, but there was this non-existent visit with Frank I was supposed to have . . ."

"You don't know, do you?" he said, cutting in. "Eckland and Grantham showed up two minutes after I got to work, Maureen. Wanted to know what the hell we were up to Saturday night."

She gasped. "What'd you tell them?"

"I didn't tell 'em dick."

"Good. Well, look, I'll talk to . . ."

"They fired me! I'm out of a fucking job!"

"What?"

"They took my fucking badge and keys! I cleaned out my fucking desk, that's how fired I am! Told I'll get two weeks severance in the goddamned mail! What the hell is going on, Maureen? What kind of game is being run here?"

Maureen swallowed, sweat breaking out on her forehead. "Listen to me, Aaron: That won't fly. You may get a couple of days off, but you will not lose your job. Do you understand me?"

Penn was silent.

"I'm gonna talk to Frank. And if they're serious about taking you out, I'm going, too. And if I go, the whole city's gonna know. So you sit tight, and calm down. You're not losing your job. You have my word, Aaron."

"All right," he said quietly. "Don't let me down, Maureen."

Janine left a message while she was on with Penn.

"Looks like the car dealers have been busy little beavers. Nothing more from Hollins, but twenty-five from Hamilton Ford, and at least ten from a dozen other folks around the state. Nearly one-fifty the last couple weeks. I don't know how Buckhalter's gonna compete, or if he'll even try. I think I can do a story comparing Frank's war chest to this point in the race four and eight years ago without compromising anything confidential that we've talked about. The difference is astronomical.

Call me. Bye."

*   *   *

She buzzed Erica inside at noon. "Food is the last thing on my mind. Thanks for coming so fast."

"No problem. What's up?"

Maureen removed a tiny cassette player from her blazer pocket. Erica's eyes widened as she rewound the tape and played back the exchange.

"Why the hell are you wired?"

She narrated quickly, realizing how far behind Erica was. Erica slumped into a chair at the dining room table, becoming paler by the minute.

"And you're gonna tape Frank? What are you gonna say?"

"I might lay everything on the line, just come right out and ask if he's taking illegal donations from the car lobby."

"And when he denies it and threatens you?"

Maureen shrugged. "I haven't gotten that far yet. But they fired Aaron this morning, Erica. Fired him! He's on the street if I don't get involved, and I wouldn't blame him if he turned on me. Ashleigh—or somebody—broke into my office and stole the Capital City file Saturday night. Somehow the security guard didn't see that, but Jerry Eckland and Craig Grantham confronted Aaron first thing this morning and knew we were up there! How the hell did they find out?"

"Just think before you do this, Mo. You're on dangerous ground if you start confronting the Attorney General, no matter how dirty he is. You've already broken into Ashleigh's computer! What if they know about that?"

"I have no choice." A pause. "Doing the right thing isn't part of this any more, Erica. It's about saving my ass."

THIRTY FIVE

Cash's receptionist pointed at the phone when he arrived the next morning. "Sonny Hollins, sir. I'll send it in there."

"Morning, Sonny," he said a minute later, loosening his tie. "How we doin'?"

"Top of the morning, Frankie. Got something real interesting in the mail just now. My service manager brought it here. Letter from Ms. Lewis, your Consumer person."

"Yeah?"

"Let me read it to you, sport."

* * *

Maureen was on a first-name basis with Jimmy Haynes, the U.S. Attorney representing the Southern District of Mississippi. She didn't have the clout to get bumped to the top of his priority list, however. She secured a few minutes with him before noon and ran errands, acknowledging a hunch which told her to stay away from the office until after the appointment. Her pager went off at nine-thirty.

"It's me," she said to the secretary, calling from the car.

"Frank wants you at his office right away."

"Do you know what about?"

"He didn't say. Just said for you to get right over."

She blanched. "I'm halfway to Magee. I've been putting off their Chamber of Commerce for months. Figured on getting back around one, one-thirty. Can you find out what he needs and call me back?"

The phone rang five minutes later. Maureen was now headed toward Highway 49, planning an unannounced hello in Simpson County to cover herself. Half an hour there might be possible.

"It's something about a letter you sent the Capital City service manager, a Mr. Gordon Smith."

She frowned. "I have no idea what he's talking about."

"He's rescheduling the rest of his afternoon to make room for you at one."

Fear stole through her insides. "Tell him I'll be there."

* * *

Rain was falling as she returned to Jackson, and her nerves became jumpy as she wove through the heavy downtown traffic and arrived at the federal building on East Capitol. She hurried up the steps and rode the elevator to Haynes' office, panic setting in. Haynes was speaking to an assistant and closing his briefcase as she approached, and this meeting was so informal he might not be able to see her at all.

"Hi, Maureen," Haynes said, a short, stocky blond man in his mid-forties. "I'm afraid I'm just not gonna have time this morning. Gotta catch a flight to . . ."

"Let me walk you to your car." The urgency in her voice caught the attention of both Haynes and the assistant. Both gazed at her, and Haynes shrugged.

"All right. Just one second." He went over instructions with the assistant. She strode away a moment later. "Follow me."

Haynes took the stairs, Maureen trailing. They dashed through what was now a thunderstorm, Haynes unlocking his Lexus with a clicker.

"Off the record, Jimmy. I'm getting ready to see Frank Cash, and I'm going to wear a wire. I'm concerned about campaign contributions from the car lobby. We found a serious scam in the garage at Capital City Motors—a mechanic came in and talked—and Frank not only pulled me off of it after he talked to Sonny Hollins, he's moved the entire jurisdiction of the car dealers to Nathan McMichael. I'm also being moved out of Consumer into a new position they're creating, and they're promoting Hamilton Dunn's daughter to Consumer Director."

Haynes frowned. "You know how involved McMichael and Dunn are with the car dealers. There'll be nobody to ride herd on them, especially if Dunn's daughter is on the other end."

"The timing is real strange. My friend Janine May at the *Times* tells me that car dealer contributions are pouring in— Frank's war chest is getting bigger by the day. Somebody also broke into my office over the weekend and took the Capital City file."

Haynes grunted. "Unless you can show there's an actual bribe taking place, or extortion . . ."

"What I have is a sworn affidavit from the mechanic. I have a copy of the tape at home Frank doesn't know about."

"And there's hard evidence there?"

"Everybody in the garage is getting rich, Jimmy. That's why I subpoenaed the billing records, which got Hollins all lathered up. He laid into Frank, and I was pulled off the case." A pause, as Haynes cranked his car. "So I'm gonna tell him about someone being in my office, and I'm wearing a wire in case anything is said."

"What I know of Cash, he's a decent, honest guy, but that doesn't mean he's pure. Sometimes the people around our elected officials are the dirtiest of all."

Maureen opened her door and popped her umbrella skyward. "I'm seeing that firsthand. Just wanted to let you know."

"I'm back Thursday. Stay in touch."

THIRTY SIX

Her heart thudded as she stepped into the foyer of Cash's office. She took in the receptionist, trying to read her face and tone. Nothing out of the ordinary.

"Come in," Cash said quickly, startling her. He was in a dark suit, the jacket off and the tie loosened. He returned behind his desk, gesturing at a chair across from him. She was taking the seat when she noticed Grantham on the couch. He gave her a nod, his poker face in place.

"I'd strongly prefer we do this alone, Frank."

She caught Grantham's frown from the corner of her eye. He didn't move. Cash gazed across the desk, surprised. "This is something I've gone over with Craig."

"No, sir," she said calmly. "Just the two of us. That's never been a problem before."

A long, cool gaze at Maureen. Then a nod at Grantham.

"We'll talk later."

Grantham didn't move. Maureen didn't look at him, but she felt his stare.

"You sure, Frank?"

"Yes, Craig. We'll talk later. Thank you."

Grantham took his time, but a moment later he closed the door behind him. Maureen sat carefully, not wanting to jar the recorder in her blazer pocket any more than she had to.

"Okay," Cash said, removing a single sheet from a manila folder. "This is a faxed copy of a letter received by Gordon Smith, the service manager at Capital City Motors. Sonny called the minute I got here this morning. He read it to me, and it was so bizarre I asked him to fax it." She started to reach, but he wasn't offering it yet. "I'm a reasonably perceptive sort, Maureen. And unless I've completely misread you over the years, this doesn't sound like anything you'd do. But it has your signature, it's

127

on your letterhead, and Craig points out that it comes at a time not long after we pulled you off the situation in their garage. So I'd like you to look me in the eye and explain what the hell you call yourself doing writing a letter like this."

He handed over the page. Her eyes widened as she read Ronnie Landrum's name in print, and she gasped as she found the outrageous request for free repair work. She read the sheet a second time before handing it to her boss. She held her temper, mindful of the fact the recorder was running.

"You think I wrote this? How stupid do you think I am, Frank?"

"It has your name, it's on your letterhead . . ."

"I want a copy of this right now! This proves someone is out to get me!"

"What the hell are you talking about?" He rapped the page. "It damn sure looks like you're out to get them!"

"The last thing in the world I would do is solicit a bribe from Capital City Motors, and why on earth would I give the mechanic's name to management? He was scared to death when he came to us! He told me a hundred times he would lose his job if his name came up. And I swore to him it wouldn't. For that reason, there's no mention of his name—or the tape—anywhere in the Capital City file, which is missing, by the way. Did you know that? Someone broke into my office and took the file!"

Cash didn't bat an eye. "Those files are for public consumption, Maureen. You know that."

"But my office isn't. Especially on a Saturday night, with me not there."

"How do you know it was taken then?"

She allowed herself a second to study him. Explain for the recorder, she reminded herself.

"Aaron Penn paged me . . ."

"What the hell was he doing there, anyway?"

"What the hell were Craig and Jerry doing firing him?"

128

Cash's eyes narrowed. "They didn't like the fact that Penn completely stonewalled when they simply asked what he was doing."

"What he was doing was fixing my computer," she said, carefully unleashing a story she rehearsed in front of Erica. "My hard drive locks up continually. Aaron spent an hour with it Friday and couldn't fix it. He brought a new one and said it would take several hours to install everything. I told him I couldn't be without a computer for half a day on Monday, and the only time over the weekend we could both be there was Saturday night. Why in the world was that a problem for anybody?"

"Why couldn't Aaron have just told them?"

"Maybe he didn't like the way they burst into his office, Frank," she said, her voice ripe with insinuation. "Maybe he was a little suspicious of them."

"What they didn't like is the fact that you guys were there 'til two in the morning!"

"Since when did that become an issue, Frank? I've spent all kinds of hours there on weekends! And how did the security guard completely miss someone in my office, but immediately get word to Jerry that Aaron and I were there and when, right down to the second?"

"I don't know, Maureen. I didn't ask." He paused, exhaling. "Look, there won't be a firing. I'll call Aaron myself. But Jerry sure thinks he's hiding something, and that really bothers me. This is an election year, for God's sake! We don't need even the hint of impropriety around here."

"Frank, here's what bothers me: The guard clearly talked to our chief of security, who got right on the phone to Jerry in the middle of a weekend so they could ambush Aaron the minute he got to work Monday morning! And what the hell was Craig doing there?"

"Maureen, none of that is your concern . . ."

"And why don't you seem the least bit upset that someone broke into my office and took a very important file?"

Cash's eyes flashed. "What are you implying?"

"Whoever did this knew exactly what they were looking for. They got their hands on my letterhead and sent a purely fictional letter meant to land in the hands of Sonny Hollins." She paused, eyeing him carefully. "Someone in this office did this, Frank. Someone who's trying very hard to get me."

Cash gazed at her. She couldn't read his silence.

"Let me be candid," she said, gently easing forward in her seat. "I know Sonny Hollins is a major player around here, and I know you go back a long way with him. I know how important Hamilton Dunn is because of his involvement in the car lobby. But moving his daughter to Consumer Director not only reeks of politics, it promises to be an embarrassment to the office. You're too smart not to see that."

She paused, taking her boss in. His eyes were hard, but nothing else.

"Is pressure being put on you by the car lobby?"

"Maureen, I don't think I have to tell you that in this job, there's pressure from all sides and then some . . ."

"Because if you were going to cut a deal, you could have told me."

Cash stood and came around to the front of his desk, never taking his eyes from her. She got to her feet slowly, mindful of the recorder.

"Who the hell would have given you that idea?"

"Nobody. But I read the newspaper, Frank. And the day I went to see Sonny Hollins, he practically foamed at the mouth at the opportunity to blow me off."

"That's typical Sonny Hollins. And you're a little naive, Maureen, if you think he's the only man in this town who thinks he has me by the short hairs."

"He just might think he does," she said, opting to narrate an exchange Tom had overheard several weeks ago. He told her about it after they read Ashleigh's e-mails. "I was at the athletic club a few days after you pulled me off him. He was there, talking to some man I didn't know about you. He said, 'You have a problem with Frank Cash, come to me. I own him.'"

A sardonic grin spread across Cash's face. "Like I said, you're naive to think that Hollins is the only one around here who thinks he has me in his pocket. That's politics, Maureen . . ."

She raised her voice the tiniest bit. "I find it interesting, Frank, that mere days after you pulled me off Capital City and deep-sixed a justified six-figure civil penalty, there's suddenly a fifty-thousand dollar campaign contribution from Sonny Hollins."

Cash's eyes widened. He bared his teeth, visibly shaking with anger. "You've had your say, Maureen, and that's enough. Nobody—and I mean nobody—walks in this room and implies that I'm taking a bribe!"

"I didn't say that, Frank! I am here to express my concern . . ."

"I think I made it clear weeks ago that you need to worry about what's in the province of your authority, Maureen, and forget the rest of it!"

". . . and I don't want to be set up! Do you hear me?"

Cash looked away, gathering his composure. A long moment passed before he spoke. "Thank you for coming in. I appreciate your candor."

The response—clearly meant to send her on her way—was impossible to read. She departed without a word.

THIRTY SEVEN

Maureen joined Janine the next day for Happy Hour at the Irish pub. They nursed beers at a table well away from the bar, trying to ignore a raucous group of men near the front who whistled and cackled each time a woman entered.

"It goes without saying that you'll have first shot at this when I go on record. But if something sinister really is taking place, I need iron-clad proof, not coincidences."

"You have evidence of a crime!"

"No, I don't, Janine. Just evidence of a scandal."

"A scandal the Attorney General is ignoring!" She paused. "Look, of course I want to blow this open. But our friendship comes first. I don't want the other shoe landing on you, and it sounds like it's in the air. Just think about it. That's all I ask."

"I will."

Janine gestured at the bar. Maureen glanced up in time to see the drunks forcibly removed from the premises. A burly manager was speaking apologetically to a trio of women in business attire.

"Reminds me of that creepy Jerry Eckland, Aaron's boss. There are a million stories about him getting loaded and hitting on every woman he lays eyes on. Did it to me at a Christmas party a couple of years ago."

"Married?"

"Except when he drinks."

Janine smiled. "Had lunch with my neighbor today. She went right to Evelyn and told her Craig was cheating."

Maureen's eyes widened.

"Evelyn apparently has Craig way up on a pedestal, even though he forced her to quit her job, ran off her friends and tried to turn her against her family. My neighbor knows her folks, and she dragged her kicking and screaming to Mendenhall. The father finally got through to her."

"How is she?"

"Pretty whacked out. They don't think she'll do anything irrational, but they're keeping close tabs on her. She has a lot of family in that area. Maybe they can get her through it." Janine sipped her beer. "This is the worst part: She was engaged to a guy right out of high school. He dumped her for someone else, and there was a suicide attempt. She was still on medication when she met Grantham."

"Oh, no."

"The mother, who also worships him, told him everything. My neighbor is afraid he'll use it in court if she files for divorce. Poor child. I wish there was something we could do."

The hint of a smile. "There just might be."

THIRTY EIGHT

Jeff and Sherry were already at their desks when Maureen arrived the next morning. Paul had car trouble, which couldn't have come at a better time.

"Let's meet for just a minute, guys."

"Miss Casual," Jeff said, smiling at Maureen's Hawaiian shirt and jeans. "The Prosecutor's Conference beckons."

"I'm not going. You are." She turned to Sherry. "Can your mother watch your child for a couple days?"

Sherry snorted. "I'm going to the Prosecutor's Conference? I'm not even a lawyer, in case you've forgotten. Mind if I ask what I'll be doing?"

"Everything said here stays here. Understand? This is completely confidential."

Both nodded.

"Craig and Evelyn Grantham have separated. Craig's been cheating on her for years." A pregnant pause. "With Ashleigh."

Shock appeared on both faces. Sherry's pencil fell to the table.

"You'll have rooms at the Belle Casino tonight and tomorrow night. You know he'll be there. And even though she's on leave, she will, too. These conferences are playtime, the biggest waste of tax dollars you could imagine. She never met one she didn't like."

"You're sure this is going on?" Sherry said. Jeff, who hated Grantham and loved juicy investigative work, was grinning.

"I have iron-clad proof." She leaned forward, a glint in her eye. "Find me something, guys. I'll be awfully generous with comp days if you do."

* * *

Jeff called from his room that afternoon, indicating that they had checked in. He called again the next morning at seven-thirty.

"We're in Magee, gassing up," he said, yawning. "Nailed 'em."

Adrenaline surged through her. "You saw them?"

"I have a tape, Maureen. Clean as a whistle." Pride was in his voice. "We'll be at the office in an hour."

"Come by here. Paul can hold the fort."

* * *

Jeff claimed to have been up nearly all night, but he looked fresher than Sherry. He handed over the small cassette and a labeled, standard-size tape. A big advantage of Jeff in the office was his knowledge of electronics; Maureen routinely sought his advice on surveillance equipment, and he'd brought his own deck from home and already dubbed the sound. This saved an uncomfortable trip to Public Integrity.

"It's cued. You'll love it."

The audio began as Grantham and Ashleigh drunkenly clambered into a room. A garment was ripped; Maureen, with her eyes closed, envisioned Grantham tearing Ashleigh's blouse or dress. Her eyes popped open when Ashleigh begged for it in the backside. Grantham climaxed loudly, repeating Ashleigh's name aloud in a chant. Oral sex then took place, with Ashleigh just as noisy. The din could likely be heard in nearby rooms.

"How the hell did you pull this off? After you left, I was thinking about how remote the chances were you'd even see them. Almost paged and told you to forget the whole thing."

"We didn't know what we were gonna do," Sherry said. "We wandered down to the buffet at dinner and there she was, already three sheets to the wind. Kept asking what we were doing there, but she was too drunk to demand a straight answer."

"We knew that was our only chance," Jeff said, leaning forward. He clearly wanted to explain. "We followed her to her room, asked if she wanted to party with us. She'd just spilled her purse, and a second room card was on the floor. Figured that one was for Craig. I picked it up when she had her back turned."

Sherry laughed. "We said we'd meet her at the bar. Never saw her again."

Jeff smirked. "You didn't. I let myself in an hour later when nobody answered. Set up the voice-activated recorder under the bed. Got it around four this morning. They were both snoring, Ashleigh on top of him. Didn't have a stitch of clothing on. You don't know what I'd give to have a picture I could download to everyone."

"God only knows what would have happened if you'd woke 'em up."

"I was more nervous setting up the recorder. The room reeked of alcohol when I went back. They were probably so drunk a bomb wouldn't have disturbed them. By the way, I tried the front desk last night and this morning. Grantham has a room but hasn't checked in. Called the Mullins household last night from a pay phone. Hung up when Warren answered."

Maureen rewound the tape. "Unbelievable. She's in a hotel room with Craig while he's up half the night with their newborn. I wonder if he has the first clue about them."

"You gonna give him the tape?" Sherry said. "Or is it for Evelyn?"

"Don't worry about that. Just check with me before you start taking comp days. You get five each. Not a word to Paul or anyone else, or I take 'em back."

THIRTY NINE

Sherry wanted vacation immediately. Maureen made the arrangements and handled phones most of the week.

"A Mr. Ronnie Landrum has called three times for you," the secretary said as she returned from a speaking engagement Wednesday morning. "Says it's urgent."

It took a second for the name to ring a bell. Then her heart sank. She dialed reluctantly.

"Ms. Lewis, they fired me! They called me in and asked how I could do such a thing. Then they handed me a check for two weeks severance and told me never to set foot on their lot again!"

The pain in his voice made her sick to her stomach.

"You promised my name would never come up! Now what am I gonna do?"

"This happened today?"

"Monday, soon as I got to work."

"Monday? Why are you just calling now?"

"I been trying to reach that woman who took your place. All I get is her recorder!"

"A woman took my place? What are you talking about?"

Landrum heaved a sigh, his frustration growing. "That

woman who called the garage! Said you'd gotten a promotion and wasn't with the Consumer department no more. Said she was in charge."

Maureen nearly dropped the receiver. "Who was this?"

"Sherry Forster, from the Attorney General's Office!"

A long moment passed. Maureen shook her head. "Go ahead."

"Ms. Forster knew all of what you and I talked about, then asked if we mechanics was still getting paid too much and if the unnecessary repair work was continuing. I told her the extra pay stopped soon as I talked to you—see, Gordon called us all together and said he knew someone talked, and we was back to our old pay 'til someone spoke. We're still doing extra work, but the mechanics don't get nothing extra, so it's horrible 'round there."

"And you told Ms. Forster all this?"

"Yes ma'am." A long pause. "Should I not have?"

"She shouldn't have called you. You did nothing wrong, Mr. Landrum," she said, softening. "This was a huge mistake made by our office." He started to speak, but she headed him off. "I know this is short notice, and I can't promise it'll help, but I'd like to get another statement. I want you to tell me—for the record—exactly what you just said."

"So I shouldn't keep trying to catch Ms. Forster?"

"No, sir. Let me handle this. I'd like to make this up to you since you were betrayed by this office, and getting another statement is the first step. You can come down here, or I can come to you. The sooner, the better."

"All right, then. Come by our place any time you want to. Wife just started today with a temp service. I'm home with my son."

* * *

She dialed Haynes' office from the car. Not only was he in town, he could see her at two. She would get the statement, then race home and wire herself before dropping in on Cash unannounced. If all went according to plan, she would have time to return home and copy the tape before seeing Haynes. She had talked Jeff into leaving his cassette deck with her without having to explain why.

The Landrum's lived in a trailer park in Pearl. Their home was modest but clean, with house plants and religious artifacts in the small living room. Landrum was reading to their toddler when she arrived. She glanced around, glad she had stopped in rather than asking him to her office. This was the type of family she had in mind when she wrote the Consumer Protection bill, folks who lived month to month and to whom a trip to McDonald's was a special occasion.

"Make yourself comfortable, Ms. Lewis. I was about to put the little one down for his nap."

He returned a moment later, grinning as the boy cried from his bedroom. "Give him a minute. He'll conk out in no time flat."

"You remember how we did this the first time," she said, placing the recorder between them on the coffee table. "No trick questions, and raise your hand if you need to stop and we'll pause the tape."

He nodded. She began the recording and identified them, explaining the purpose. Landrum was relaxed this time, calmly answering her questions and painting a clear portrait of the morning he heard from the woman who identified herself as Sherry Forster. Ten minutes later she stopped the tape.

"So you're still Director of Consumer Protection, and not Ms. Forster?"

"I'm in charge until July." She permitted herself a smile. "You remember the day you and your wife talked to us, in my office. Remember the woman who was with me?"

"A black woman."

"That's Sherry Forster."

Landrum's eyes became the size of saucers. "A white woman called me, Ms. Lewis! Said she was Sherry Forster, plain as day."

"First of all, Sherry wouldn't call you. She's one of my investigators, and there would never be a situation in a case I'm handling where she would talk to you without a request from me. Second, she's on vacation. I don't expect her back until next week."

"So who called me?"

"I have a pretty good idea. It wasn't Sherry, though. I can promise you that."

He wanted to ask more questions, but she got to her feet.

"That's all I can say. But you shouldn't have gotten a call from our office, and you shouldn't have been fired."

"You gonna try to get my job back?"

"I'll clear your name. That way the firing won't hurt you down the road. If I were you, I would talk to a lawyer."

His eyes narrowed. "You telling me to sue Mr. Hollins?"

"I would talk to a lawyer, Mr. Landrum, that's what I'd do. Fact, while your child is asleep, write down everything that has happened to you, from the day you started with Capital City until now. If you do take action, that would be very helpful." She handed him a business card. "In the meantime, go find another job, and if the firing stands between you and something else, call me. I'll talk to the employer myself."

"That's mighty kind of you, ma'am. My wife and I are grateful for everything you've done."

"Least I can do. You deserve better. Talk to a lawyer, Mr. Landrum. And make notes on everything you've gone though. Do it right away, so you'll have everything."

"Yes, ma'am."

* * *

She called Sherry from the car.

"I'm breaking my own rule, disturbing someone who's on

vacation," she said. "I'll be brief. I hope I didn't get you in the middle of anything."

"Just got back from the grocery. Got back from Georgia last night, matter of fact. What's up? Need me to come in?"

"You won't believe this. Remember Ronnie Landrum?"

"Sure, the mechanic from Capital City. What's he done now?"

"He lost his job. Someone identifying herself as Sherry Forster called him Monday, then ratted him out to management."

"What?"

"Whoever did this knew we taped him. He called me today after getting your machine a bunch of times."

"What the hell is this about, Maureen?"

"I know you didn't do it, Sherry. Just tell me, for the record."

"Of course I didn't! I was in Macon on Monday!"

"I know that. That's all I wanted to hear." Reassurance was in her tone. "I just took another statement from him. He'd forgotten who you were until I reminded him who was with me the first time. He 'bout fell on the floor. He said a white woman who knew all about the stuff in the garage called him. Told him that I had been promoted, and that she was now in charge of Consumer."

Sherry gasped. "Ashleigh?"

"That's what I'm thinking."

"Oh, shit. What do you want me to do?"

"Not a thing. Enjoy your time off, then come back to work like nothing happened. I'll handle this. Fact, I'm gonna see Frank today."

* * *

She wolfed down a sandwich at the apartment, then removed her blouse and ran a wire across her chest. She tested the equipment, satisfied it would work again. She dressed and hustled to

Gartin. A television crew was getting a sound bite from Cash when she arrived. She leafed through a magazine, trying her best to appear casual. Twenty minutes later Cash's door opened. He frowned when he saw Maureen.

"Five minutes, Frank. I know I didn't call, but . . . "

"This is a very busy day."

"Five minutes. That's all."

Cash frowned, then ushered her in. She had the Attorney General to herself.

"I got a very disturbing call this morning. Ronnie Landrum, the mechanic at Capital City we took the statement from, was fired Monday." She paused. Cash frowned but didn't respond. "Mr. Landrum received a call from a woman who identified herself as Sherry Forster."

"Why would Sherry call the mechanic?"

"She didn't, Frank. Sherry's on vacation this week. I just talked to her. She was in Macon, Georgia on Monday."

"Can somebody confirm that?"

Maureen's eyes narrowed. "I just took another statement from the mechanic. He said a white woman called him at the dealership. A white woman who said that she had taken over Consumer Protection and was getting caught up on my cases. A white woman who seemed to know an awful lot about the affidavit sworn out by the mechanic. That sounds a lot like Ashleigh Dunn to me."

"Look, I know you don't like the fact that Ashleigh is taking over Consumer, but there's no reason to immediately make the assumption that . . ."

"Oh, for God's sake, Frank! Nobody knew the mechanic's name until I turned that tape over to Craig!"

Cash looked frightened. Aware he was losing his cool, he turned away.

"Listen to me!" Maureen said, slamming her hand on the Attorney General's desk. Cash whirled. "Did you give Ashleigh the name of the mechanic?"

"No! And you don't raise your voice at me, not if you want to work in this office!"

Her eyes locked on his. She spoke slowly, malice in her tone. "If you didn't give her the mechanic's name, who did?"

Cash sighed. "Craig, I guess."

Her fists were now clenched. The only thing maintaining her self-control was the recorder. "Tell me you're kidding."

"He must have," Cash said, looking away. "You gave him the tape."

"I fully expected it was going to you!" she said, trying to keep from shouting. "Why on earth would he talk to Ashleigh about it? She's on maternity leave, Frank! Since when did she become part of this investigation?"

"I don't know that he talked to her, Maureen, and you don't, either . . ."

"That's just great. A man lost his job over this, and you're pleading the fifth? Maybe you need to keep a better eye on things around here. Sounds like there's a lot going on you don't know."

Sweat was on Cash's brow. He leveled a finger at her. "I'm warning you: If you expect to keep your position in this office, you'd better watch your mouth. You are walking a very fine line, Maureen. Do you understand?"

Cash's phone speaker buzzed.

"They're waiting, sir."

He acknowledged his secretary, then faced her. His eyes were hard. "If you'll excuse me."

FORTY

Jimmy Haynes told his secretary not to interrupt unless there was a crisis. He listened to Maureen's cassette, which now clocked in at thirty minutes. He gave her a wan smile when it was over. Her heart sank.

"You don't have enough to indict, do you?"

"There's just not evidence of Cash accepting a bribe, no matter how dirty his office is. The F.B.I. might see fit to wiretap his phones, if you want to go that route."

"He's too smart to say anything, especially now."

"I'd agree. Where does this leave you with him?"

She shrugged. "I'd fire anybody who talked to me like that."

* * *

She shuffled papers the rest of the afternoon, making sure each investigator was out of the office. The solitude gave her time to think, but it didn't change her mind. She typed a brief resignation letter, then drove to Gartin.

"Craig's in with him," the receptionist said. "Do you want me to interrupt?"

"No," she said, handing over a folder. "Give this to Frank. Please make sure it gets in his hands, even if you have to barge in there. It's very important."

She paged Janine from her car. The call was returned a minute later.

"I'm ready to talk. On the record."

* * *

Janine left the apartment ninety minutes later. Maureen dialed the ABC affiliate after the six o'clock news. She waited out the automated switchboard and was transferred to the newsroom.

"Carolyn Davis, please."

"She just stepped out. Can I take a message?"

"Maureen Lewis, with the Attorney General's Office. Please page her. This is very important. Let me give you my home number."

The call was returned five minutes later.

"You said to call if I had a scoop, Carolyn. I have a big one."

*   *   *

Carolyn and a photographer arrived twenty minutes later. Maureen was miked and told her story, omitting only the affair between Grantham and Ashleigh and the firing of Tom. They left before eight. Carolyn called an hour later and put her on with the news director, a man whose voice had a Cajun feel to it.

"Maureen, what you'll see first is a four-second I.D. which says, 'What's under the hood at the Attorney General's Office? Find out tomorrow at ten.' First play is at the end of our late newscast, going into *Nightline*. That's an hour and a half from now."

"I'll be watching."

"It'll play all day tomorrow. The Promotions department will also put together a fifteen-second spot beginning around noon, just in time for the block of soaps. It'll run all afternoon and evening. Let me read the script to you." He cleared his throat. "'A department head at the Attorney General's Office mysteriously resigns. An alleged scam at a car dealership is ignored, while campaign contributions from that dealership pour into the Attorney General's Office. Carolyn Davis finds out what's under the hood, tonight at ten.'"

Maureen waited him out, adrenaline pouring through her.

"That audio will be cut tomorrow. We can tailor this to make sure you're comfortable with it, but Carolyn and I wrote it based on your sound bites."

"It's fine." She sighed. "I'm dead once it hits the air, but I've already resigned."

"We couldn't reach Cash. We'll talk to him tomorrow. By the way, Carolyn said the *Times* has this tomorrow morning."

"You guys are the first TV station . . ."

"Believe me, we appreciate it. I say that because we have a blurb of tomorrow's *Times* headlines just before the end of the late news each night. It'll be mentioned there, too, since it's a front- page story."

* * *

The late newscast was on when she got off the phone. Nerves chattering, she poured herself a glass of wine. Her head was against Tom's chest as the news neared its end, a tape already rolling in the VCR. The black male spoke first.

"A quick look at tomorrow morning's *Jackson Times* headlines," he said, a graphic filling the screen. "Why the rash of Metro bank robberies, and what you can do to protect yourself."

"And just what's under the hood at the Attorney General's Office?" the white female anchor said as the shot dissolved back to the set. She turned to her counterpart. "This is a story you'll only see here, and Carolyn Davis is putting it together as we speak. Should be quite interesting."

The black anchor nodded and faced the camera. "That's our news at ten. We'll see you tomorrow night. *Nightline* is next."

A commercial break ran. Then the I.D. played, just as it was described.

"Whoa!" Tom said, leaning forward. "Rewind that."

The audio was authoritative and left a clear question mark. The video was a collage of a car lot, a fistful of greenbacks and Frank at a press conference. The images had been altered, creating a haunting effect.

"My God," she said, plopping on the couch. "I'm really doing this."

"Want your phone back on?"

"No. And I wouldn't mind if you'd stay tonight."

145

FORTY ONE

The ABC affiliate's morning show had no mention of the story, although another I.D. ran just before *Good Morning America.* Maureen made coffee and awakened Tom, her stomach tight after checking her voice mail.

"Frank called last night while Carolyn was here. No way he'll accept my resignation. Said the whole thing has been a big misunderstanding and wants all of us to sit down, including Ashleigh. He won't after he reads the paper."

Her hands were shaking as she opened it. She gasped as she discovered photos of Cash and herself below the fold on the front page. The story continued on another page.

A.G. DEPARTMENT HEAD RESIGNS
By Janine May, Jackson Times Staff Writer

Two months ago Governor Bobby Greene signed into law the Consumer Protection Act, which afforded Mississippi consumers far more clout against deceptive advertising campaigns and con artists than ever before. Maureen Lewis, Consumer Protection Director of the Mississippi Attorney General's Office and author of the bill, resigned yesterday at 5:00 p.m., effective immediately. She cited a series of events which has left her questioning her job security and the sanctity of the office.

"Days after the bill became law, I visited Capital City Motors after receiving complaints about overcharging and unnecessary work in their service department," Lewis said. "Several days later a mechanic with the dealership swore out an affidavit and alleged on tape that a huge scam was taking place in their garage.

"We subpoenaed their billing records, and I was prepared

*to demand a $100,000 civil penalty based on what I consid-
ered to be numerous, blatant violations of the law. The
Attorney General is an old friend of the dealership's president,
and not only was I told to back off completely, this case—and
all other cases concerning automobile dealerships around the
state—was transferred immediately to (Motor Vehicle
Administration Executive Director) Nathan McMichael.*

*"While McMichael technically regulates the car dealers,
my department has always stepped in when we felt further
action was necessary. I was never given a straight answer as
to whether action of any kind would be taken against Capital
City, and I've been flooded with calls since then from consumers who claim all they get from McMichael is an answering machine."*

*Lewis said she was forced from her position barely a
month after Governor Bobby Greene signed the Consumer
Protection act into law.*

*"I was offered a different position in the office May 1, a
job the Attorney General and his Chief of Staff claimed they
created especially for me. I had a lot of questions about it, and
while I wouldn't call it a demotion, I would have been
watched closely, and my trial work would have been carefully monitored. It was obvious that I wouldn't have any say in
cases which came through Consumer Protection. When I said
I wasn't interested and would prefer to stay in Consumer, I
was told that wasn't an option. The decision to replace me
had already been made, and my successor had already been
chosen."*

*Lewis's replacement is Ashleigh Dunn. Dunn, currently
on maternity leave, reports to her new assignment July 1. She
has spent six years with the Attorney General's Office, the last
two as a staff attorney under Lewis. She is the daughter of former Madison County Senator Hamilton Dunn, now a government lobbyist highly involved with the automobile indus-*

try around the state.

"I'm excited about the opportunity," Dunn said last night by telephone. "I'm grateful to Frank Cash for his confidence in me. I plan on being a friend to our state's consumers, someone the people can count on."

Cash had no comment about the resignation of Lewis, referring all inquiries to Chief of Staff Craig Grantham.

"Maureen Lewis is a talented and hard-working attorney, but her ego trips and self-absorbed behavior have become more destructive to the Attorney General's Office than we're comfortable with, especially in light of the unwarranted harassing of area car dealers," Grantham said.

"We sincerely hoped Ms. Lewis would remain with the office in the position we created with her strengths in mind. We're confident that Ashleigh Dunn, who has a wide array of experience and is an equally competent prosecutor, will continue to raise the level of excellence in this critically important department."

Lewis strongly defended her actions. "The idea of me harassing car dealerships—or any business of any kind—is absolute nonsense. We don't issue subpoenas unless the circumstances involved absolutely demand it. My record of loyalty and integrity to the businesses and consumers of this state speaks for itself, as does my contribution to the Attorney General's Office. It speaks volumes, if you ask me, that my replacement is the daughter of the state's biggest automobile lobbyist."

Lewis says that while she feels politics played a major role in the promotion of Dunn, the frightening part was only beginning.

"My office was broken into, and the Capital City file was stolen. Two days later the Attorney General called me in and made me aware that a letter—on my stationery and supposedly signed by me—had been mailed to the dealership's service manager. It said that in exchange for free service on my own car, I would turn over the name of the mechanic who made us aware of the scam. I was stunned. There's no way I would solicit a bribe from Capital City Motors, and the last thing in the world I would do is turn the name of the mechanic over to management. He was afraid to talk to us for fear of losing his job, and I promised him his name wouldn't be revealed."

Lewis says the mechanic was fired immediately. She took a second statement from him.

"He called me two days after the firing. He said a woman with the Attorney General's Office called him and identified herself as the new Consumer Protection Director. The problem is, the woman who made this call used someone else's name. The woman whose name was used was not only on vacation when this call took place, she's black. The mechanic said a white woman called him, a woman who claimed she had taken over as Consumer Director and was catching up on my cases."

Dunn denied making the call, but knew about the letter to the Capital City service department. "I have no idea what Maureen Lewis is talking about, with respect to calling a mechanic. I just had a baby. I start back to work in July. Now, I did hear about Maureen's letter to Capital City. Based on that, I'm not surprised she's resigning. It's unfortunate that these things happen, because it gives our entire office a black eye. But like I said, I'm looking forward to the opportunity and will be a friend to the state's consumers, not someone whose primary goal is seeing herself on television."

Lewis says the real question is how the person who called the mechanic became aware of his identity.

"The Attorney General admitted to me that he gave the mechanic's name to one of his high-ranking people," she said, refusing to call the staffer by name. "No one else should have had it. Also, the agreement I had with the Attorney General *was that I would brief Ms. Dunn on my cases when she returned from maternity leave, which is several weeks away. I have no proof Ms. Dunn called the mechanic, but whoever made the call lied about her identity, which I can prove. And whoever made the call sure knew a lot about this case for someone who should-n't have been privy to inside information."*

Lewis says she resigned because she feels she is being set up. "I was stonewalled in my attempts to pursue a business which is clearly breaking the law, and I was replaced in my job by someone who not only is politically well-connected, but who may be using the position for personal gain and the destruction of others."

When asked about skyrocketing contributions from statewide car dealers—reported twice in the Jackson Times *recently—Attorney General Frank Cash had no comment. A South Mississippi car dealer did, however.*

"None of that surprises me," he said, speaking on condition of anonymity. "I'm sick and tired of hearing from (Mississippi Vehicle Association President and Capital City Motors President Sonny) Hollins and being told how much money we need to throw at Frank Cash."

Hollins was unavailable for comment, but Irv White, a spokesman for Capital City Motors, denied any wrongdoing.

"I know I can speak for Sonny in saying that Frank Cash is a fine and honorable man, and he's never given us any kind of break in terms of something illegal," White said. "If campaign contributions are pouring in, it's because of the man's integrity and record. He hasn't been elected Attorney General three times for nothing."

Nathan McMichael, Executive Director of the Motor Vehicle Administration, also defended Cash and casts doubt on Lewis's allegations.

"I don't know where Ms. Lewis gets the idea that we're up to no good in my office. When someone gets the voice-mail, it

means I'm already on the phone with one of our state's fine consumers. Not all complaints are valid. We always get both sides of the story before taking any action, which it doesn't appear Ms. Lewis did before shooting off her mouth. As far as Frank Cash is concerned, he's an honest, decent man with roots in the community and love for the people of our state. I'd certainly trust his word over that of a selfish, disgruntled employee."

"At this point I'm finished in the legal community," Lewis said. "I have no idea what I'll do or if I'll even stay in the area. But I felt it necessary to come forward with this information before my name became tied to anything unethical and possibly illegal."

Maureen had showered and dressed by the time Tom finished the article. "Did Grantham talk to Janine last night?"

"Sure did. Her pager went off in the middle of the interview. I called her right after leaving my resignation with Frank's secretary, and I'm guessing Craig and Frank talked and decided to call Janine. They know she's written about campaign contributions, and it's no secret we're friends." She grinned. "I don't know how ethical it was, but since she called Craig from right here, she asked if I wanted to respond to what he said."

"You're really thinking about leaving town?"

"I wasn't exaggerating, Tom. Short of begging the Public Defender for a job, I'm finished. I don't know anyone in the legal community who'd hire me now, especially if there are any political ramifications."

"My dad knows a lot of people. Here and in Columbus."

"Mom and Dad are getting old. I might go back home. Never thought I'd hear myself say that." She kissed my cheek. "Let me clean out my office while I can still do it in peace."

FORTY TWO

Joyce Cash had already seen an I.D. on the ABC affiliate by the time her husband emerged for breakfast. She had prepared toast, fruit and coffee. She had also retrieved *The Jackson Times* from the driveway. It was beside his plate. Eyes widening, he read quickly. Joyce watched, waiting for an explanation, but he grabbed his cell phone and walked outside. He dialed Grantham.

"In my office in half an hour."

* * *

Grantham, who didn't have Evelyn to awaken him any more, slept late and was caught off guard by the call from his boss. He flipped on *Good Morning America* to catch the headlines and saw an I.D. just before leaving the house. He gasped when he saw the pictures of Cash and Maureen on the front page of the paper. Now frightened, he took an extra five minutes to read the article. His cell phone rang the minute he hit the heavy downtown traffic.

"What is this shit in the paper? That bitch did a hatchet job on me, and Maureen comes off smelling like a fucking rose!" Ashleigh said angrily. "You said you were going to handle this, Craig!"

"Don't yell at me!" he said, nearly plowing into a car at an intersection. "I told you five hundred times it was under control, but you had to do everything you could to fuck Maureen Lewis. That letter was the height of stupidity, Ashleigh. I thought you were a little smarter than that. And if you were going to call the mechanic, why the hell didn't you just make up a name?"

A pause. "You just remember that there'll be hell to pay if I get fucked over, Craig. And you'll be right in the middle of it."

* * *

Grantham stalked past the receptionist and rapped on Cash's door. The Attorney General closed it behind him. He took Grantham by the lapels.

"I warned you about Ashleigh. I warned you, you moron!" he said, shoving him away.

Grantham straightened his clothes, then sat across Cash's desk. Cash poured himself a cup of coffee, remaining on his feet.

"This will not impact Washington in any way, Frank . . ."

"So help me God, Craig, it better not. Now I have to get to the national press and smooth this out before they get it and blow me out of the water! I'll be on the damned phone all morning! What the hell was I thinking about when I let you talk me into moving Maureen Lewis?"

"I'll get dirt on her, you just wait. I still want to know what she was doing with Aaron Penn."

Cash leveled a finger at him. "No, you won't, Craig. Damage control is your mandate now, not scorched earth. Do you understand me?"

Grantham looked away. "Yes, sir."

"And stay the hell away from Ashleigh. She's out of control. I haven't decided what to do about her." Grantham nodded, starting for the door. Cash stopped him. "I'm in Grenada today, so you're in charge. Use your head," he said, enunciating each syllable.

FORTY THREE

"Erica called right after you left," Tom said an hour later, lingering in the apartment doorway. "And Janine just called. Wants you to page her."

Maureen grinned. "You make a good receptionist."

"Thought I'd head up to Columbus. Dad's full of good ideas." He embraced her. "I know the last thing on your mind now is us, but I'd like to keep seeing you, wherever we wind up. You're a special lady."

She kissed his cheek. "You're a sweet guy. Let's see what happens."

"By the way, the folks get your station on the cable. We'll be watching."

*   *   *

She talked to Janine twice that morning. The second time was while receiving a massage at the athletic club.

"Grantham has called an eleven-thirty press conference on the front steps of Gartin."

"Craig? What in the world about?"

"The press release was vague. Also, my boss and I just got out of a meeting. Seems that Hollins pulled his advertising and is demanding a retraction."

"For what?"

"A rush to judgment," Janine said, laughing. "That's what his lawyer said. Screw him. But our sales manager says Capital City is responsible for almost twenty percent of the entire paper's revenue by themselves. The lawyer for the dealership implied that the other big car dealers might pull out, too."

"Oh, bullshit, they will not!" She whirled and covered her mouth. The young woman giving the massage grinned.

"A lot of it was just posturing. But it got pretty heated. The heads of state are going to talk some more. The sales manager said he understands they made the same threat to Channel Four. They must have heard the blurb before *Nightline* last night."

Maureen shook her head. "How did your boss handle it?"

"I was real proud of him. Got right in the sales manager's face and said we would all walk before we kissed up to Sonny Hollins to save someone's ad budget. Let me run. I'll call you after the press conference."

*   *   *

Grantham's interns coordinated with the media, then rang his desk. He appeared two minutes later, smiling for the gathering. It was warm and sunny, a beautiful late-spring day.

"Good morning. Attorney General Cash is on a fact-finding mission in Grenada today concerning the proposed juvenile detention facility site, which—in light of the success the project has had in South Mississippi—is something he's very excited about. He regrets he can't be here."

He paused, glancing around. "He and I felt it imperative, however, that we address you in the media and rebut what we consider a totally unwarranted and uncorroborated attack on this office from a disgruntled employee."

Hands shot up, but Grantham continued. He was clearly reading a statement. "Attorney General Cash and Sonny Hollins are close friends, and they go back a long way. But for Maureen Lewis or anyone else," he said, searching the gathering until he made eye contact with Janine, "to imply that their professional relationship is anything other than pure is unconscionable. Mr. Cash and I both regret that Ms. Lewis shot her mouth off and hinted otherwise before coming to us to check out the facts.

"Furthermore, Nathan McMichael at the Motor Vehicle Administration is a trusted friend of the residents of this state, going back many years to his glory days in a baseball uniform at Mississippi State. Mr. McMichael has given us his word that he is doing everything in his power right now to watch over our state's car dealers. He asks—and we do, too—that you understand this is a transitional period, and if you get his cotton-pickin' answering machine, leave a message and he swears he'll call you back!" Grantham said, attempting a laugh. It was met with dead silence, and he continued without missing a step.

"In trying to anticipate your questions, let me touch on the subject of Ashleigh Dunn. As you read in this morning's *Jackson Times*, it was implied by Ms. Lewis that Ms. Dunn made a phone call to a mechanic at Capital City Motors, and that she wrote a phony letter to the Capital City service department. Ms. Dunn denies any involvement with either, and let me remind you that this letter—in which Ms. Lewis asked for free service on her own car—was sent on Ms. Lewis's stationery and signed by Ms. Lewis. While it is common knowledge that Ms. Dunn is the daughter of former state lawmaker Hamilton Dunn, let me assure you that her ascension to the position of Consumer Protection Director is indeed warranted, just as Ms. Lewis was promoted to that position with similar credentials seven years ago."

He glanced at his notes before continuing. "Let me underscore the fact that Ms. Lewis, in turning in her resignation, is forfeiting a sizable promotion to a position we created especially for her, based on what she told us she wants to accomplish in her career. Ms. Lewis, as I said in the paper, is a bright woman and a competent attorney, but the side of her you haven't seen in the media is someone who is self-absorbed and power-hungry and who didn't feel she had enough control of our state's businesses."

A smirk appeared on his face. "We find it most interesting that after Mr. Hollins sent a copy of this letter to Attorney General Cash, Ms. Lewis immediately resigned and started making all these accusations."

Janine's mouth fell open. She started to speak, but a burly, prematurely-gray man wedged forward.

"Mr. Grantham? Walter Jett, Coast Daily Leader . . ."

Grantham held up a hand. "That is all. Be aware that Attorney General Cash will want to speak with you regarding his trip to Grenada when he gets back . . ."

"Mr. Grantham . . ."

"Mr. Jett, I'm not taking questions at this time . . ."

Jett shoved forward again, drawing the ire of a television photographer as he bumped him aside. "Do you confirm or deny a long-running affair with Ashleigh Dunn?"

Grantham rolled his eyes and broke into a grin, stepping away from the podium. "I have work to do . . ."

"Do you confirm or deny . . ."

"I've never had anything other than a purely professional relationship with Ms. Dunn, Mr. Jett," Grantham said, stepping back to the podium. He grinned, trying to hold his temper. "I don't know why this kind of stuff—the politics of personal destruction, as someone once said—has to take place, but . . ."

"Sir, do you confirm or deny you spent the night with Ms. Dunn at the Belle Casino in Gulfport this past Wednesday, at the Mississippi Prosecutor's Conference?"

The gathering buzzed. Grantham did his best to retain his cool. "As I said, Mr. Jett, Ms. Dunn and I have had a purely professional relationship over the years, and she is a talented attorney with a bright future . . ."

Jett moved to within six feet of the podium. "Did this affair have anything to do with Ms. Dunn's promotion?"

"I told you there was no affair!" Grantham said in blind rage. He quickly stepped within a foot of Jett, who held his ground. He lowered his voice and leveled a finger at the reporter, who grinned and shrugged. Grantham's interns herded him into Gartin before anything further developed.

* * *

"Me again," Janine said. "Grantham lost it at the press conference. After this long, rambling statement where he defended Cash, Hollins, Ashleigh and McMichael—and painted you as an egotistical control-freak—Wally Jett of the Coast Daily Leader asked if he could confirm or deny he was having an affair with Ashleigh."

Maureen gasped. She was at home, in the middle of a carry out plate from the neighborhood grocery.

"He knew they were at the Belle. Who'd you send?"

"Sherry and Jeff. Shit! I'll call you back."

Jeff returned her page five minutes later. She filled him in on the press conference, then confronted him.

"I did it," he said, returning to the phone after closing his door. "Jett and I are old friends. Went to college together."

She closed her eyes. "Do you realize what Craig will do to me?"

"Maureen, Wally is every bit as trustworthy as Janine May. Craig'll never know where it came from. After reading the paper, I just couldn't let them get away with it. It's high time somebody stood up for you. I wish I could do more."

"Thank you," she said, softening. "Watch the late news on Channel Four tonight. I can't wait to see what's done to them."

FORTY FOUR

"So what are you gonna do?" Erica said for the third time. They were in her kitchen after supper.

"I don't know, I told you. I'm tired of talking about it. I thought my father was gonna go into hysterics." She gestured at the living room. "I thought we were gonna play Chess."

Erica set up the board. "What did Graham say?"

"That I was really screwing up. That I was throwing away a bright future with a politician who was clearly going big places. Used the words reckless and irresponsible. I don't know if I'm more disappointed or pissed off, Erica. I fully expected a speech about morals and ethics and how I was doing the right thing by going to the press with this stuff. Made me wonder if what's most important to him is being able to brag about his daughter in front of his Yacht Club buddies."

"I can't believe that. What did Tom say?"

"He was real supportive. But he's unemployed, too."

"Does he know what he's gonna do?"

"His dad has an ad agency. He went up there to see them." She managed a smile. "Said they get the station on the cable. They'll be watching tonight."

"He say anything about wanting to stay in touch?"

"He did," she said, waiting for Erica to begin the game. "Still wants me to meet his folks. Wants to come to the Bay, too."

"What did you tell him?"

"I think my exact words were, 'Maybe so.' Can we play now?"

Erica shook her head slowly. She made no move to start the game. Maureen looked up. "I don't understand you. All your life you've wanted a nice guy without your father in the middle of it. Now you have one, and if I know you, you left Tom twisting in the wind."

"I'm still getting to know him! He spied on me, for God's sake! And with all due respect to our friendship, if I wanted your opinion about this . . ."

"Is it fear of commitment because of your dad, or some irrational search for perfection?"

Maureen's jaw tightened. "This is not the time to push, Erica. Please hear that before you continue and I really lose my temper."

They played in silence for ten minutes.

"I don't know what I want with Tom. And I don't think being rushed into a decision will help either one of us."

"I respect that," Erica said, contemplating her next move. "But as someone who loves you and knows your deepest, darkest secrets, I think I'm qualified to speculate. And I think you're so brainwashed about your vision of Mr. Right you wouldn't know it if he knocked on your door."

Maureen sneered. "Oh, you're suddenly the expert, now that Keith put a ring on your finger?"

"I'm no expert, Mo. But falling in love with Keith was as much about making a new friend as anything else. Tom wants to be your friend. Let him."

* * *

She settled in Erica's recliner an hour later and watched as the ABC affiliate led with an update on a deadly hit and run. Then Carolyn Davis loomed in the background of the studio. Maureen raised the volume as the male anchor tossed to her.

"Tonight, in a report you'll only see on NewsCenter Four, we look at a major increase in campaign contributions to Attorney General Frank Cash from the state's car lobby, possibly in exchange for turning a deaf ear to a scam taking place in the garage of a major Jackson dealership."

The shot in the studio, which displayed Carolyn against the same background featured in the promotional I.D., dissolved to Maureen on her couch.

"Governor Greene signed the Consumer Protection Act in March. It gave us a great deal more latitude than we'd had in the past in terms of sanctioning con artists and fraudulent business-es. In the first few days after the bill was signed, I received a number of complaints about service at Capital City Motors," she said, car lot footage now running. It had been altered to elimi-nate the possibility of identification.

"I visited the site and spoke with management, and several days later a mechanic with the dealership contacted me. He swore out an affidavit and alleged on tape that a major scam was taking place there. I presented this information to the Attorney General and subpoenaed the billing records from the dealership," she said, now back on camera.

"My staff and I determined that given the amount of over-charging, a substantial civil penalty was in order. I suggested $100,000, along with restitution to the consumers who were overcharged. According to our figures, the dealership was on a pace to make over one million dollars in unnecessary and incorrectly diagnosed repair work over a twelve-month period."

A fast-moving transitional graphic followed, as a fistful of dollars flew through the air against a blue background. The sound of a cash register was heard. Then Sonny Hollins was on camera. Maureen's adrenaline flowed.

"Yes, we got a rather bizarre subpoena from Ms. Lewis referring to a scam a few weeks ago. We also got a letter from her asking for free service on her car, if you're interested in getting both sides of the story," Hollins said, cornered on the dealership lot. "I categorically deny that anything illegal is taking place in our garage. We would never knowingly charge any of our fine customers a nickel more than what the repair calls for. Fact, we try to cut 'em a break every once in a while so they'll keep coming back," he said, forcing a smile.

"As far as Frank Cash is concerned, the Attorney General is a fine and honorable man, a man I consider a friend as well as a most trustworthy politician. Our relationship has always been above board, and I told the Attorney General that I didn't appreciate his Consumer person throwing a bunch of unwarranted accusations at me after all the things my family has done for this community."

The shot dissolved to Frank, who was in a golf shirt and khaki's. The television crew had found him in Grenada with a group of construction workers in the middle of a bulldozed field.

"Let me make myself perfectly clear: I have never accepted illegal contributions from Sonny Hollins or anyone else. All contributions are reported, and the timing of the one Ms. Lewis spoke of is purely coincidental. Again, everything in our dealings with the car lobby and everyone else is above board. It always has been, and always will be."

A dissolve to Carolyn in the studio. "But the issues surrounding this case don't stop there. Maureen Lewis was suddenly told she was being transferred to another department. And days later her office was broken into. The Capital City Motors file was stolen," she said, as altered video of someone entering a room aired, followed by a file being removed from a cabinet.

Maureen was back on camera. "I was called in May first and offered a different position in the office. When I said I wanted to stay in Consumer, I was told that wasn't an option."

"Were you told why?" Carolyn asked off-screen.

"No. I was simply told that I was being replaced, and that a new position had been created for me."

"But you say it wasn't anything you wanted. Why not?"

Maureen stared, remembering how carefully she'd chosen her words.

"Because I didn't feel I'd have the freedom to pursue the best interests of our state's consumers."

"Were you still in charge of Consumer Protection at that point?"

"Yes. Ashleigh was to take over July first. I was in charge until then."

Back to Carolyn in the studio. "Ashleigh Dunn was a staff attorney supervised by Maureen Lewis for two years. She joined the Attorney General's Office in 1994 and worked in Opinions and later in Criminal Appeals before moving to Consumer Protection in 1998." File footage of Hamilton Dunn on the Senate Floor was next. "Her father is former Madison County State Senator Hamilton Dunn, now a government lobbyist with strong ties to the state's automobile industry. We spoke with Senator Dunn by phone this afternoon."

A telephone graphic emerged with Dunn's name and credentials. His familiar southern drawl boomed:

"For Maureen Lewis to imply that the Attorney General and Sonny Hollins are in cahoots is mud-slinging at its worst. This is clearly a case of an angry, jealous woman who's resentful that my daughter is getting the same chance she got several years ago. She oughta be ashamed of herself."

Maureen flashed her middle finger at the screen as the shot dissolved back to Carolyn.

"But Ms. Lewis is deeply concerned about a letter written to Capital City Motors two days after the Capital City file was stolen from her office." Altered video of a cassette being placed in a tape deck followed. "This letter, which revealed the name of the mechanic who swore out the affidavit and warned of the scam, was sent to management. It cost the mechanic his job."

Maureen was back on camera. "I got a frantic call from the mechanic. He said that a woman with the Attorney General's Office had talked to him and identified herself as my replacement in Consumer. Said she was already in charge. Later that day he was fired. He called me, because his calls to the woman who supposedly called him were not being returned. But the woman who supposedly called him was not only on vacation at the time, she's black. The mechanic confirmed that a white woman called him, a woman who knew a great deal about our investigation and shouldn't have had his name."

Carolyn, off-screen: "But you were still in your capacity as Consumer Protection Director, were you not?"

"That's correct. As I said, Ashleigh Dunn was to start July first."

"Do you think she called the mechanic?"

"I don't know. I have my suspicions, but no proof."

"How did the person who called the mechanic get his name?"

Maureen raised the volume. Her heart had pounded as she gave this answer.

"The Attorney General's Chief of Staff asked for the tape as soon as I told him the mechanic had talked to us. Only the three of us knew it existed at that point. You'd have to ask the Attorney General if he gave it to anyone else."

A cutaway to Cash, in the field. He was upset, a far cry from his usual cool in front of the press.

"I entrusted the tape to the possession of my Chief of Staff

Craig Grantham, who was to then hand-deliver it to Nathan McMichael with the Motor Vehicle Administration. This is standard operating procedure. There was clearly a breakdown in communication . . ."

"Why was Mr. McMichael put in charge of the car dealers, when Maureen Lewis is your Consumer Protection Director?" Carolyn said, off-screen, stepping on Cash's words.

"That's why the Motor Vehicle Administration was set up, Ms. Davis, to investigate complaints against our state's car dealers. Now, if you'll please excuse me. I have nothing further to say."

"Did Mr. Grantham give the mechanic's name to anyone else?"

"I told you, I have nothing further to say!"

A cutaway to Grantham, behind his desk. His smile was in place. "It's unfortunate that the identity of this mechanic has created such a gross misunderstanding. As I said earlier today, Ms. Lewis is a disgruntled employee who clearly didn't understand the big picture concerning our consumers, and in my estimation, there was a breakdown in communication between Ms. Lewis and Ms. Dunn, which doesn't surprise me since . . ."

"Did you give the name of the mechanic to Ms. Dunn?" Carolyn asked off-screen, stepping on Grantham's words.

"No, I did not. And if you want to know the truth, I've heard the mechanic was fired because he didn't know what he was doing. That makes a lot more sense than these wild allegations by someone trying to save her reputation, don't you think?"

"It has been alleged that you and Ms. Dunn were having an affair. If so, did this affair prompt her promotion to Consumer Protection Director?" she said, video of Grantham in Jett's face airing. An angry Grantham was back on camera a moment later.

"I will say this for the last time, Ms. Davis: There is no affair. And as far as Wally Jett is concerned, he's a publicity-hound with strong ties to the Republican Party who's never stopped looking for ways to savage Frank Cash's reputation. It's unfortunate that the politics of personal destruction have reached such a peak in this day and age."

Carolyn back on camera: "The biggest issue here is the prospect of questionable campaign contributions. According to two recent articles by *The Jackson Times*," she said, as actual copies of the articles superimposed onto a blue background aired, "Attorney General Cash has received over $900,000 in contributions from the car lobby alone since the beginning of this year, bringing his war chest to nearly two million dollars. Is it a coincidence that Maureen Lewis was relieved of her duties as Consumer Protection Director mere weeks after attempting to fine a local dealership $100,000 for illegal business practices?"

Maureen back on camera. "I'd sure like to know."

"I demand a full investigation into this!" Brandon Buckhalter said. He was a short, stocky man in his early forties, the Vicksburg lawyer who was running against Cash and hopelessly behind in the polls. "It reeks of good-old-boy, back room politics, the kind of stuff this state has a history of and will always pay a price for. Know what it reminds me of: Washington, for the past eight years. If you're accused of something, deny it, spin it the other way, then attack whoever made the allegations. If something illegal is going on and the Attorney General knows of it, I hope he'll come forward immediately."

Carolyn was now at the anchor desk, part of a three-shot with the anchor team.

"We will watch this situation carefully. I might add that Ashleigh Dunn was unavailable for comment, and Maureen Lewis resigned her position with the Attorney General's Office effective yesterday."

"Nice work, Carolyn. Thank you," the male anchor said, turning to the camera and teasing the next story before the commercial break ran. Maureen turned off the television, armpits wet and mouth dry.

"Wow," Erica said. "That's good television."

Maureen burst into laughter.

"I'm serious. I can't remember the last time I was on the edge of my seat during a local newscast. People will be talking about that all over the city tomorrow."

"Maybe."

Erica tented her fingers. "I bet Ashleigh's gone."

"He'll never fire her because of Hamilton. The guy running Opinions couldn't stand her, so they moved her to Criminal. The woman there hated her, so Frank moved her to Consumer."

"Grantham, then."

"Not the Golden Boy. He'll smooth it over, like he always does."

"Somebody's gonna answer for this. You take one of those Mason-Dixon polls now, I bet Cash's favorability drops twenty percent." She paused. "You were excellent on camera, by the way."

"I wasn't trying to play the victim."

"You were, though, and somebody will have to answer for it."

* * *

Frank Cash's phone was ringing before the story was over.

"Goddamn it, Frank!" Sonny Hollins said, yelling so loudly Cash had to hold the phone from his ear. "Those bastards just raked me over the fucking coals!"

"I'm watching, too," he said, trying to hold his temper. Joyce was staring from the other side of the bed. "I can't do anything right this minute."

"Well, you best repair any damage to my reputation as soon as you drag your happy ass into that big, fancy office of yours tomorrow morning. Otherwise Uncle Sonny's gonna be out for blood!"

Hollins hung up. Cash placed the receiver in the cradle. Joyce touched his shoulder, her normally warm face grim.

"I want to know what's going on, and I want to know now."

"No, you don't. You just pray this doesn't ruin Washington."

He strode downstairs and dialed Grantham, getting his machine.

"I just watched the news. In my office, at seven-thirty. Don't be late this time, Craig. You understand me?"

FORTY FIVE

Cash was waiting alone in the foyer the next morning. He didn't speak until he and Grantham were in his office. A copy of *The Jackson Times* was on his desk. A huge photo of Grantham in the face of Walter Jett adorned the front page. Cash held it aloft, then tossed it aside.

"Nice going, Craig. That's just great. I told you to use your fucking head!"

Grantham had never been this unsure of himself around his boss. He lingered near the desk, eyes on the floor. He didn't dare take a seat.

"You're resigning, effective immediately. I'll have a press conference later today."

Grantham's head snapped up. "Frank, please think about this!"

"I can't have this kind of crap going on around here. I'll keep open the option of bringing you to Washington, if that hasn't been completely destroyed. That's the best I can do."

"But . . ."

"That's the best I can do," Cash said again, his voice carrying a warning.

"Yes, sir."

"Did you give her the name of the mechanic?"

Grantham nodded, his eyes again on the floor.

"Why, goddammit?"

"She wants Maureen's blood. She badgered me about it for weeks. I had no idea she'd write a letter!"

"She broke into Maureen's office, and not only signed Maureen's name to a letter she obviously wrote, she called the mechanic and said she was Sherry Forster! My God, Craig, do you realize how stupid that was?" Cash exhaled, then slumped into his chair. "I told you long ago that what you did on your own time was your business. But every time Ashleigh has batted those baby-blues and spread her legs, you've come running. And because of it you've made some very stupid decisions."

Grantham looked away, humiliated.

"You're a skillful and resourceful politician, Craig. But you're going to have to use better judgment if you want to work for me. This kind of thing in Washington is practically Watergate."

"Yes, sir."

"I'm sorry about having to do it this way. But I can't bring you to Washington unless I get there myself. And if you want to come, you best get rid of her."

* * *

Grantham finished clearing his office an hour later. Chief of Security Tom West was alongside when he turned in his badge and keys to Cash. Eyebrows went up all over Gartin as Grantham made several trips to his Explorer, but he spoke to no one. Cash simply regarded him with a nod as he departed.

"The mail just ran. Maureen sent this," West said, a dark-haired, big-gutted man of fifty. He displayed her badge and keys.

"You canceled her access to the network, didn't you?"

"As soon as you called. Eckland did it."

"Good. Have him cancel Craig's, too."

"Yes, sir." West smirked. "What a way to start the day."

"The fireworks are just beginning."

168

*   *   *

Ashleigh checked her lipstick a final time in the elevator two hours later. She wore a navy dress with matching heels and had baby pictures at the ready. It was her first visit to Gartin since March. She was greeted warmly by the receptionist and others in the hallway, despite the tension in the air.

"Good morning," Cash said, showing her in. His poker face was in place. He remained on his feet when Ashleigh settled on the couch. She crossed her legs and gave him a big smile.

"I assume you want to talk about the TV report. Pretty creative. I saw the paper, too. Craig wasn't exactly the picture of cool, was he?"

"Craig has turned in his resignation. That's an offer I made him earlier this morning." A pause. "It's the same offer I'm making to you."

Ashleigh's jaw fell slowly. It was a full five seconds before she spoke. "You think you're gonna fire me?"

"You have the option of writing a resignation letter, which I hope you'll do."

Ashleigh got to her feet. She stepped toward the Attorney General and glared at him. "I realize you have a reputation to save, but maybe you need to look at the big picture a little better. Before you make such rash decisions about the people closest to you."

Cash leveled a finger at her. "We don't use the power of this office to carry out vendettas, young lady, and your vendetta cost an innocent man his job. It also cost me one of my most loyal department heads, and I've gotta stand in front of the press and try to convince them I have a handle on what's going on around here!"

Ashleigh gazed around the room, a coy smile playing across her lips. "You sure you don't want to think this over?"

"It's done. As I said before, you have the option of writing a resignation letter. I'll take your badge and keys at this time."

She paused, then removed the items from her purse. She tossed both into the large waste can adjacent to Cash's desk. "Is there anything else you'd like to say? I'll give you one last chance to admit that you need to get your shit together before making a decision like this."

Cash's eyes narrowed. "My advice to you is to grow up. Business isn't done this way in the real world."

Ashleigh bared her teeth. "You've got some nerve to talk to me about the way business is done, you gutless son of a bitch. My advice to you is to watch your back."

FORTY SIX

The media assembled on the front steps of Gartin that afternoon. Many were buzzing, as rumors about Cash's staff had circulated. Cash appeared on time, Joyce at his side. Both looked relaxed.

"Good afternoon. We'll see if we can make this pretty quick, since it looks like rain. Briefly, the trip to Grenada was fruitful. Ground breaking ceremonies will take place in the next several weeks, and I'm pleased that our lawmakers saw fit earlier this year to give us the means to build the kind of juvenile detention facility in North Mississippi which has been so successful in the south part of the state."

Hands were already up. Cash ignored them, gazing at the gathering of approximately one hundred.

"I've decided to make a couple of changes. I'm here to announce the resignation of Craig Grantham, my Chief of Staff, and the resignation of Ashleigh Dunn, who was slated to take over as Consumer Protection Director in July. Both have resigned effective immediately."

Cameras clicked. The group murmured. "Does this mean Maureen Lewis will be reinstated?" said a man from the Mississippi Network.

Cash preferred to read his statement or make comments uninterrupted, then open the floor for questions. He frowned, trying to hide his irritation.

"I've had no contact with Ms. Lewis since her resignation. Ms. Lewis was a trusted friend and a valued member of our team. That doesn't mean we always saw eye to eye, but I thought enough of her to create a position which I felt would greatly enhance her career. I'm honestly sorry she turned it down and wish her well in her future endeavors."

More questions, but Cash forged ahead. "Sonny Hollins is an old and trusted friend. I'm grateful for his contributions, and I'm appreciative of those from his fellow members of the Mississippi Vehicle Association. As I said recently, these contributions are above board and a matter of public record. It goes without saying that I would never, ever turn a deaf ear on any crime being committed by anyone while in office." He glanced at the sky. "I'll take questions at this time, in case there are any of you who haven't already shouted yours."

The veteran reporter from Channel Two wedged forward, bumping several people aside. "It has been alleged that a six-figure penalty was in the early stages of being pursued against Capital City Motors. Can you comment as to where an investigation stands, or is one taking place?"

Cash didn't bat an eye. "It has always been policy in this office not to comment on whether or not an investigation is taking place."

"Mr. Cash?" Walter Jett said loudly, drawing the ire of several as he shoved forward. "Are you reassigning Mr. Grantham or Ms. Dunn, and can you confirm or deny that an alleged sexual relationship between them is the reason for their resignations?"

"Both have resigned, effective immediately. I have no further comment about either one."

Janine wedged in behind Jett. She caught Cash's attention. "Your comment on the car dealer in South Mississippi who says he's tired of being told by Sonny Hollins to contribute to your campaign?"

Cash gave Janine a weary smile. "Janine, I'm surprised you'd print that. Thought you needed two sources before you went with something that off the wall."

Much of the gathering laughed, and Cash called on Carolyn Davis.

"Have you considered resigning?"

"Of course not."

"What about speculation that you'll be asked to replace the U.S. Attorney General if his health problems cause him to retire?"

He laughed. "Let me say this for the record: I'm a Mississippi boy. I'm committed to the people of this state, and I'd like to be Attorney General as long as our folks want me in office."

Cash took several more questions, using the opportunity to hold forth about the importance of the juvenile detention facility. He halted the proceedings when rain began to fall. He gripped his wife's hand as he departed up the stairs.

FORTY SEVEN

Maureen flipped through the classified ads later that afternoon. The one bright spot was her financial situation. A shrewd investor like her father, she had saved a great deal of money over the years. Crunching numbers, she estimated that she could survive six months before things would get tight. She checked the e-mail before logging off. A pair of jokes forwarded by Erica were alongside something from an anonymous address.

You were close. Don't stop now.

Maureen stared at the message. It was from a Hotmail address, which meant it could have come from anywhere. Thoughts raced through her head. Who would have her personal address and not reveal his or her identity? She hit the reply key and typed:

Please identify yourself.

FORTY EIGHT

Cash swung by Lake Caroline on his way home. Sonny Hollins was waiting for him in the game room, nursing a drink. It was almost nine.

"Frankie," he said, slipping an arm around the Attorney General. "You've had a long day. Brandy, my good man?"

Cash accepted the drink and selected a pool cue. Hollins set up the table. "Glad to see you get rid of Grantham. Arrogant little fuck, you ask me. Fear any retaliation?"

"Nah. He knows he fucked up."

"What about Ham's daughter?"

Cash glanced at him. "How well do you know Hamilton?"

"Round of golf, drinks here and there. Lot of hot air, you ask me. Has some deep pockets, though. Why?"

"In strict confidence, Sonny," Cash said, eyeing the older man, "Ashleigh came to me when the divorce was final, seven or eight years ago. Turns out Hamilton touched her in the wrong places a few times growing up. Said Eleanor really cleaned him out when she found he was cheating. The deal included a ton of money and an agreement that if he ever made trouble, the little family secret would be revealed. The ladies keep him on a pretty short leash, apparently."

"Jesus. Didn't know anything about that."

"I hardly know Eleanor at all. What about you?"

Hollins shrugged, sipping his drink. "Socially. Wife says her drinking has gotten way out of hand. There's been a scene or two."

"I've heard that. You know my history with the daughter, of course. I've never gotten any sense as to whether Hamilton knows or not. Or if he knows that I know about him."

"You're asking me? I haven't got a clue."

"I got the impression Ashleigh doesn't have any dealings with her father, but he calls me each time she fucks up and asks me to help. Hell, nobody can stand working with her. I've had to move her twice since I hired her."

"You think Eleanor makes him do that? You think he's under her thumb to that extent?"

"That's my guess."

The hint of a smile appeared on Hollins' face. "The way you're talking about the daughter worries me, Frank. You think she'll fuck everything up for us?"

Cash looked up, his eyes narrow. "No, Sonny. She won't be a problem."

"Maybe throwing her out wasn't such a smart idea."

"Read my lips, Hollins! She won't be a problem. Got it?"

The men finished the game in silence.

"By the way, Janine May asked if I cared to comment on the car dealer in South Mississippi who was tired of being told by Sonny Hollins to contribute to my campaign. Any idea what that was about?"

Hollins looked up. "I bet I find out."

*   *   *

Joyce was in the kitchen when Cash arrived. She waved off his apologies for being late.

"Supper can be reheated, if you're hungry. By the way, somebody called and hung up a bunch of times tonight. Caller I.D. said 'Pay Phone.'"

"My advice to you is to watch your back."

"Probably kids. Turn off the ringer."

FORTY NINE

Maureen and Tom were on their way to a movie Friday night when her cell phone rang. Tom watched as her face fell. She talked quietly, then made a U-turn in a crowded intersection.

"My father had a heart attack. He's at the hospital. They don't know if he's gonna make it. I'd better get down there."

Tom squeezed her hand. "Want some company?"

Memories of her father—intertwined with the disastrous memory of his encounter with Richard—flashed before her. She started to turn him down. Then she heard Erica's words.

"Please."

*   *   *

The cell rang again ninety minutes later. By then they were gassing up in Hattiesburg. Maureen's body language was an indication things were better.

"Everything's stable. He's alert." She shook her head, a half smile on her face. "Already wants to go home. Wouldn't be one of his nurses for the moon."

Tom went inside for a soft drink. She was doubled over when he returned, tears streaming from her eyes. She brushed him away but was unable to get back on the road. He reached for the keys.

"Let me drive. Close your eyes and rest."

Half an hour later she looked around. The last sunlight was fading from the sky. Traffic was thickening along Highway 49 as they approached Gulfport. Teenagers in convertibles were everywhere, and music blared as the cars roared past.

"Get some sleep?"

"No. I've been debating what to share about my dysfunctional family, since you're about to meet them."

"All families are dysfunctional. I could tell you some stories."

"Dad is a bank president. Spent years preparing my brother Jack to take over, and Jack told him to shove it. Punches were thrown the last time they were around each other, which was over a decade ago."

Tom said nothing, waiting her out.

"Mom drives to Nashville every few months and sees him. He's a psychologist, got married ten years ago. Lot like Dad, actually—a perfectionist and very stubborn. Mom said her worst fear was that something would happen to Dad before anything was resolved between them."

"You and your brother close?"

"We were growing up." A sigh. "Dad tried to push a career on him. He's tried to find me a husband. I came to Jackson because Erica was already there and had heard good things about Frank. But it was also to get away from home. I worked in the Hancock County D.A. office the first two years after Law School, and Dad ran off each guy I met because he didn't think they were good enough for me. One of the girls in Medicaid Fraud introduced me to Janine, and she set me up with a music professor named Richard. Divorced, kids were in their early teens then. He had a boat, and he'd take me sailing."

Tom turned onto Highway 90, now just minutes from the hospital. The water was to their left. The resistance to share this story was powerful. Again she heard Erica's words.

"He was my first. We got serious real fast. Lasted about six months. Mom and Dad used to drop in unannounced back then, and they picked a weekend we were cooking out at his house. Not only were his kids there, but also the ex, who he was friendly with. He was in jean-shorts, sandals and no shirt, drinking beer and laughing with his ex, while his kids were playing frisbee and climbing trees. Mom handled it okay, but Dad wouldn't shake his hand, eat, or speak to the kids. Called him a hippie. Richard told him to get lost. Dad looked at me, and I will never forget this as long as I live," she said, her voice hollow. "'Maureen Nicole, you weren't raised to be in the company of a man like this.'"

She shook tears out of her eyes. "I can still feel the shame I felt when I looked at my father. I was a grown woman, and I felt like a little girl. I couldn't even look at Richard. We left. I sent my parents home when we got to my apartment—which resulted in a huge fight with my dad—and went back to Richard's house. He wouldn't let me in. Told me right then it was over. Said he didn't need a lady in his life who couldn't stand up to her father."

They drove in silence, Maureen staring out the window.

"That's why I haven't dated. No matter how lonely I've been, no matter how angry I've gotten at my father over the years, I could always bury my head in my career and escape. Now I can't even do that."

Tom frowned as teenagers in a Camaro flew past and flipped them off for no apparent reason. "You and your mom close?"

"Yes and no. I don't respect her. You can't meet a nicer person, but what's important to her is being liked by everyone. But then I'm too hard on people. Like Dad." A long pause. "We never talked about what happened. At this point I'm afraid to. Don't know what would come out of my mouth."

Tom sighed. "My father says the hardest thing to do as a parent of a grown child is keeping your mouth shut while you watch them make mistakes. He said he knew my ex was trouble after spending five minutes with her. But he had to stand back and let me do what I had to do."

"Thing is, I've always wondered if he was right about Richard."

He met her eyes. "Maybe. He's not right about everybody, though."

"But he's gotten inside my head. That's what it comes down to, Tom," she said plaintively, tears streaming down her face. "I can't even meet a man now without wondering what Dad will think of him."

He gripped her hand, glancing at the highway before turning to her. "Whatever happens between us, Maureen, your father will never run me off. Promise."

She smiled through her tears. "Thank you."

FIFTY

Graham wasn't allowed visitors until the next morning. By then Jack and his wife had arrived. Jack, a tall, bearded man with a strong facial resemblance to his father, paced and said little, uncomfortable and deep in thought. June was emotional, giving and receiving hugs from the array of family members who had driven in from points along the Coast.

Maureen entered Graham's room with Tom at her side. Cards and flowers were everywhere. He was conscious but weak, each breath and heartbeat carefully monitored by machines which would sound alarms at the slightest irregularity. A series of scenes flashed through her head—the day they appeared on the local ABC morning show after she set a county record for Girl Scout cookie sales, the pride on his face at her Law School graduation when the Dean bragged on her to Graham, the awful day in Richard's yard. She broke down as she gripped his hand. Graham opened his eyes and touched her cheek.

"This is Tom, Dad." Tom stuck out his hand. Graham's eyes opened wider. A smile formed. He returned the handshake as best he could.

"Have to go out and play eighteen when you're back on your feet, sir. Understand you're quite a golfer."

"Always ready to play," Graham said, his voice a whisper. He turned to Maureen. "Got your resume updated?"

She patted his hand. "Don't worry about that. Just get some rest."

Graham was asleep a minute later. Maureen took Tom's hand and left the room.

* * *

Erica arrived at noon. She took June, Tom and Jack's wife to lunch, giving Maureen and Jack some privacy. They strolled along a winding sidewalk on the hospital grounds, stopping at a bench shaded by a clump of pines. It was quiet and peaceful, the smell of freshly cut grass in the air. Maureen grimaced, however. She and her mother had walked this very path ten years ago when June's father was stricken by a heart attack and hospitalized here. He didn't make it.

"How you been, kid? Mom says they screwed you at the A.G.'s Office. Anybody you want me to beat up?"

She laughed. "I think everybody's gotten their flogging in the press. Thought about teaching, actually. Might just get out of

179

law altogether."

"I always thought you'd make a good teacher."

"I'm glad somebody thinks so. Dad said I was nuts."

Jack sighed, watching a pair of squirrels dart from the path of a woman pushing a stroller. "When Sharon and I talked about marriage, I told her I didn't want kids. Fine with her, since she had the two from her first. But I'd told her all about Dad, and she said to make sure that choice wasn't because of him."

Maureen met his eyes. "Was it?"

"I've never been able to decide." His tone was so like that of their father it sent chills down her spine. "I got his letter. He said some nice things, sounded honestly sorry things worked out the way they did. I wrote back and expressed my appreciation, but explained that I was on no timetable to start up this big, loving relationship with him. We'd do it when it was right for both of us. If it was right."

Maureen hid her surprise. Nothing had been said about Graham's letter since the discussion on the porch several months ago. She assumed her father had discarded the idea.

"You look great, Mo," Jack said after a long pause, gazing at the woman pushing the stroller. "You're prettier each year."

A blush. "Aren't you sweet. Thank you."

"I was looking at those pictures in the hallway this morning. Me in high school with that shag haircut . . ."

"Me in my fat stage when I ate a hundred pounds of M&M's a day . . ."

She didn't realize he was crying, and she turned when he sniffed back tears.

"All the years we've lost. God, I'm sorry," he said. "I can't put into words how much I miss you. But I just can't handle the family crap."

She gripped his hand. "Jack, there are all kinds of other things we can talk about."

"But it hangs there, Mo—it just does. Besides, it's easier to bury myself in my work, be Sharon's husband and a step-father to her boys. Try not to be to them what Dad was to me." He wiped his eyes. "Sharon always said to take some baby steps with Dad before it was too late."

"The doctor said . . ."

"I know. He may live another ten years. But he's through running the bank and taking Mother to St. Thomas and holding forth at the Yacht Club with his buddies. He's through being the big, strong man who was right about everything and knew what was best for everybody." Jack paused, meeting Maureen's eyes. "That was the man I needed to confront. I put off doing it for years because I was a coward. And I'll never have the chance now."

Maureen wiped her eyes.

"We made some small talk. He got this little grin on his face and said, 'Mo has a boyfriend. Surprised she brought him.'"

"I almost didn't."

"You guys serious?"

"I told him about me and Dad—and about you and Dad. Guess that says something." Her stomach growled. "Let's go have lunch. I'll tell you about the office."

FIFTY ONE

Cash sat on his deck Sunday morning, reading the newspaper and drinking coffee. The hang-up calls had continued, and Joyce discovered a pair of panties in the mailbox. The mood turned tense, and Cash called their daughter at school and told her to postpone her visit until the following weekend.

Joyce appeared after clearing the dishes, still in her bathrobe.

"I take it we're not going to church?"

Cash exhaled. "Come sit down. We need to talk."

* * *

That afternoon Sonny Hollins joined Frank on the deck. Joyce was probably with her sister, who lived across town. She had stormed out of the house in tears, giving no indication when she would return.

"You sure you want to do it this way?" Hollins said, sipping bottled water.

"I don't think I have a choice, Sonny. She's unstable."

"But the other night you said . . ."

"I know what I said, damn you. This is the best way to handle her. Trust me. I know what I'm doing."

"She's out, then?"

Cash sighed, staring into the distance. "Haven't decided yet. That's complicated. I'd welcome some input."

"Your call. You're the boss." A snicker. "She's a bright kid, isn't she?"

"Nothing more than blackmail. Like she's been doing for years."

"Like you've done to people for years, Cash. But you call it politics." Hollins' smile faded. "Speaking of which, I don't want any surprises tomorrow."

"There won't be. How's your service manager?"

"Pissed. But he'll live. He has my word he won't be prosecuted."

Cash nodded. "Let the smoke clear, then ease him back in, Sonny. Three, four months, tops."

"Exactly what I said."

"And one more thing: Huff and puff all you want in the press, but when you do something crazy like driving to Billy Redden's place . . ."

Hollins was on his feet immediately, his jaw set. "Now don't start lecturing me, buddy boy . . ."

Cash stood, leveling a finger at him. "Sonny, if the Feds start in on you, there's not a goddamned thing I'll be able to do about it. I'm just giving you fair warning. Keep that macho streak of yours on a leash."

Hollins gazed. "Duly noted, counselor. You just mind the store."

FIFTY TWO

Grantham contacted a realtor and listed his home the following day. He was told that he had picked a great time of year to sell and could expect a contract within a month, if not sooner. Upbeat, he watched the local news at five. Frank Cash was again the lead story. Curious, he raised the volume.

"You fucking bastard!" he said a moment later, suddenly pacing around the room. He shook with adrenaline. "What the fuck are you doing? Washington is gone, you worthless son of a bitch!"

FIFTY THREE

Graham was out of the woods by that evening, although the cardiologist warned that a complete recovery was unlikely. Maureen and her mother were home, discussing the changes that would have to be made in his lifestyle when her cell rang.

"It's me!" Janine said. Excitement was in her voice. "Where are you?"

"Bay St. Louis."

"I left three messages at your apartment. Somehow I totally blanked out on your cell and couldn't find it until now," she said, her words coming out in a rush. "I tried Erica and got her voice mail, too. I was even going to dig up Tom . . ."

"They're both here. Dad had a heart attack."

A long pause. "Oh, Maureen, I am so sorry. Is he going to make it?"

"He's out of intensive care. He was about fifty-fifty the first twenty-four hours, but he's doing a little better. This was a big one, though. He's already been told he's through at the bank," she said, mouthing Janine's name to her mother. June smiled and gestured for her to take the call where she could have some privacy.

"Is there anything I can do, hon'?"

"Pray for him. That's what we're all doing." She stepped outside, gazing across the highway at the water as she breathed the humid, salty air. It was almost completely dark, and a lone couple walked at the water's edge. "So what's up? This must be a big deal for you to start calling my friends."

"You sure this is a good time to talk?"

"It's fine, Janine. Be nice to talk about something besides my father's long-term health needs."

Janine told the story. Maureen's eyes widened. Her jaw fell open. She collapsed into the porch swing, barely able to hold on to the phone.

FIFTY FOUR

Grantham slept little. Still furious the next morning, he drove to Castlewoods subdivision near the Reservoir and parked at the clubhouse. He watched the golfers in the chilly sunrise and checked his watch. Cash jogged this route three times a week and would appear momentarily. Grantham had run it with him before, once minutes after sex with Ashleigh in his Explorer.

There he was, like clockwork. He was shirtless, wearing a thick headband, navy shorts and expensive shoes. A small water bottle was held to his waist with velcro. Grantham waited until he was fifty yards away, then emerged.

"Top of the morning, Counselor!"

Startled, Cash glanced around. He frowned when he saw Grantham and slowed reluctantly.

"Hello, Craig."

"Thanks for the warning, Frank. You realize you've completely killed any hopes we had of going to Washington."

Cash glanced around again. "Craig, some things in life are more important than . . ."

Grantham's fist met Cash's jaw, sending the Attorney General reeling backward to the pavement. He got to his feet slowly, his eyes hard.

"I busted my ass for you," Grantham said. He didn't try to keep his voice down. "For twelve years you've come first. This is the thanks I get, and I find out on the fucking news?"

"I realize you aren't pleased, but as I said, there are things more important than . . ."

Grantham stepped closer. "You've got some nerve to lecture me about Ashleigh when you were fucking her as a teenager, you pompous ass!"

"I don't blame you for being angry . . ."

185

Grantham swung again. This time Cash grabbed his arm and kneed him in the groin. Grantham crumpled to the ground in agony.

"... and I know you're hurt that I didn't ask your advice, but my marriage and family come first."

"You don't fool me," Grantham said hoarsely. He struggled to his feet, wincing in pain. "What have you gotten yourself into, Frank? What made you run to the press?"

Cash went to his poker face. "I appreciate your loyalty and hard work. But maybe it's time we went our separate ways."

Grantham stared. He retrieved his keys and limped away when Cash didn't respond. "You screwed up, Frank. You'll be sorry you did it this way."

"That a threat?"

Grantham smiled over his shoulder, beginning to catch his breath. "No, it's not a threat. I'm the least of your worries. I don't know what you're hiding, but I bet you just made the smoke a lot thicker. Enjoy those sleepless nights. And don't ask me for any favors, you ungrateful bastard."

FIFTY FIVE

A loud radio in a passing car awakened Maureen the next morning. She opened her eyes, feeling the cool chill of the morning air through the open window. Tom was still asleep in the twin bed ten feet away. She felt refreshed, a far cry from the previous two days. She was debating a walk on the beach when her eyes opened wide. She threw on her robe and dashed down the stairs, retrieving the newspaper in bare feet. A huge picture of Frank Cash adorned the front page. Her heart pounded, even though Janine had practically read the story to her last night.

ATTORNEY GENERAL ADMITS AFFAIR
By Janine May, Jackson Times Staff Writer

In an extraordinary turn of events which sent shock waves through the state, Attorney General Frank Cash admitted to an extramarital affair before he ran for office. He also released the findings of an internal investigation, confirming that a complicated and lucrative scam was taking place in the service department of Capital City Motors.

Cash revealed shocking details of an affair with Special Assistant Attorney General Ashleigh Dunn, who resigned last week from the Department of Consumer Protection. He stated that he and Ms. Dunn, the daughter of former state Senator Hamilton Dunn and the controversial replacement for Maureen Lewis as Director of Consumer Protection, consummated a relationship in 1987, when Ms. Dunn was a nineteen year old sophomore at Mississippi College.

"This was a consensual, sexual relationship which took place before my first run for the office of Attorney General," Cash said, flanked by his wife Joyce and his attorney. "Ms. Dunn was nineteen when it began. It ended a year later. I maintain that the relationship had no impact on her hiring in 1994, nor did it have anything to do with her resignation last week. I apologize to the people of our state and beg your forgiveness."

Cash dropped another bombshell minutes later, confirming that an alleged scam was taking place in the service department of Capital City Motors and announcing the termination of a supervisor.

"We have confirmed what (former Director of Consumer Protection) Maureen Lewis feared was taking place," Cash said. "Her findings, thanks to an internal investigation in our office, have been proven correct. We have concrete proof *that over a million dollars would indeed have been made over the course of this year in unnecessary repair work caused by negligent and purposely incorrect diagnoses.*

"I have spoken at length with (Capital City President) Sonny Hollins, and he steadfastly maintains that he was completely unaware of this situation.

"Mr. Hollins has terminated the employment of his service manager and is in the process of reaching an agreement with our office so that restitution can be awarded to our state's consumers who were taken advantage of."

As reported in yesterday's Jackson Times, *Billy Redden, President of Gateway Motors in Collins, went on record with claims that Hollins has put pressure on him each of the last two years to increase contributions to Frank Cash's re-election campaign. Cash, when responding to Redden's comments and the prospect of criminal wrongdoing, stunned the gathering at his press conference with his response.*

"I've decided, as of today, that because of the appearance of impropriety, donations from the car lobby will no longer be taken," Cash said. "Full refunds will be sent to all members of the Mississippi Vehicle Association, including Sonny Hollins and Billy Redden."

Cash offered a smile when it was pointed out that eighty percent of his campaign contributions over the last four months have come from the automobile lobby. "We'll be out well over a million dollars," he said. "But we're confident that with hard work we'll raise that money again and win the election."

Cash said he has no plans of stepping down, although several groups—including the Southern Baptist Convention—are demanding his resignation. Brandon Buckhalter, Cash's opponent in November, blasted the Attorney General.

"This is a disgrace. It sounds just like Washington. Did I hear the Attorney General say he never had sex with that

woman? I guess because he cares about our children and wants criminals off the streets, we're expected to forget the integrity issue completely and understand that everybody does it, right? What I can't figure out is why the Attorney General, after categorically denying any funny business about campaign contributions just last week, is suddenly returning a million dollars to the car lobby! What else is going on that he doesn't want us to know? I wish the man would air all his dirty laundry at once."

Sonny Hollins referred all inquiries to his lawyer, L. Gregory Flannigan of Jackson. "Mr. Hollins will cooperate fully with the Attorney General's Office. However, he maintains his innocence and points at a long history of charitable contributions and service to the community when responding to his detractors," Flannigan said.

Cash indicated that the original civil penalty of $100,000 will be pursued against Capital City Motors and hopes for a settlement.

"It is my hope that Mr. Hollins, now faced with cold, hard evidence of a major scam within the confines of his operation, will do what's necessary to make this right and regain the trust of his customers. We will also launch an investigation into possible intimidation of members of the Mississippi Vehicle Association, in light of Mr. Redden's comments."

Ashleigh Dunn also refused to comment, referring inquiries to her attorney, Carl Schoenweis of Jackson.

"We are pursuing our legal options," Schoenweis said. "It is an unconscionable invasion of Ms. Dunn's privacy to have this information made to the general public in this nature."

Jeff Garland, an investigator under former Consumer Protection Director Maureen Lewis, was named Interim Consumer Protection Director yesterday. Cash stated that a search for a permanent replacement for Lewis was underway. He had no comment when asked if Lewis would be considered *for reinstatement in her old position. The search for a new Chief of Staff is also continuing, following Craig Grantham's resignation last week.*

Maureen read the article a second time, then dialed Janine.

"It's me. Wake you up?"

"Course not. You still on the Coast?"

"We're coming back today. Just read the story. I'd have fallen off my stool if you hadn't warned me."

"I forgot to tell you this last night: Off the record, Billy Redden's house is being watched."

"Did Hollins threaten him?"

"Sure sounds like it."

"Goodness. I loved Buckhalter's comments, by the way. 'Did he have sex with that woman?'"

Janine laughed. "That's what I could print. They did some good damage control, though. Frank talked so much about doing right by the Capital City customers you practically forgot he and Ashleigh were an item. I'm also wondering if this Redden thing is going to bite Hollins. That's a lot more serious than the crap in the garage."

"Maybe. He shelled out some bucks for that Flannigan guy, I know that. He doesn't come cheap. What I'm wondering, though, is why Frank told the world about Ashleigh."

"I'm wondering who else has had her. Maybe the whole legislature."

Maureen couldn't stifle a giggle. "Seriously, Frank's a smart man, no matter how much of a slime ball he is. Maybe Ashleigh has something serious on him, something he thought it was best to trump by running to the press."

"If that's the case, he hasn't heard the last of her."

"I bet I haven't, either."

FIFTY SIX

A stack of mail, an abundance of voice mail messages and a full litter box awaited Maureen when she arrived home. Alone, she drew a hot bath and poured a glass of wine, soaking to Dan Fogelberg in soft candlelight. She checked her e-mails after a second glass. There were more forwarded jokes from Erica, a confirmation that a book was on its way, and two notes from the Hotmail box. The first was several days old, a reply to the inquiry she'd nearly forgotten she made.

Who I am is unimportant.

She stared, then opened the second. It had come earlier today:

Don't let what's in the newspaper stop you. This isn't over.

FIFTY SEVEN

M aureen updated her resume the next day. She took steps toward obtaining a teaching certificate, although she was far from convinced that it was the right move. Returning to the Attorney General's Office, as Janine suggested, was totally out of the question. She admitted to Janine that the practice of law had lost much of its luster in recent weeks.

She met Tom's parents, joining them for lunch that Friday. Warm and outgoing, they issued an open invitation to Columbus for when things settled down. She left for Bay St. Louis after the meal to help June with Graham's arrival. He was frail and cranky, alternately wanting attention and privacy.

"You've lost weight," he said Sunday morning, clad in his bathrobe. They were playing Chess at the dining room table. "You're not eating well, are you?"

"Dad, I'm fine."

"How's the ulcer?"

She grunted. "Manageable. How's the pacemaker?"

"Good thing we don't have a garage. Interviewing yet?"

"You won't stop, will you?"

"Let me make some calls, Mo. You'd knock 'em dead down here."

"I'll think about it."

"You're not serious about teaching, are you?"

She looked up wearily. "If you had discovered the entire banking industry was a fraud, you wouldn't have wanted to return to it."

"This is one politician and his cronies, Mo, not the whole legal profession. And with your reputation and credentials—especially in light of what's going on in that fool's office—you won't be blacklisted there or anywhere else."

"I'll keep you posted. Let's leave it at that."

A pause. "Tom seemed like a nice young man."

"He is."

"What does he do?"

"Advertising," she said, her eyes on the board. "He worked for the dealership we were going to bust. Lost his job when management found out we were seeing each other."

Graham's jaw dropped open. "You can't be serious."

"And they say politics aren't personal."

"Sorry to hear that. Bring him back down sometime. Like to visit with him when I'm not flat on my back with a bunch of tubes sticking out of me."

"I'll do it." Maureen moved the chess pieces. "Checkmate."

A grin formed on Graham's face. "Two out of three."

FIFTY EIGHT

S he checked her e-mail as soon as she returned home. A new note from her anonymous pal awaited her.

Clear your name before they get you.

She called Erica immediately. "What do you think?"

"Ashleigh?"

"She isn't that subtle. There would be a mention of Tom, perhaps the mechanic who got fired."

Erica groaned. "You're gonna run with this, aren't you? I can hear it in your voice."

Maureen laughed. "I promise I'll be safe."

She replied before going to bed:

Your clues are too vague! Give me something I can work with.

* * *

Her phone rang before eight the next morning. She checked the bedside Caller I.D. and frowned. It was someone from the Attorney General's Office.

"It's Jeff. Sorry to call so early, but the public defender has been looking for you. The secretary finally put him on with me. He wouldn't say, but word is he has an opening."

"I'll call him. Thank you." A pause. "So how are things, Mr. Interim Consumer Director?"

Jeff laughed. "Chaotic. Let's catch lunch before long."

* * *

She went for a walk after breakfast. There was another new note from the Hotmail address when she returned.

193

You know who's involved.

This made her even more curious. She decided not to reply right away. She phoned the public defender, then paged Jeff. He returned the call immediately.

"Can you have lunch today?"

"If you don't mind eating late. Several fires to put out before I do anything else. I'll call your cell when I'm done and we'll pick a place."

"Let's eat here. Call when you're on your way and I'll pick up a couple of deli plates."

* * *

"Public defender offer you a job?" Jeff said two hours later, sipping sweet tea from a Styrofoam cup.

"I'd be second only to him." Maureen paused, her mouth full of Salisbury Steak. "More money than I expected. Said I'd think about it, but it took two minutes to realize I'd starve before I did defense work. Too many stories about thugs calling in the middle of the night with their tales of woe."

"You wanna come back? Bet Frank would take you in a heartbeat."

She gazed at him. "Did you plant that rumor in Janine's mind?"

"No. I just know how much he needs good press. And Sherry and Paul and I would love it."

She smiled. "Thanks, but no thanks. He can't trust me any more."

"He can't trust anybody, Maureen. You know how politics is. What's your take on Ashleigh and him? And Hollins?"

"Maybe I'm just naive, but I was totally shocked about him and Ashleigh."

"All of us are."

"Far as his future, there were always rumors about him going to Washington, but that's dead now. He can still beat Buckhalter, although if the Republicans had a better candidate they'd really have a shot. The Hollins thing pisses me off since it was our investigation, but that's politics. I'd be surprised if those customers ever see a dime, you wanna know the truth."

"Agreed. Offering to refund the donations was shrewd, though."

"Makes me think there's merit to the Redden complaint." She pushed away her food. "I'm getting anonymous e-mails at home, Jeff, and I think they're coming from the office."

He didn't change expression. "You're asking if I sent them?"

"Did you?"

A smile. "No. You gonna tell me what they're about, or is that off-limits?"

She sized him up. "Can I confide in you? And get your help?"

"Absolutely."

Twenty minutes later the entire story was told, concluding with the e-mails. By now both had finished their meals. Jeff nursed his tea.

"What we're hearing through the grapevine—Hillary Bankston, to be honest—is that Warren is divorcing her and wants the baby. Ashleigh moved in with her mother for the time being. I'm sure you're the least of her worries, if you think it's her."

"I should leave it alone, but if someone's after me, they aren't going to stop now."

Jeff's smile disappeared. "You and I didn't always see eye to eye on everything, but I really wanted to kick someone's ass after seeing you on TV that night. I'll do anything I can to help you sink those bastards."

Maureen gazed at him. "Then let's find out what's going on."

FIFTY NINE

Tom joined her for supper, which was Hamburger Helper and steamed broccoli. He had completed his first day selling local cable advertising.

"Pretty good account list. Walker Brothers is the big dog. A third of what I'll make comes from them, so tell your buddies at the A.G.'s Office not to mess with 'em."

She laughed and told him about lunch with Jeff.

"Cool! I've always wanted to be a private eye."

"You just took a new job, Tom! I don't want you putting it in jeopardy."

"A little snooping won't hurt anything. Fact, I know where Eleanor lives. Let's ride out there. Come on," he said, reaching for his keys.

"Now? What on earth for?"

"Just to show you where. Then we'll find somewhere quiet to relax. Your shoulders are due to be rubbed."

* * *

The sun was almost gone when they reached Clinton. Tom directed them to a posh neighborhood on the west side of town.

"Wow," Maureen said softly, slowing the Civic. "Most of these are probably worth half a million dollars. Hell, the lots are probably a hundred grand. How do you clean a house so big?"

"That's Eleanor's place," Tom said, pointing at a Victorian-style home with a long, semi-circular driveway in front. The lawn was lush and green. Perfectly-trimmed rose bushes were near the front door. A swimming pool could be seen through the open gate of a wooden privacy fence. A BMW was parked in front of the closed garage.

"There's Ashleigh's car."

"Sure is," Tom said. "I'm tempted to talk to her. Or her mother."

"Please don't."

"Let's go, then, before I do."

* * *

They drove up the Natchez Trace as far as Ratliff Ferry, then turned around and returned to Jackson. They were a mile from I-220 when Tom spoke.

"Go to Clinton."

"We are not going to confront them, Tom."

"One more ride through the neighborhood. Please?"

She sighed, then drove to Clinton. Another long gaze at Eleanor's house. Floodlights bathed the front yard. Poolside lights were now visible.

"Interesting. Ashleigh's gone. Wonder who's watching the baby."

"I'm sure her car is in the garage, Tom. Can we go now?"

"I suppose so."

Maureen made a U-turn at the end of the street. She was doubling past Eleanor's home when Tom whirled.

"The garage door is opening."

Irritated, Maureen slowed. A car backed out, made the loop through the driveway and headed the opposite way.

"I suppose you want me to follow them."

He grinned. "At a discreet distance."

She picked up the car as it left the subdivision. "What is it? A Porsche?"

"A Jaguar." The driver moved into the turn lane as they approached a traffic light, but Tom motioned for her not to follow. "That's Sonny Hollins. I know the plate."

Maureen turned to him in surprise. "Hollins? That's just great. God only knows what he and Ashleigh are up to."

"I don't think he was there to see her. Wonder if he and

197

Eleanor are involved."

She laughed. "Now you're getting a little carried away."

"Maureen, if he's there on business with either one of them, he parks by the front door. Think about it—two hours ago Ashleigh's car was there. Now it isn't, and Hollins leaves from a closed garage? Bet Ashleigh left to give them some privacy, and he parked inside because he didn't anyone to see his car."

SIXTY

She checked her e-mail when she got home and was disappointed when nothing from the anonymous writer appeared. She opened the most recent message and typed a reply:

> *You know more than you're telling. I can't go forward without an idea of what I'm looking for. Please help me.*

She sent the message and was reading a joke from Erica when the computer beeped. The message was from the Hotmail box. Adrenaline surging, she clicked open the message.

> *I can't afford to lose my job. Use your head and piece it together.*

Maureen's eyes widened. Sounded like the person was with the office. Had he or she meant to give this away? She took a deep breath, then replied.

> *Do you work in Gartin or 802?*

She sighed when there wasn't an immediate response.

Twenty minutes later she was playing Solitaire when the message alert beeped again.

If you must know, I'm in Administration. This is positively all you will find out about me. If you persist in determining my identity, I will cease communication with you.

She gasped. Lisa McNulty was the division chief, a pleasant but all-business sort whose hands wouldn't be dirty and had no reason to get her. She typed a reply:

Please tell me what you know. I swear I will not try to find out who you are. I am definitely not going to the A.G. this time.

Back to the Solitaire game. She switched to Chess a short time later, then Monopoly. No reply from the Hotmail box. At midnight she logged off, frustrated.

SIXTY ONE

She called the public defender the next morning and turned down his offer. She washed clothes and read the newspaper, then went to the grocery store. With no more errands to run and nothing to do, she reluctantly logged onto the computer. The anonymous author had written.

Okay, okay. I'll write back tonight and tell you what I know. I'm taking you at your word that my identity will not be sought.

It wasn't even ten o'clock. She faced the bathroom mirror, smiling sadly at the fact that with no job, her life now revolved around clues from someone too scared to talk to her about something taking place where she no longer worked.

*　*　*

Supper was at Janine's house. She passed on a movie, too preoccupied to concentrate. She trotted into the apartment and logged onto the computer. No new messages. She called Tom, then tried again. Nothing. She watched the late news, then hoped the third time would be the charm. She wasn't going through another day of waiting helplessly for an e-mail.

It was there.

> *You know who my boss is. That person and I have always gotten along. One of my duties was to reconcile the collection numbers from Consumer. I signed off on paperwork showing where the money came from and where it was going once it was collected. Then I submitted it to Boss for approval.*
>
> *Early in April I took a week of vacation. While I was gone, a memo went out stating that Boss would handle Consumer collection paperwork effective immediately. I didn't see the memo until later, so I had no idea. I returned to work and tackled the in-box like I always did.*
>
> *Later that day Boss was looking for a file and was frantic. Boss went ballistic when she discovered I had it. Kept screaming about the memo. I was crying. Boss finally calmed down when I swore I knew nothing about the memo and was following S.O.P. as I knew it. The new policy didn't strike me as anything out of the ordinary. But Boss's reaction did. Boss used to be easygoing and fun to work with, but is now very stressed out all the time. Boss spends much more time with A.G. than I remember.*

This still wouldn't have made an impression, but when I saw you on TV, I realized the events you described matched perfectly with when the memo went out. The person who was going to take your place talked to Boss a lot around then. This is everything I know. Good luck.

Maureen drummed her fingers next to the keyboard. Then she took a deep breath and replied:

I have proof that Ashleigh was warning Frank that I was about to land on Hollins right after the Consumer bill was passed. I probably got too close to something illegal, which is why I was moved from Consumer. Am I in some danger? Please help me.

Ten agonizing minutes passed. Then the beep.

The names all fit, based on who was calling or seeing Boss at that time. I wrote in the first place because I overheard Boss mention your name in a recent phone conversation. Boss was upset. This concerned me, although I didn't know the context. I don't know if you're in danger. Since you resigned, you would seem to be in the clear. The female you referred to was in Boss's office the day she resigned. Voices were raised. I don't know the context. I wouldn't have thought twice about it, but A.G. announced her resignation later that day.

Maureen replied immediately:

Do you think the person we're talking about would threaten or extort Boss?

The wait stretched into an hour. Maureen paced, played Solitaire, nibbled on leftovers and played more Solitaire. She was beginning to think her pen pal had logged off when the computer beeped.

The answer to your question is yes. This is the last time you will hear from me. If you pursue this, be careful. Good luck and goodbye.

SIXTY TWO

She didn't check her voice mail until the next morning. Graham had called last night, informing her that he had a chance encounter with a partner at a prominent Gulfport law firm. The man was an old friend, and it turned out that the firm would have a late summer opening due to a retirement. Graham had promised that Maureen would call in the next twenty-four hours.

"Hi, Dad. I don't think your doctor's advice was to find me a job."

"They think the world of you over there, Mo! How could I not mention your plight when he asked how you were doing."

"I'm just not sure I want to work in private practice. It has nothing to do with him."

Graham took his time. "I see. So should I call back and tell him that even though you have no job and no idea what you're going to do, you're not interested in even talking to him?"

She gritted her teeth. "All right, I'll call down there and talk to him . . ."

"Oh, let me," Graham said, clearly insulted. "Since I overstepped my bounds, the least I can do is handle it. While you go about whatever it is you're going about."

"What's at stake here, Dad, my future or your ego?"

"You don't talk to me like that, young lady!"

"Don't give me that! What I could use is your support!"

"You have my support, Maureen Nicole! Do you want a list of all the things . . ."

"Don't even start! I put myself where I am, thank you! Your primary concern is bragging to your Yacht Club buddies about how important your daughter is! Don't even try to deny it."

The silence grew uncomfortable. "I really resent that, Maureen."

"Know what I resent, Dad? Everything I know about ethics and morality came from you, and I thought you'd be proud of the fact that what's right and wrong is more important to me than power and status! That's why I went to the press and sacrificed my job. But your advice is not to rock the boat with Frank Cash because my ticket to the big-time will go down the drain. You've shown your true colors, and I don't ever want to hear one of your sanctimonious speeches about ethics again."

Graham hung up without a word. Maureen slammed down the phone, tears welling in her eyes.

* * *

Three hours later Janine arrived with a sack of Krystal hamburgers. Maureen recounted the conversation, spraying bits of meat, bun and tea as she did. Anger and guilt alternately fueled and slowed her tirade.

"I don't have to like him. This is why I moved up here, after all." She handed over the updated stack of e-mails. "Read the last two pages carefully."

Janine whistled as she looked up. "Could she threaten the administration person into helping her get you?"

"That's what I'm wondering. By the way, Jeff heard that Ashleigh has moved in with Mommie Dearest. Tom knows where she lives, so we rode through the neighborhood the other night. Hollins was leaving Eleanor's house." She paused. "Pulling out of the garage."

Janine's eyes widened.

"I thought he was there to discuss something with Ashleigh. But Tom figured something might be going on between Hollins and Eleanor. I blew it off, but now I'm inclined to agree."

"What I'd think, if he was quietly leaving from the garage. Sounds like he didn't want the neighbors to see him."

"And don't forget why Tom lost his job. Eleanor saw us at the mall, and the next day Hollins called him in on the carpet."

"Trust your hunch. You were right the first time."

SIXTY THREE

Late that afternoon Maureen flipped through old planners, trying desperately to find Lisa McNulty's home phone and address. She eventually paged Jeff.

"The husband is named Mack, isn't he?" she said, the phone book open.

"Nickname. Real name is Darren or Dan or something."

"Here's a Donald McNulty on Broadmeadow."

"That's him. You going over there?"

"Sure am."

* * *

Broadmeadow Drive was in a middle class North Jackson neighborhood fifteen minutes away, the houses generally twenty-five years old and surrounded by pines and redbuds. Maureen found the house in the remaining sunlight and parked along the curb. A young man of perhaps thirteen opened the door and frowned when she asked for Lisa.

"Wait here," he said awkwardly, leaving the door ajar. A minute later a stocky, clean-shaven man in jeans and a yellow Polo appeared.

"Hello, Maureen," he said. A forced smile was on his face.

"Hi, Mack. Looking for Lisa."

"Can I ask what about?"

"It's office related."

An uncomfortable pause. "She's not here. We've separated."

"Oh, dear," Maureen said, her eyes widening. "I'm sorry."

Mack nodded. "We're hoping it'll be short-term."

"You mind telling me where I can find her?"

He gave directions to a nearby apartment complex. Maureen nodded, familiar with the place. "Sounds like the A.G.'s Office has turned into a zoo. I want her to leave, but she's determined to stay. I can't imagine why. It never seemed all that important to her before."

* * *

The sun was gone by the time Maureen reached her destination. It was off Old Canton Road, and there was nothing fancy about the place. It sure wasn't convenient to the office. She found the building and was starting up the stairs when a tall, attractive blond in a suit brushed past her. The woman went straight to the apartment and let herself in with a key.

Maureen hesitated, suddenly unsure. She sat in her car for ten minutes, then climbed the stairs. She heard raised voices as she approached the second floor. The voices were coming from Lisa's apartment. They quieted when Maureen knocked. A long moment passed before the door opened.

"Maureen?" Lisa said in surprise, holding a cigarette. She was in jean shorts and a tank-top, a short blond in her early forties. Lisa had always been slender, but Maureen didn't recall her being this thin. She didn't know Lisa smoked, either. "What are you doing here?"

"Got your address from Mack. I hate dropping in unannounced . . ."

"Let's talk about this another time," the woman in the suit said, grabbing her purse. She shot Lisa an angry look, glared at Maureen and marched down the stairs.

"Wait!" Lisa said in frustration, following to the head of the stairs.

"You have company!"

"She won't be long, I'm sure . . ."

The woman turned, now at ground level. The tension was palpable. "Another time. Good night."

A moment later she was gone. Lisa took a deep drag from the cigarette, tossed it down the stairs and returned inside, head down. Maureen followed into the living room, glancing around. The place reeked of cigarettes and was sparsely decorated, as if she didn't plan to be here long.

"I'm sorry. He didn't give me a phone number."

Lisa looked up, her eyes heavy with emotion. It was apparent what Maureen had interrupted.

"Quit apologizing. You're here," she said. She forced a smile. "Sit down. A drink? A beer? Forgive me if I have another cigarette."

"I'm fine," Maureen said, trying to focus. A headache was already forming from the smoke. This would have to be done now, regardless of how uncomfortable it was for either of them. "Again, I'm sorry about you and Mack . . ."

"That's not why you're here."

"Has to do with the office."

Lisa frowned. "Maureen, everybody knows you got screwed. I told Frank and Craig they were making a huge mistake when they decided to move you. But I have as much clout as the man in the moon. If I were you, I'd get on with my life. You're as smart as anybody up there and can probably snap your fingers and find a job."

Maureen studied her. Lisa was scared. "I swear to you everything said stays here."

"Look, I don't have time for . . ."

"I've gotten a series of anonymous e-mails from someone who claims to work in Administration. Says the fallout isn't over yet. And that I need to watch my back."

Lisa jumped to her feet. "Look, you did drop in at a bad time. I don't know what in the world you're talking about, but it's best if you go," she said. She gestured at the door. "Please. I have a lot to do."

Maureen didn't move. She explained the content of Ashleigh's e-mails, then recalled the chance meeting with Eleanor at the mall. By then Lisa had made a drink. She slumped onto the couch, her hands shaking.

"If you know something, tell me, Lisa. For your sake and mine."

Her hands shook so badly the drink spilled down the front of her shirt. She set it clumsily on the coffee table. She stubbed the cigarette in a cheap plastic ashtray, spilling ashes.

"I don't know who's e-mailing you," she said. "I really wish you'd leave."

Maureen waited her out, but she said nothing else. "Lisa, Ashleigh will stop at nothing. Take my word."

Lisa took a deep breath and wiped her eyes. "Okay. Jen and I are involved—the woman who just left."

Maureen nodded, her suspicions confirmed.

"Mack and I have had some problems. We've stayed together because of the kids. Jen and I met a few months ago in a tennis league. Never attracted to a woman before, not in my wildest dreams. She's divorced, easy to talk to. Has a condo not far from the office, and I got into the habit of telling Mack I was working late and stopping a couple times a week. We were careful as we could be, never went anywhere together. And one day Ashleigh came into my office."

Lisa lit another cigarette. "This was in April, the day Greene signed the Consumer bill. She talked about how much more money would be coming in once your staff really started shooting its guns." A pause. "Said I'd be keeping a second set of books under a false name."

Maureen gasped.

"The regular set is still business as usual. The second has all the money coming from Consumer divided between her, Frank and Sonny Hollins, the car guy."

"What? Lisa, that money is supposed to be split evenly with the state and the A.G.'s Office! It goes into a general fund!" she said frantically.

"There isn't a dime in there. Hollins has somebody in the state audit department in his pocket. Nobody finds out, and they all get rich. Over two hundred thousand dollars has come in since the bill was signed, and they've gotten every penny of it."

Maureen tried to take this in. She got to her feet and stepped away from the cloud of smoke, her head throbbing. "The e-mailer overheard my name in a conversation you were having," she said. "What was that about?"

Lisa met her eyes. "The bonus I got—a measly ten thousand dollars—was to help her backdate and forge information to drag your name into it. At some point—she won't say when—she'll pull the plug."

"Expose the scam?"

"And you."

Maureen's mouth fell open. "Why didn't you tell me, for God's sake?"

"Maureen, the day she explained this, I was laughing. I said, 'This is great. You oughta write for *Saturday Night Live.*' Ashleigh didn't crack a smile. Walked behind my desk and pointed at the picture of Mack and the kids. Said, 'I know who Jennifer Green is. I know where she lives and what you dykes do in her bed. This is real, and if you don't go along completely, not only will I gut your job, I'll make sure your husband knows everything.' You should have seen the look in her eye. It still gives me chills."

Maureen looked away, speechless.

"I peed in my pants when she mentioned Jen. I was already in love with her, so I'd been sneaking around and lying to my husband and kids. That made it even worse. Moved here last month, told Mack I needed to find myself. It was so we could be together, since I don't dare go to her place any more."

"So Mack doesn't know about the scam. Or her."

"No. He's very trusting. He deserves better. So do the kids," she said, choking up.

"Level with me, Lisa: Does anyone else know about this?"

"I don't know. I swear I don't. I've just tried to keep my mouth shut and do what she says."

"Is Grantham in on this?"

Lisa shook her head. "Craig's name has never come up. Just Frank, Sonny and Ashleigh."

Maureen screwed up her face. "No Grantham, even though he all but wiped Frank's ass, and Ashleigh is still in, even though Frank fired her?"

"That's the only time he acknowledged this was going on, and he really didn't do it then. Said to keep taking her calls. I hear from her every couple of days."

"Does Frank know she's trying to get me?"

"I don't know that, either, Maureen. The last time your name came up, I told Ashleigh this would be a hell of a lot safer—as well as easier—if you weren't involved. Maybe that's what that person overheard. Ashleigh went ballistic. Repeated her threat about going to Mack."

Maureen glanced at the cigarette pack. She had several with Janine a few days after parting company with Richard, bought more the next day and came very close to becoming hooked.

"A friend and I did a little snooping of our own. We saw

Hollins leaving Eleanor Dunn's house the other night. We got the distinct impression they're involved."

"Who?"

"Ashleigh's mother and Hollins. He was pulling out of the garage."

Lisa closed her eyes. "That's all I need to hear. One tightly-wrapped little nucleus, extorting and destroying everyone they can get their hands on." She wiped a tear away. "I can't live like this any more. I can't sleep, I can't eat, I'm smoking again, I'm drinking too much—I'm a nervous wreck. But I come forward, I lose my husband, my kids, my job and my lover. She's leaving town, by the way. Says it isn't worth what we're having to go through."

Maureen got to her feet. "Give me the diskettes, and I'll call my lawyer. He and I will meet with the U.S. Attorney first thing tomorrow morning. We'll bust the whole thing open. I can't make any promises, but if you come forward, you can probably cut a deal and get away unscathed."

The phone rang as Lisa started to respond. She answered and spoke in hushed tones. A moment later she hung up.

"Maureen, I have to go."

"Lisa, this is a bomb waiting to go off! You think for a second Ashleigh won't sabotage you when she tells the world?"

She grabbed her purse. "Write down your number and I'll call you first thing tomorrow morning, soon as I get to work. All the books are on diskette, and everything is locked up in my desk. Nothing'll happen to them tonight."

SIXTY FOUR

Maureen had just made coffee the next morning when the phone rang.

"It's Lisa. They're gone! Both sets of diskettes!" she said, whispering fiercely. "All the paperwork, too! The whole file cabinet is empty!"

"Oh, shit! I told you we should have . . ."

"I know that, Maureen! But what do I do now? Tell Frank? Tom West?"

"No, don't get West involved," she said. "Tell Frank, and document the exchange, word for word."

"Then what?"

"I don't know." She gave Lisa her cell number. "I'll page later on. Keep your cool. We'll get out of this."

She hung up and paced. Then she called Erica.

"Mo, go to Haynes! I'm begging you!"

"It'll have to come from Lisa to carry any weight."

"Talk to her, then. Scare her!"

"She's already scared."

"Scare her some more!" Erica said, shouting. "Ashleigh Dunn is about to take you down, maybe send you to jail, and this woman—who can blow all of it out of the water—is gonna sit by and let it happen because she doesn't want to lose her dyke lover!"

Maureen went for a walk. The more she thought about it, the more Erica was right. She paged Lisa and spoke casually when she called.

"I think I have a plan. Let me give you directions to my apartment."

SIXTY FIVE

Lisa appeared just before noon. She wore a plaid sundress and sunglasses, hiding dark circles under her eyes. Maureen was again struck at how much this woman seemed to have aged in recent months.

"What did Frank say?"

"He's out all day. It'll be tomorrow before I can see him. So what's the plan?" she said, fidgeting. Smoke was on her breath.

"You're coming forward."

"I can't, Maureen! I told you that last night!"

"Lisa, this isn't going to just go away!"

"She said as long as I played by the rules everything would be fine!"

"She's lying! She'll go right to your husband!"

Lisa looked away. "Jen wants me to come with her. Says it's over if I don't. I haven't decided yet, but I'll have to tell Mack about us eventually . . ."

Maureen placed her hands on Lisa's shoulders. "Listen: I'm not going to prison over this. Now get yourself a lawyer . . ."

"I can't!"

"Yes, you can, and you will! Go see the U.S. Attorney! We'll do it together, Lisa! But I'm not taking the fall for this, understand?"

* * *

That night, on the tree-lined walking track at Rankin Medical Center in Brandon. It was quiet and safe, and Maureen had been too apprehensive to sit still in the apartment. Tom was having to work to keep up with her, despite his long legs. She rounded a curve and kicked a pine cone away. Light rain was falling, and they had the place to themselves.

"You think she'll show tomorrow?"

"Yes, for the tenth time. She has no choice. If she leaves town without telling anybody, the family will start looking for her."

"I don't have a good feeling about this. Maybe I was too hard on her."

"I don't know why you care about her feelings. She should have told you weeks ago. You wouldn't even know if it weren't for those e-mails!"

"I don't care about her feelings, Tom. She's a stupid, selfish fool, scared of her own shadow. I'm just afraid I frightened her even more."

"She'll be there, trust me. There's no other way out."

* * *

Maureen's lawyer was an old friend from Law School who practiced with a Jackson firm. A short, brown-haired man in a charcoal suit, he met Maureen on the front steps of the federal building the next morning. It was humid, and the bright sunlight was offset by gathering storm clouds. A sneak peek at another sweltering Mississippi summer.

"My air conditioning is out," he said, wiping his brow as he shook Maureen's hand. "Let's wait inside."

"I said I'd meet her here. She may not go through with it if she doesn't see me."

"Come on," he said, taking her arm. "She'll be right up."

Haynes appeared a few minutes after ten. He explained that an appointment was running late and directed them to a conference room. Maureen's lawyer doodled on a legal pad. Maureen stared into space, checking her watch every few minutes. She tried several times to reach Lisa. The receptionist eventually poked her head in, stating that Haynes was wrapping up. The door opened again two minutes later. Maureen looked up, fully expecting to see Lisa and her lawyer. It was Haynes, toting a tape recorder. A man in a suit was at his side. Haynes introduced him as an F.B.I. agent who would also be asking questions.

"We're missing Ms. McNulty, aren't we?"

"No answer at work or at home. Not answering her pager, either."

"What do you want to do?"

Maureen sighed. "I'll tell the story, but it won't matter unless it comes from her."

SIXTY SIX

Maureen and her lawyer parted company an hour later. Frustrated, she promised to call him if anything new developed. It was the same thing she told Haynes, who again stated that there was nothing he could do until an actual crime was suspected.

She logged onto the computer, hoping her mysterious friend had written and could shed light on why Lisa didn't show. Only a message from her mother awaited, however.

Maureen,

Your father is very upset at the way you talked to him. Whether you want to work down here or not, you should certainly acknowledge his attempt to help find you a good job. As you know, he is recovering from a serious heart attack and does not need to be this stirred up. I hope you'll reconsider some of the things you said and apologize. I can't believe you talked to him like that after all he's done for you.

Mom

Furious, she hit the reply button and typed:

Mother:

If you want to help, tell Dad to let me sink or swim on

214

my own, which I'm certainly capable of doing. Since you're obviously not going to do that (since it would involve confrontation), please stay out of it.

Maureen

* * *

Tom whistled when she recounted the exchange that night. Maureen, who now regretted it, lowered her head.

"Their whole world revolves around them. They have no idea what I'm going through."

"And they won't unless you tell them."

"Sure, and get another lecture about making things right with Frank! For the sake of my career, of course, not so the elite of Bay St. Louis can stroke him."

He embraced her. "Give 'em a few days. They'll cool off."

She sighed. "I'll call Dad next week. Once we're speaking again, Mom'll be fine. If Graham's happy, she is. That's the way of the world."

The phone rang, startling her. She grabbed it without checking the Caller I.D. unit.

"Maureen? Mack McNulty. Have you seen Lisa?"

Her eyes widened. "Uh, hi, Mack . . ."

"She was supposed to take our youngest to a soccer game tonight and didn't show. I had a hunch she wasn't coming—tried to call all day, and she never answered. Receptionist said she never came in. I went by her apartment twice, and she's not there."

Maureen sat and closed her eyes.

"Do you mind telling me why you wanted to see her?"

"It was office related. That's probably all I should say right now . . ."

"Look," he said, cutting in. Frustration bordering on panic was rapidly ebbing his patience. "The boys are scared. Hell, I am, too. If you know something, Maureen, please tell me."

"I told her to get a lawyer," she said. "We were supposed to

215

see the U.S. Attorney today. She didn't show."

"Oh, my God. What on earth for?"

"It's a long story, but she was put in a bad spot."

"Does this have anything to do with that crap you were on television about?"

"I don't know. Mack, call the police and file a missing persons report. And when she turns up, tell her she's gonna have to come forward, no matter how scared she is."

SIXTY SEVEN

Maureen awakened early the next morning and made coffee, tuning in the ABC affiliate. The weatherman she met at the miniature golf course that night was droning about the humidity. She thought about how much had happened since she met him and his wife. He bantered with the young female anchor, who then introduced a breaking story. She tossed to Carolyn Davis, who was live at the scene. Frowning, Maureen raised the volume.

"I'm at the Natchez Trace Parkway where it dead-ends into I-55," Carolyn said, the camera shot widening to show the interstate in the pre-dawn light. "A highway patrolman discovered a grisly automobile accident here about three-thirty this morning," she said, continuing as file footage from the middle of the night was shown. Maureen's heart sank at the crumpled wreckage of a small car. A granite barricade which separated drivers from a field below had a lengthy crack.

"The driver was pronounced dead at the scene by the Madison County coroner. I'm told that an autopsy will be performed, and that the identification of the victim is being withheld pending notification of family," Carolyn said, now back on camera.

"The Mississippi Highway Patrol has closed this exit until the accident site has been cleared and urges motorists to take an alternate route into the city. We will update this story as further information becomes available, and we'll have full coverage at five, six and ten."

Maureen dialed Janine.

"I'm watching. The other stations also have it."

She recounted the events of the last two days. "That sure looked like the car in front of that apartment building."

A long pause. "I sure hope you're wrong, hon'. I'll see what I can find out and call you later this morning."

*   *   *

Maureen was running errands when the cell rang.

"It's me. Off the record, the coroner says the deceased is Lisa McNulty. That's her, isn't it?"

"Yeah," Maureen said, fear spreading through her insides. "Oh, Jesus."

"No evidence of foul play, no sign of a struggle. No weapon."

"Suicide, then."

Janine lowered her voice. "It'll be several weeks before toxicology tests come back, but that's what he thinks. The front half of the car was completely caved in, and the wall has a perfect imprint of the front end. He thinks she was going at least a hundred when she hit."

Maureen recounted Mack's call.

"He'll know soon, if he doesn't already."

*   *   *

Janine's story ran the next day. It was on the front page of the State/Metro section and didn't imply a connection to previous events at the office, but a sense of doom enveloped Maureen. Mack McNulty's first message was left that night while she was out with Tom. He tried again the following night, which was

Friday. She was walking out the door to Erica's and ignored the call, opting to retrieve it in the car.

"Maureen, it's Mack. This is the second time I've called," he said. Other voices could be heard in the background, and she imagined a house full of grieving friends and relatives. "Lisa's funeral is tomorrow, and I don't think I have to tell you what we're going through over here. It's very important to the boys and me that we have some closure about this. I need you to tell me why you needed to see Lisa the other night and what you talked about. Please call when you get a chance."

* * *

Maureen didn't attend the funeral. She phoned Jeff that afternoon, guessing correctly that he was among many from the office who attended. She described the calls from McNulty.

"He was in pretty bad shape. So were his kids."

"Was Frank there?"

"He talked to Mack for a long time. Even gave him a hug."

A hollow laugh escaped her.

"I don't know what to tell you. I'm sure Mack wants answers, and I don't blame him. But I wouldn't say a word in your shoes. Send him to Haynes."

"I may do that. But it doesn't help us with those damned diskettes. With Lisa gone, I just know Ashleigh is about to make her move."

* * *

Another message from McNulty Sunday night. He had spoken to one of Lisa's neighbors and was aware that Jennifer had visited several times during her short stay at the complex. Maureen decided to return the call, since it didn't appear he was going to leave her alone.

"Hi, Mack, Maureen Lewis. I've been out of town," she said softly. "I'm so sorry. Is there anything I can do?"

"I apologize for leaving so many messages. I'll make this quick. When you went to Lisa's apartment, was a woman there? Tall, blond, nice-looking?"

"She was by herself," she said without hesitation. "I was only there fifteen, twenty minutes."

"Do you mind telling me what it was about? You said it was office related."

"I was trying to get her to see the U.S. Attorney. I told you that."

"How'd you know she was involved in anything?"

She answered carefully: "I got an anonymous tip. I know that sounds strange, but someone e-mailed me. I'm still trying to find out who."

"They said Lisa was in trouble?"

"Implied she was. Didn't call her by name. That's why I went to see her."

"In trouble how?"

Maureen exhaled. "Mack, the best advice I can give you is to go to Andrew Haynes. He's the U.S. Attorney. I told him everything Lisa told me . . ."

"What did Lisa tell you, damn it? Who are you trying to protect? Frank Cash?"

She snorted. "Can I say something to you in confidence? I wouldn't trust anything Frank Cash says. Not a word."

This slowed him. "He said some really nice things at the funeral . . ."

"I wouldn't trust that man as far as I can throw him. Not any more. Whatever you do, please don't talk to him, Mack."

A long silence. "So Lisa's death does have to do with that stuff in the paper."

"I have no proof. And because I don't, I can't start dropping names and speculating on things. Talk to Haynes. I'm begging you."

SIXTY EIGHT

A storm swept through during the overnight hours. A clap of thunder awakened her, interrupting a dream involving Warren Mullins. She got to her feet and focused, trying to remember why it was so important to see him. Then it dawned on her. She plugged in the headphones and listened to the cassette from the casino. She slept little the rest of the night and paged Jeff before eight.

"Are you where you can talk?"

"I'm in traffic. What's up?"

"Two things: Try to get with Frank today, preferably this morning. I'd love to know if he knows the diskettes and files in Administration are gone. I'm not sure Lisa had a chance to talk to him."

"Good idea. Even if I can't see him, I'll wander through Administration."

"Excellent. What have you heard about Warren Mullins lately?"

"Lots of gossip. Sounds ugly with Ashleigh."

"Would a copy of the casino tape do Warren any good? I'm serious," she said when Jeff laughed. "I'll bet the mortgage Ashleigh has the diskettes."

"If you're thinking about Warren getting them for you, don't hold your breath. Sounds like they're barely allowing him to see the kid. I'll drop in on Lisa Vick when I'm at Gartin. I think she still plays tennis with Ashleigh. Maybe I can pry something out of her."

"Call me. If you get the voice mail, try the cell."

* * *

Maureen drove to the athletic club, too fidgety to relax. She was finishing her session on the treadmill when she spotted Craig Grantham. She walked to the window overlooking the basketball court and watched him sink a shot. Then he disappeared, emerging a moment later in the adjacent weight room. He made himself comfortable at a Nautilus machine and began pumping iron. She draped a towel around her neck and trotted downstairs, doing her best to appear casual as she approached.

"Well, what a surprise! Howdy, stranger."

Grantham looked up and grinned. "How are ya?" he said, panting. "I'd stick out my sweaty hand, but I don't think you want to shake it."

Maureen smiled. His greeting indicated that he viewed them as old friends. If she cared to get into it, he would likely chalk up their stormy past to politics. That was just his way.

"What are you up to? Heard you put your house on the market."

"Got a contract this morning," he said, getting to his feet and wiping his face. "Probably go into private practice, much as the idea repulses me."

"Around here?"

"Nah. Had my fill of Jackson. New Orleans, I think. Got an offer from a firm the other day. They're flexible about the start date."

She didn't ask which, and he didn't volunteer. There was an awkward moment.

"Heard about Lisa?"

Grantham's face clouded. He glanced around. "That's bizarre. She weirded out the last couple of months I was there. Real uptight. Last time I saw her was right before Frank asked me to resign. She was late with some data, and I got on her pretty good. She started screaming at me, absolutely flew off the handle. So I'm not completely surprised. Something had gotten to her. I just don't know what."

"Talked to Frank lately?"

He took his time. "I don't think we'll be exchanging Christmas cards."

A grin. "Bad breakup?"

"There was a bit of an altercation. I told him what I thought of his disclosure." He laughed to himself and kicked at the floor. "But maybe it was a wake up call. I'm not sure he's running on all cylinders, either. You know what they say about getting out while the gettin's good."

An argument between two men on the basketball court caught their attention. Maureen was grateful for the interruption. She looked in that direction, considering what to say. He didn't seem to know anything about the scam and might be infuriated at Cash for leaving him out. The reference to Ashleigh was interesting; it was amusing to hear him chastened after using people so readily for so long. But would he care enough about getting even with them to help her? And could she trust him? There was no way to know.

"How much longer you gonna be in town?"

He watched an employee break up the dispute before responding. "Two, three weeks. Maybe a month. I'll be making periodic trips up here to see my lawyer." He rolled his eyes. "Sure you've heard about that."

She permitted a smile. "Not going quietly, huh?"

"Have as big a laugh as you want, Maureen. I'd just love to know who clued her in."

She went to her poker face. "Let's have a drink before you split. There are some things we should talk about."

Grantham eyed her. Then he retrieved a business card from his wallet and scribbled his cell on the back. She smiled and walked away.

SIXTY NINE

Her own cell rang a moment later. She answered when Grantham was completely out of sight.

"Frank had Tom West in his office the whole time I was there," Jeff said. "Never got in."

"Oh, boy. Wouldn't you love to have been a fly on the wall."

"Did walk through Administration, though. Tense, although there was no way to know if it was Lisa or the missing diskettes."

"Bet somebody went to Frank when they couldn't find anything, and Frank went to Tom. He can play dumb and launch one of those infamous internal investigations. Might even put you in charge."

Jeff laughed. "Spent a few minutes with Lisa Vick. She's nice enough, but don't tell her anything you don't want the whole world to know."

"What did you find out?" Maureen said, ducking into a quiet corner of the dressing room. Two young women in aerobic tights were twenty feet away. They were engrossed in animated conversation and unable to hear her.

"She and Ashleigh had lunch yesterday. Lisa McNulty's name came up—that's how I got Ashleigh's name into the conversation—and Vick said Lisa was stepping out on Mack. She found out from Ashleigh."

"Great."

"Vick asked with who, and Ashleigh just gave her a little smile," he said, disgust in his voice. "But Ashleigh supposedly acted like life was great. Said she had a couple of things up her sleeve, whatever that means."

"God only knows."

"I don't think she told Vick. This may interest you, though: Ashleigh and Eleanor are going on vacation tomorrow, the Virgin Islands or somewhere. They'll be gone at least a few days."

Maureen's heart jumped.

"Far as Warren is concerned, he'd probably take any help he can get. He wants custody. It sounds like he's concerned about his son's safety at Eleanor house—Eleanor's drinking is legendary, apparently—and he's offered Ashleigh an exorbitant amount of money. Vick said Ashleigh couldn't care less about custody, and she sure doesn't need the cash. She's getting her jollies watching Warren so jacked up. Has her lawyer call his every couple of days with different demands."

"Did my name come up?"

"No. I doubt they talked about you. If Ashleigh really is after you, she's not gonna chance her gossip buddies spreading around her schemes."

She glanced around. She had the room completely to herself. "I ran into Craig Grantham just now. He was actually very nice. Almost forgot how much I hate him. Suggested we have drinks."

"Who did?"

"Me. If I know him, there has to be an axe to grind with Frank, both for gutting his future and telling the world about Ashleigh. I got the impression he found out about them when everyone else did, and he doesn't seem to know about the embezzling. He's moving to a private firm in New Orleans in less than a month, by the way."

"Vick says he has a new girlfriend. He may want to put the whole thing behind him."

"I told him we had some things to talk about. He sure looked interested." She paused, forcing a smile at an employee who walked through with a load of fresh towels. "So is it worth looking up Warren Mullins?"

"All he can do is tell you to get lost. Just watch what you say to Grantham. I wouldn't trust that bastard as far as I can throw him."

SEVENTY

She drove in the general direction of downtown, in no hurry to get home. The thought of Ashleigh breaking the news to Mack McNulty that his wife was having a lesbian affair was nauseating. Worse, Ashleigh could sabotage Maureen further, perhaps implying to Mack that she was up to something. Mack was devastated by his wife's death and totally frustrated by the circumstances surrounding it, which the conversation with him made clear. If Ashleigh played on his paranoia, she might talk him into going to the police and dropping Maureen's name.

She turned off the radio, trying to concentrate. She suddenly wanted to know what Lisa's friend knew about the office. If they were intimate—especially with the prospect of Lisa being extorted—the woman might know a great deal.

". . . I know who Jennifer Green is, and I know what you dykes do in her bed."

Maureen thought back to the night at Lisa's apartment. She remembered the woman, a blond who was clearly upset at her intrusion. She was reasonably attractive and appeared to be athletic.

". . . We met in a tennis league a few months ago. She has a condo not far from the office, and I got in the habit of telling Mack I was working late and stopping a couple of times a week."

Maureen turned around and started home. Ashleigh had barged into Lisa's office and threatened her, prepared to exploit her relationship with Jennifer. How did she find out about their involvement, and how did she know where Jennifer lived? She paged Jeff. He hadn't responded by the time she reached the apartment. She paced, then impulsively flipped through the e-mails from Ashleigh's computer. She raised an eyebrow as references to tennis were made. Ashleigh had bragged endlessly about winning a city tournament a couple of years ago. Would she be in the same league as Lisa and Jennifer? Little light was shed on who played whom until the last note. It was from Hillary Bankston.

"*. . . Have to find a new tennis buddy with you out or I will gain the weight back. That Jennifer chick from our league moved in next door, the one so chummy with McNulty. Maybe I'll talk to her.*"

Maureen's eyes widened. She was reading the message a second time when the cell rang.

"Sorry for the delay," Jeff said. "What's up?"

"I was trying to figure out how Ashleigh could have known about Lisa and Jennifer, and I realized it's the tennis league! That's how Lisa met Jennifer, and one of the e-mails we printed off Ashleigh's computer was from Hillary Bankston. She talks about playing with the 'Jennifer chick who moved in next door and is real chummy with McNulty.'"

Jeff gasped. "They were all in the same league?"

"It sure sounds like it. Do this for me: Call Lisa Vick, since you just talked to her. I know she and Ashleigh play. Tell her your wife is interested in signing up. Find out where they play, and I'll take it from there."

He called back ten minutes later. "They play at Parham Bridges. Vick hurt her elbow and sat out this league, but she knew a lot about it. The pro is named Shelly and works in the clubhouse. That's who I'd try first."

* * *

Parham Bridges Tennis Center was at the corner of Ridgewood and Old Canton in North Jackson. The tennis courts were next to the tree-lined walking track, a public portion of the park which she had used many times before. She found her way to the pro shop and glanced around. An attractive, fortyish brunette in tennis clothes was behind the counter.

"Hi. I'm trying to find Shelly."

"I'm Shelly," the woman said, an artificial smile immediately in place. "Can I help you?"

"My name is Maureen. I'm interested in joining a league. Could I get some information?"

"Sure. The summer league has already started, so you'll have to wait 'til the fall," she said, pulling a red binder from behind the counter. "I hope that's not a problem. We'd love to have you."

"I'm a little rusty, so that actually would work out fine."

Shelly explained when the next league began and the costs involved. She described most of the players as professional women, although a fair amount were at home. It sounded like a lot of country club types, nobody she cared to spend time with.

"Everybody gets along great and has a lot of fun, and at the end of the league there's a party for the players."

"I assume they're separated by rankings?"

"That's correct. Have you played in a league before?"

"I was a three-five before I moved here," she said, lying. "On the Coast."

"Very good." She smiled, lowering her voice. "Some women tell us how good they are, and we put 'em in leagues and find out they've never played organized tennis. Makes the rest of us who are serious about it pretty upset."

Maureen contemplated her next move. "Is there a roster of players I could look at?"

Shelly flipped through the binder. She slid it around so Maureen could view the names.

"Ashleigh Dunn is our top female," she said. The phone number alongside her name was the North Jackson listing Maureen was familiar with, which indicated that no one here knew about the separation from Warren. "She has gotten so good I was only beating her about half the time before she got pregnant. She'll be back before long, though. She's won several tournaments."

Maureen scanned the names, recognizing none. "Can I look through these?"

"Help yourself," Shelly said. She was already making her way to a handsome male customer.

Maureen flipped the pages quickly. Ashleigh played in the 4.0 league, of which there were two dozen women. The 3.5 section had four groups of twelve, including Lisa Vick and Joyce Cash. The 3.0 had six groups. She was scanning the last one when she found Hillary's name. Just below it was Lisa McNulty. She looked for Jennifer's name but didn't find it.

"I can get you signed up right now, if you want," Shelly said, suddenly at her elbow. "There's no rush, but it would be one less thing you'd have to fool with at the last minute."

"Let me practice a few weeks before I commit to a league. I may start at 3.0." She hesitated, then gestured at the page as she handed over the binder. "I played with a woman a couple of months ago named Jennifer. I thought she was in this group. I was only around her once and don't know how to get in touch with her. Good player. Gave me a lot of tips, told me to call if I wanted to play."

Shelly frowned. Maureen grimaced internally, fearing her cover was blown. "Oh, I know who you're talking about," she said, smiling in recognition. "The woman from Dallas. She's real good. She walked right through 3.0 in the spring. Some of the girls think she sandbagged, but like I told them, a 3.0 game there might win the 3.5 league here. When Ashleigh's playing again, I'm gonna try to get them on the court together. That would be something to see."

Maureen barely suppressed a laugh. "Do you know how to get in touch with her?"

Shelly flipped pages. "Here we go. Jennifer Green. Let me write down her phone number."

"Can I look through this one more time? There was a brochure which caught my eye."

"Help yourself. Just leave it on the counter when you're done," Shelly said, waving at another customer. "Nice meeting you. Let me know when you're ready to sign up."

She waited until Shelly was several steps away, then flipped pages until she found the roster which included Lisa and Hillary. She looked around, then copied Hillary's number. She placed the binder on the counter and strode out.

SEVENTY ONE

F iftcen minutes later she logged onto her computer at home and ran a reverse trace on the Internet, something she had done many times while researching businesses in Consumer. She typed in Jennifer's phone number. A moment later an address came up.

3646 Meadowbrook Road, #17—Jackson, MS 39211

Hillary's number was next. A moment later another address came up.

3646 Meadowbrook Road, #18—Jackson, MS 39211

". . . She has a condo not far from the office, and I got into the habit of telling my husband I was working late and stopping a couple of times a week."

Maureen gasped. Hillary lived next door to Jennifer? If that was the case, it didn't take a leap of faith to presume she found about Jennifer and Lisa, then told Ashleigh. And if Ashleigh had plotted the Consumer scheme, the knowledge was probably a pivotal part of her plan.

She drove north on State Street, reaching Meadowbrook Road in five minutes. She turned east, wound through the older neighborhoods and approached the interstate. She sat at a traffic light, taking in the private elementary school which occupied a full block of Old Canton Road. Jeff said he went to school there. Across the street was a small, gated community, with half a dozen houses which easily cost half a million dollars each. As the light turned green she glanced to her left. A large, recently-completed development disappeared down a winding, woodsy drive. Curious, she crossed over the interstate and turned around on a side street, returning a minute later. She edged into the cobblestone driveway, taking in the large marble sign on a small hill.

The Woods North—3646 Meadowbrook Road

The security gate was open. A spectacular canopy of trees held her attention for the first two hundred yards, but the trees ended abruptly once the interstate was no longer visible. Maureen snickered, discovering attractive but somewhat ordinary condominiums bordered by a lengthy privacy fence. The covered parking spaces were assigned, and she spotted a gray Lexus with Texas plates. She parked fifty feet away and approached quietly. Jennifer opened as she prepared to knock. She was in a sports bra and running shorts, a Walkman in hand. Her hair was shorter than Maureen remembered, and her angular face was pretty despite the lack of make up. There wasn't an ounce of fat on her. She had initiated the relationship from what Lisa implied, and Maureen found herself wondering if she would have suspected that this woman was a lesbian.

"Yes?"

"Jennifer Green?"

"Yes? Can I help you?" A frown spread across her face as she recognized Maureen. "What do you want? How'd you find me?"

"My name is Maureen Lewis. I used to work with Lisa. Can I come in?"

Jennifer didn't budge. "I know who you are. I asked how

you found me. Do I need to call the cops?"

Maureen glanced around. "The woman next door to you also works at the Attorney General's Office. Her name is Hillary Bankston. She's in your tennis league."

A frown. She poked her head out and glanced at the neighboring home. "Hillary lives there?"

"She does. And it's my hunch that she tipped Ashleigh off about you and Lisa. I assume Lisa mentioned that name to you."

Jennifer's eyes hardened. She gestured for her to step inside. The interior was a lot like Maureen's apartment, with Berber carpet, crown molding, modern appliances and a fireplace. Moving boxes were piled high, however. Maureen remained on her feet.

"I don't have a lot of time. And quite honestly, I don't feel much like talking about Lisa," she said. Pain, which she was trying to conceal, was in her eyes for the first time. "So make it quick."

"Did she tell you about the embezzling?"

"She told me everything. I know all about what happened to you. You'd talked her into coming forward, but she flipped out when the diskettes disappeared."

"What has she told you about Ashleigh?"

Jennifer sighed. "The firm I work for sent me here on a year-long project. I met Lisa playing tennis. Things didn't get complicated until Ashleigh threatened her."

"Did Lisa know Hillary lives next door?"

"I don't know. It's sure news to me. This is the woman from the tennis league? Forties, brown hair, little heavy? Runs her mouth all the time?"

Maureen nodded. "She and Ashleigh are friendly. Do you think there's any chance Hillary saw Lisa here?"

"I suppose. That's why Lisa got the apartment, because somebody found out about us and she was scared to come back over here. I've never seen Hillary here, though. I didn't try to meet any neighbors since I knew I wouldn't be here long." She started to add something, then changed her mind. Maureen assumed it had to do with Lisa and moved ahead before the moment became awkward.

"You must have talked to her playing tennis."

"Briefly," Jennifer said, drumming her fingers on the glass coffee table. "She and another woman accused me of lying about how good I was so I could win the league, which wasn't true. But that shouldn't have been enough to make trouble." A pause. "Are you friends with this woman?"

"Hillary? She's no friend of mine. She's not as ruthless and psychotic as Ashleigh, but I could see her being jealous of your tennis game and the car you drive. Once she realized you lived here and saw Lisa coming and going, she probably got right on the phone to Ashleigh and her other gossip buddies."

"I may just look this Ashleigh chick up and have a word with her."

"Please don't. She'll know I put you up to it. I don't want to go into detail, but I'm getting ready to make my move, and that would blow it out of the water. Would you be willing to see the U.S. Attorney?"

Jennifer got to her feet. "I won't have time. I'm catching a flight this afternoon, and I'm leaving town next week. And honestly, I'm not sure that'll accomplish anything. The way Lisa talked, those people are above the law."

"Assuming Ashleigh is charged with embezzling and extortion, which I'm confident she will be, the F.B.I. will want to talk to everyone who knew anything. If Ashleigh found out about you guys through Hillary, and Lisa killed herself because of the extortion threats, the police may want to talk to Hillary. I'm just speculating, but she might get scared and tell them anything Ashleigh confided about the crimes. It sure couldn't hurt."

Jennifer stared. Hatred was in her eyes. She retrieved a business card from her briefcase. "If it'll help put Ashleigh behind bars, I'm all for it. Lisa was scared to death of her. I wish I could spend ten minutes in a locked room with her."

* * *

"So that's how Ashleigh knew about them," Janine said late that afternoon. She and Maureen were having a beer at the Irish pub. This time they practically had the place to themselves. "Now what do you do?"

"Don't know. I couldn't get Jeff, and I want to run everything by him." She sipped her beer. "I'm tempted to contact Warren Mullins and offer the casino tape in exchange for his help. It wouldn't be admissible in court, but I don't have to tell him on the front end."

"What kind of help?"

"Getting the diskettes! You know as well as I do Ashleigh has them, and I was told she and her mother are going out of town for the weekend."

Janine gasped. "Maureen, don't tell me you're going to break into Eleanor Dunn's house."

"I've thought about it all afternoon. I'm a prosecutor, and here I am actively plotting a crime. Erica really let me have it. Like I told her, I wish this stuff would just go away so I could get on with my life. But there's every indication Ashleigh is trying to sabotage me. I'm liable to be charged with a crime if I don't fight back, Janine."

SEVENTY TWO

"Warren Mullins." His deep, southern drawl had a weary edge.

"Hi, it's Maureen Lewis," she said, straining for an

air of calm as her heart pounded. It was the next afternoon.

"This is a surprise," he said neutrally.

"Like to see if we could sit down and talk."

"May I ask what about?"

"Honestly, I'd rather save that until we're face to face. Won't take long."

There was a delay, as he replied to someone in the office. "Okay, I suppose. When? Today?"

"Yeah. Somewhere we could have a little privacy."

"Come by here, then. Everybody will have cleared out by five-thirty."

"Tell me how to find you."

*   *   *

She changed into a navy suit and drove to East Capitol Street. A leggy receptionist was lingering in the lobby and showed her to his office. She announced that she was setting the security alarm and closed the door behind her.

"Hi, Maureen," Mullins said, offering a handshake and a forced smile. He gestured at a seat across his desk. He was a tall, dapper ex-jock who kept himself in good shape and maintained an aura of self-importance. His office was decorated with plaques, citations and pictures of Ashleigh. Pictures of the new-born were on his desk, and CNBC was on a small television behind him. "What can I do for you?"

"I don't know how to go about this without being terribly blunt. Please forgive me."

A quick nod.

She glanced around, then faced him. "Ashleigh, Frank and Sonny Hollins are embezzling from the Attorney General's Office. The woman from Administration told me two nights before her death."

Shock appeared on his face. If he knew about this, he was an awfully good actor. "You think Ashleigh killed her?"

"No, I think it was suicide. Several months ago Ashleigh ordered her to use two different sets of diskettes to chart where the money was going, and offered her ten grand to make it happen. But if she didn't go along, Ashleigh would go to Frank and gut her job. She'd also done some spying, found some things out and was prepared to go to Lisa's husband and bust up their marriage."

Mullins' jaw dropped open. She recounted the meeting with Lisa.

"I don't suppose you know why she would have such an axe to grind with me, do you?"

He took his time. "Maureen, I honestly don't. She complained about you, but she bitched about everybody. I'm discovering there's a lot I didn't know about her. A whole lot."

Maureen nodded. "I wanted to go to the U.S. Attorney and had Lisa talked into going with me, but she called the next morning from the office. Said both sets of diskettes and a file cabinet full of paperwork had disappeared without a trace."

Mullins was turning paler by the minute.

"I think Ashleigh has the diskettes. I know she's living with her mother, and I've been told they're going to the Virgin Islands this weekend."

"You know more than I do," he said angrily. He bit his tongue, clearly wanting to say more.

"I still have friends at the office. And I'll tell you the same thing I told Lisa: I'm not going to jail for something I didn't do."

Mullins snapped his fingers. "I just thought of something. There was a white box on the kitchen table marked 'Administration' the other day when I went to see my son. I didn't think about it at the time, but she grabbed the box and took it to a different part of the house. She was mumbling something that didn't make sense, like her resume was in there and she needed to put it in a safe place."

Maureen's heart leaped. Mullins held up a hand.

"I can't just go get it, Maureen. We're on very poor terms.

Eleanor is even worse. I'm doing well just to get in there."

"I'm not asking that. But in exchange for something you could use, I'd like some help getting in." She glanced around. "An alarm code, for example. A place where I might find a lock box. I have to get those diskettes, Warren. There's a chance I'll go to prison if I don't."

Mullins sized her up. The time had come to make the offer.

"I found out about Ashley and Craig Grantham a while back. I assume that's why you guys separated."

He said nothing, but the anger in his face made it clear she was correct.

"There was already evidence that she was out to get me, so I sent a couple of people to the prosecutor's conference to look for them."

She removed a copy of the tape from her purse and held it aloft. Mullins squirmed in his chair, barely able to contain himself.

"They don't know I have this. Tell me how to get in and where to look, and it's yours."

* * *

She left twenty minutes later and paged Jeff.

"Warren has a copy of the casino tape, and I have what he thinks is the alarm code to Eleanor's house. He saw a box marked 'Administration' the last time he was there, so I'm sure the diskettes are somewhere in the house. Be thinking about what night we can go."

A long moment passed. "You're serious, aren't you?"

"Jeff, I'm dead serious. I'll do it myself if I have to."

"No, I'm still in. Just a little apprehensive, that's all."

"We'll plan everything to the letter. Tom will be with us, I'm sure. No way he lets me go out there alone. I'm about to call Craig now. If you don't hear back from me tonight, expect a call in the morning."

Jeff laughed. "Tell him Walter Jett said hello."

She hung up and dialed Grantham's cell, trying to sound calm. "It's Maureen. Wanna have a drink?"

"We can, I guess. I've got 'til about seven-thirty."

"Chili's at Briarwood in half an hour?"

"Yeah, I suppose so."

She hung up before he could change his mind.

SEVENTY THREE

She pulled into the Chili's parking lot exactly thirty minutes later, having changed into jeans and a pink, sleeveless sweater with a t-shirt underneath. Grantham was approaching from the other direction, also dressed casually. He started for the bar, but she requested a table. They had beaten the dinner crowd and were seated immediately. The mouth-watering smell of sauteed onions emanated from the kitchen.

"Understand you have a new honey."

A frown, barely discernible behind the smiling facade. "Word gets around."

"I won't even ask who. But it's safe to say you and Ashleigh are no longer involved?"

A flash in his eyes. "You wearing a wire?"

Maureen laughed. "No. Just trying to get a feel for where your loyalties might lie."

Grantham leaned forward. The smile was gone. "I got the impression you knew something about Evelyn's lawsuit. That's why I'm here. I take it I was mistaken."

She smiled, relishing her moment of control. "Evelyn only figures into this peripherally. Your new flame doesn't figure at all. And since you don't have a lot of time, I'll cut right to the chase."

He nodded, gazing into her eyes. She glanced around before continuing.

"Level with me, Craig. How much did it bother you that Frank Cash killed your chances of going to Washington?"

Grantham's eyes became hard. He looked directly at her. "I could kill the son of a bitch."

"What about Ashleigh? She may have been a little smarter than you thought."

"What do you mean by that?"

"She was in on some things you didn't know about. Some pretty big things. So was Frank. If I know you, you would have blown them both out of the water if you'd known what they were up to."

"What the hell are you talking about?"

Maureen smiled and sipped her beer. "We have to agree on something first. I'll talk to you in confidence. But I have something on you, Craig. Something that'll mess up your future, and I won't hesitate to use it if you screw me. And since you're moving to New Orleans," she said, raising her voice when he tried to cut in, "I took it upon myself to share this information with Wally Jett. Our agreement is that he keeps quiet as long as you're cool. But you screw me, everybody finds out. I'll wait until the time is right, then blast you. Understand?"

Grantham wasn't used to being threatened. He stared in a mixture of anticipation and anger. "I'm listening."

She glanced around a final time. "Ashleigh, Frank and Sonny are embezzling from Consumer, to the tune of two hundred thousand dollars at last count. Its been going on since April."

For a nanosecond she feared the joke was on her. But something in Grantham's eyes finally gave the impression that this was news to him. He gazed back, waiting for her to continue. She told the story, leaning forward to emphasize the part she rehearsed in the car.

"You were left out because Ashleigh wanted it that way. She

used you, Craig. She played you like a stringed instrument. Think about it. How else would Evelyn have found out about you guys?"

He didn't reply, but he shifted in his seat.

"She might have told her about the video. That's pretty racy stuff. Maybe that's why her attorney is making it so complicated for you."

The remark hung in the air. Maureen prepared for an eruption.

"How the fuck do you know about that?" he said with gritted teeth, trying to hold his voice down. Fury was in his eyes.

"At the risk of sounding coy, Craig, I'm a prosecutor. I investigate crimes," she said. "And I've found out a lot of things about Ashleigh. I honestly don't know what she's capable of. But I'm going to get those diskettes and clear my name, no matter what I have to do." A pause. "And if I know you, you'd like nothing more than to help take her down. You'd also bury Frank Cash at the same time."

He looked into the distance.

"You don't know anything about them, do you?" he said at length.

"Who? Ashleigh and Frank?" she said, thrown. "Just what was in the paper."

"Do you even know about Eleanor and Sonny?"

"I just found out. They're having an affair, aren't they?"

"That's been going on years. Long before Frank was in office. I haven't known very long."

Horror spread across her face. "Are you saying Frank doesn't know?"

Grantham finally met her gaze. "I honestly don't think he does, believe it or not. I've done some snooping, too. Recently and in the past. The Sonny and Eleanor thing is guarded pretty carefully. I just stumbled onto that. But I've known some of the Dunn secrets for a long time. You talk about a dysfunctional family."

Maureen waited him out. Expectation was in her eyes.

"That's not anything you need to know," he said, now regarding her with a slight air of amusement. He knew he had gained back control of the discussion.

"Why protect them?"

"I'm trying to protect you. You exploit their skeletons and the gamesmanship would cease. Ashleigh and Eleanor would hunt you down and put a bullet in your head." He paused. "And at the risk of sounding melodramatic, it wouldn't be the first time."

Maureen's eyes widened, but Grantham held up a hand. "I know a lot of folks are delighted to see Evelyn sticking it to me. But that's small potatoes. Where I really screwed up was devoting over a decade of my life to a politician who is used like a pawn by a small group of people."

"You swear you didn't know about him and Ashleigh?"

"Not until I saw it on the news." He sipped his beer. "Sure, my ego took a pretty major hit, but I realized right then how truly little I knew about things around here. That's when I began poking around, asking some questions. You're right—Ashleigh played me like a cheap fiddle. Just like she's playing Frank Cash."

"If Hollins is having an affair with Eleanor, Ashleigh certainly knows about it, right?"

"Of course. The picture I'm getting is Hollins playing along with Frank like they're big pals, then plotting against him with Eleanor and Ashleigh. Scary, isn't it?"

She mulled this over. There was no way to know how much of this—if any—was true. "Why would Frank be involved, anyway? We're not talking about millions of dollars from Consumer, Craig. You know that."

Grantham glanced around. "I've heard rumors about Frank's gambling. But I've heard rumors about lots of things, a lot of them from political enemies. Like the governor. Hollins is well-connected, though, and the Dunn family is practically a small Mafia. I know Frank, and what I saw in those sound bites was fear. Maybe Ashleigh threatened him when he fired her. Maybe she went to Joyce. Maybe Eleanor did. But running to the press about the affair wasn't smart, and I told him so. If Ashleigh has the goods on Frank, that won't make it go away. It'll make it worse."

Maureen exhaled slowly, trying to slow the flow of adrenaline through her body. Her stomach needed milk, not beer. "Does Hamilton figure into this at all?"

"Let's just say that he, too, has a history. He's a player, all right." Grantham got to his feet. "I took an interest in Ashleigh all those years ago to get back at him. I thought I was a pretty cool cat. I didn't know shit."

"Let me walk you out," she said hastily, dropping a ten dollar bill on the table. She spoke at his car. "I'll do whatever I have to do, Craig. If I'm being set up, I'm not going down without a fight. Tell me about Eleanor's house. Specifically how to get in, and where I'd find a safe or lock box."

"I've never been out there. Swear to God."

"Damn it, Craig . . ."

"I can tell you this, though: I was with Ashleigh once at an ATM. She'd had too much to drink and made a big deal of her password, said she and her mother use it for everything." He smiled. "Three-six, two-four, three-six."

Maureen shrugged, not getting it.

"Thirty-six, twenty-four, thirty-six. Just like her. And Eleanor."

"Come on," she said, laughing in spite of herself.

"Bet it works on the security system. Two of the vainest broads I've ever met."

She quieted, her eyes widening.

"No guarantees. I've heard they're making it real hard on Warren. Might have changed the code because of him."

"I hope not."

He climbed into his Explorer. "Be careful, Maureen. You're into a lot more than just politics now."

SEVENTY FOUR

She paged Jeff the next morning. It was over an hour before he returned the call.

"Sorry for the delay. Frank called me in—he's found someone to run Consumer. Some guy who's moving from Memphis. He'll start in August. Anyway, tell me about last night."

She recounted the discussion with Grantham.

"Wow," he said. "You still want to go through with this?"

"Sure do. Warren Mullins just called with some critical information. I really think we'll find what we're looking for. Let's plan on tomorrow night."

* * *

Erica called the next afternoon.

"Keith and I are in the mood for Mexican tonight. You guys wanna come?"

"Not tonight," she said casually. "One night this weekend?"

"That'll work." A pause, as she spoke to someone in her office. "Haven't talked to you in a few days. Please tell me you're not playing private eye any more."

Maureen felt guilty lying to her friend. "Just reading classified ads. Making daily trips to the athletic club so I won't balloon. Didn't realize how susceptible I am to snacking when I sit around here all day."

"I know the feeling. Save some calories for this weekend, okay?"

SEVENTY FIVE

Jeff arrived at the apartment at nine. He was in jeans, as was Maureen.

"Told the wife I might be late, made up this last-minute project for Frank. She's a lot more understanding now that he hired someone." He grinned. "I come bearing good news. All your Consumer files are still backed up."

She looked at him blankly.

"One of the furniture stores is up to no good again, and Frank, of all people, said you'd popped them a couple of times. It occurred to me that as thorough as you were, you probably backed everything up each night because the network was always going down. I took a shot, and there it was on your computer. The same one I'm using now."

She was unable to speak, although she was beginning to understand.

"Ashleigh—or somebody—erased your files on the network and stole the paper trail from Lisa's office. She covered herself perfectly there. But she forgot your hard drive, Maureen! I spent ten minutes looking at backup files on the C: drive. There's a whole directory of memos you sent to Administration whenever a check from a business came in. Goes back several years."

She sat, trying to take in this incredible break. "How could someone—or several people—go to such lengths to savage me and forget something so obvious?"

"You may have touched on it right then. If several people are involved, it may have just slipped through the cracks. Remember, Ashleigh hasn't been there in weeks. She may have told Lisa to take care of it, or someone from Accounting. Who knows why. It just didn't get done."

Maureen managed a smile. "And because of it, there might

just be a way out."

"We ready, then? I want to do this before I lose my nerve. I don't break into houses every day."

"Soon as Tom gets here."

The intercom buzzed on cue.

SEVENTY SIX

They took Jeff's minivan to Clinton. He slowed as they reached the neighborhood.

"There's a clubhouse right around the corner," Tom said, leaning forward from his perch in the middle seat. "Let's park there. Won't look nearly as suspicious as the driveway."

"More than just a pretty face," Jeff said with a grin, winking at Maureen. She forced a smile, by now barely able to sit still. "What did Warren say?"

"Last time he was there, the lock on the sliding glass door going to the pool didn't work. A short broomstick was keeping it closed, and Warren thought there might be enough room for someone to squeeze through. The keypad is in the kitchen, next to the door going to the garage. It sounds like your typical security alarm, which means thirty seconds to turn it off. Can you believe this combination: Three-six, two-four, three-six."

Both men chuckled.

"If it doesn't work, we're screwed. We haul ass back to the van and get the hell out of Dodge before anybody sees us. But maybe that won't happen. We have Warren's blessing, for what that's worth. He has the baby, and it would be fine with him if we firebombed the place."

"So we look for a box with 'Administration' written on it?" Jeff said.

"We look for the safe. Warren said Ashleigh was gone at least five minutes when she left with the box. That would have given her enough time to put the diskettes somewhere else, hopefully the safe. He's not sure, but he thinks it might be in the closet in Eleanor's bedroom. If that combination gets us in the house, he thinks it'll surely get us in the safe."

They quieted as Jeff arrived at the clubhouse. Maureen handed out small flashlights and rubber gloves. She took a deep breath and signaled for them to follow. Eleanor's street was two hundred yards away. They reached it quickly, pausing to check for traffic.

"Heads up!" Jeff whispered fiercely. They dashed across the street and into a clump of pines. A patrol car passed slowly, its lights on high beam.

"Quickly, guys," Maureen said when the officer was out of sight, emerging from the cover. "I doubt we'll get a second chance if this goes wrong."

Eleanor's house was a quarter-mile from the intersection. She had more privacy than most of her neighbors, thanks to the curve of the road and a pair of large oaks near the edge of the property. They dashed toward the trees as another car approached. It was barreling along and clearly wasn't law enforcement.

Maureen squinted, looking at the fence. "The gate is on the other side, damn it. We'll be right out in the open trying to get over to that side."

"We don't need to be fooling with a gate," Tom said. "I'll hop the fence, then open the front door when I get inside. You're right—chances are a lot better we won't be seen if we stay on this side."

Maureen met his eyes. She flashed back to his initial phone call, then the night he admitted Hollins had put him up to the ruse. She had forgiven him, but he clearly hadn't forgiven himself. He was volunteering to take on a dangerous role in a serious crime, part of a never-ending attempt to prove his character.

"It'll be a snap. Trust me."

She gripped his hand. "Be careful."

* * *

Five agonizing minutes crawled by. Maureen and Jeff remained motionless, waiting for any sound to indicate that Tom was inside the house. The chirping of a cricket startled them, but it was quiet a moment later. Then the soft click of a dead-bolt was heard. The door opened a crack. The flashlight beam hit the welcome mat for a split-second, the signal that he had successfully disabled the alarm. Maureen and Jeff trotted to the front door and disappeared inside.

"Anybody see you?" Jeff said.

"I don't see how. The lights at the pool are dim," Tom said, steadying his breathing. "That guy wasn't kidding when he said there might be enough room to squeeze through. Getting my head through was the hardest part. I was afraid I was going to set off the alarm, then get stuck."

"Warren said the safe might be in Eleanor's bedroom closet," Maureen said impatiently. "We don't have much time. Let's go."

The house had a large formal dining room and an even bigger great room. It was hard to see in the darkness, but the china cabinet and antique furniture made it hard to imagine a baby playing here. It was a split plan, with a pair of bedrooms on the west side. Jeff went that way. Maureen and Tom disappeared down a hallway in the other direction, flashing the beam on thick Berber carpet. She snapped her fingers a moment later. Jeff hurried through the house.

"This has to be Eleanor's room," Maureen said, stepping over the threshold. She took a second to inspect the antique brass bed. It was covered by an equally elderly canopy. Tom walked through the bathroom, which was highlighted by a huge, heart-shaped Jacuzzi tub. Maureen followed, stepping ahead of him into a large, walk-in closet. Miles of expensive clothes from top designer names were neatly arranged, with a wicker cabinet sporting a variety of shoes.

"The life of luxury," Tom said to himself.

"It's not in here," Maureen said, ignoring him. She strode to the other side of the house, the men following. Two smaller rooms opened from a short hallway.

"Ashleigh and the baby are in here," Tom said, pointing at a crib and playpen.

Jeff tried the last door. It was locked. He glanced at Maureen, then applied a bit of force. It opened.

"Did you break it?"

"No. Must have been stuck. No walk-in closet in here."

The room was a study. Maureen looked over a Gateway computer while Jeff and Tom searched the room. They didn't find a safe.

"Great!" She strode for the master bedroom. "It has to be somewhere. You don't think they took it to the Virgin Islands, do you?"

"I hope not," Jeff said, opening the walk-in closet again. He sifted through the formal dresses, stopping at the shoe rack. Maureen stepped forward, nudging it with her foot. A pair of black flats, carefully balanced on top, fell backward. Her eyes snapped up as they hit metal.

"Help me with this," she said fiercely, grabbing the rack. A moment later the safe was revealed. It stood on a pair of cement blocks. She looked at Tom. "Stand near the door. You're the lookout."

Jeff knelt and tried the combination. It didn't work. Maureen tensed, now hunkered down beside him.

"I don't think I quite hit the numbers. You know how precise these things are," he said calmly, trying the combination again.

"Could we carry it out?"

"I don't know how we'd get it all the way to the van without . . ."

Click.

"Oh, my God!" she said as the door opened. She snapped her fingers. Tom appeared a moment later. She flashed him a thumbs-up. He nodded and returned to his perch.

"This is loaded. Be careful," Jeff said, beads of sweat dripping from his forehead as he carefully removed a .38 from the safe. A large stack of legal envelopes were below. A small envelope fell when Jeff removed them.

"What have we here?" Maureen whispered, opening the envelope. Three computer diskettes were held together by a rubber band. Two more were alongside.

"If that code got us in the house and in here, it really might get us on the computer, Maureen . . ."

Tom appeared in the doorway, terror on his face. "Somebody's here! The garage door is opening!"

Maureen scooped up the diskettes. Jeff grabbed her arm and herded her into the hallway. They trotted into the great room, Tom in the lead. Their footsteps were mercifully silent on the thick carpet. They wedged behind the large, leather sofa just as the door to the garage opened. Maureen was shaking in fear. She tried to collect herself, knowing they would likely get one shot at an escape, if that.

The door opened. There was a pause, then an audible click. Maureen froze as she realized someone had a gun. Footsteps could be heard in the kitchen—sounded like the floor might be made of marble—then again on the hardwood in the foyer before fading. She guessed the visitor was checking the front door.

"Eleanor, how many times have I told you not to forget the fucking alarm?"

Tom's eyes widened. "Hollins," he said to Maureen, mouthing the word. Jeff glanced their way, thrusting his hand palm-down toward the floor. Be still.

The footsteps increased in volume, then faded as Hollins hit carpet and strode toward the two bedrooms on the west side of the house. They all got a quick look at him, and Maureen felt her heart skip a beat when she saw his firearm. He came back through a moment later, now on his way to Eleanor's bedroom. Suddenly Jeff was moving. He tried the sliding glass door, but it didn't move. Panic appeared on his face, but Tom dove and grabbed the broomstick.

It banged against an end table. A lamp overturned.

All froze as Hollins, who was discovering the open safe in that instant, darted back toward the living room. Jeff ripped open the sliding glass door and grabbed Maureen, meaning to shove her through first. The chivalrous gesture backfired as her foot tangled with his. The delay allowed them to escape into the backyard, but Tom was forced to hold back. Pool side lights gave him a dim view of them. Hollins would see them soon, if he didn't already.

"Who's here?" Hollins said loudly, ten feet away. "I have a gun!"

He worked his way toward the sliding glass, coming within five feet of Tom. Tom, able to see the older man's shadow, crawled around the end of the sofa. He grabbed the broomstick and crouched, ready to strike. Hollins paused, squinting into the darkness.

"Don't fuck with me!" he said, keeping his voice low. "I'll shoot!"

Hollins stepped forward. Tom jabbed the broomstick, catching his foot as he started outside. He fell forward onto the marble walkway. The gun discharged and clattered away. Maureen screamed, darting for the house. Jeff followed close behind. Hollins dove for the gun. He got his hands on it just before Maureen reached him and pointed it at her. She backed away, terrified.

"I'll kill both of you. I swear I will."

"Put it down!" Tom said, his voice hard as he stepped onto the walkway. He was five feet from Hollins and closing.

"You!" Hollins said angrily, pointing the gun at Tom. It was a small caliber revolver. "You're a dead man, you son of a bitch!"

"Put it down . . ."

"Take one more step and I'll shoot, goddammit . . ."

Maureen froze as Hollins aimed between Tom's eyes. Jeff, who was shielding Maureen, lunged and threw a forearm into Hollins. The gun went off, shattering glass thirty feet away. Hollins drew back to shoot Jeff, but Tom landed a quick blow to his head. Staggered, Hollins tried to regain his footing. He reached for Tom, but Maureen, finally breaking out of her trance, kicked Hollins' wrist as hard as she could. The effort knocked her down. It also sent the gun clattering away. Hollins turned just in time to see Tom coming at him. He tried to duck, but Tom hit him low and knocked him down. He yanked Maureen to her feet.

"Go!"

Jeff was already approaching the sliding glass. He opened it wide. The three of them had just darted inside when the door exploded. Maureen screamed, fully expecting to see Tom down. But he was hot on her heels, shoving her toward the front door. A moment later they were sprinting down the street.

* * *

"You okay?" Tom said, his arm around Maureen inside the van. She clung to him, weeping into his chest. She managed a nod.

"Have the diskettes?"

She held the envelope aloft.

"Jeff, you all right?"

"Not a scratch. What about you?"

"A little bruised, but I'll live." A pause. "I think we got

away. We're on the interstate by the time the cops get here."

"Hollins isn't calling the cops. His prints are all over the place," Maureen said shakily, speaking for the first time. "A neighbor will have to do that."

"A light was on across the street when we ran by."

"They're too far back from the road to have gotten a good look." She took Tom's face in her hands. "You saved my life."

He kissed her. "I thought I was a goner. He was shooting at me when he hit the sliding glass. He had a wide open shot. I don't know how he missed."

Jeff looked at them in the rear-view mirror. "I nearly did all three of us in, sending us into the backyard. I just didn't see how we'd have all gotten out the front without one of us getting shot."

"We're safe now," Maureen said. "Let's go print this stuff out. I pray these are the right disks. We're really in the soup if they're not."

SEVENTY SEVEN

The security guard at the Attorney General's Office was an older black man. He nodded and smiled when Jeff showed his badge.

"Make yourselves at home. Don't work too hard."

They made their way to the Consumer suite. Maureen flipped on the dingy fluorescent lights and strode to her old desk, noticing absently that the room looked and smelled absolutely the same. She unwrapped the rubber-banded diskettes and inserted the first one into the floppy drive.

"I hope WordPerfect can read these," she said, staring at the screen. "That's about as computer literate as I've gotten over the years."

"Open the directory," Jeff said.

CONSUMER1.XLS

"One file, in something I've never heard of. What the hell is XLS?"
"Try to open it."

CONSUMER1.XLS - Unknown Format

"That's just great!" she said, slapping the desk with her palm. "What do we do now? Call Aaron Penn?"
Tom leaned over her shoulder. "That's Microsoft Excel. Probably a spread sheet, if you can get into it."
Maureen turned to him. "Do you know how? I sure don't."
"You need someone who has the program."
"I realize that," she said, trying not to take out her frustration on him. "I don't know anyone who has it. If you do, speak up. I'd love to talk to him."
"Bet WalMart has it," Jeff said. "The one in South Jackson is open twenty-four hours."
"Try the Microsoft web site," Tom said. "See if you can download it."
Five tries and ten minutes later, Maureen wrung her hands in frustration. "Damned Internet. Any other night I'd have no problem getting on. What the hell are we going to do?"
Jeff grabbed his keys. "You guys sit tight. Back in half an hour."

*   *   *

Tom was rubbing Maureen's shoulders when Jeff returned. "What do I owe you?"
"Three hundred bucks," Jeff said, grinning.
Her jaw fell. "Are you serious?"

"Don't worry about it. I know where petty cash is. If they stole that, you can buy me a deli plate once a week for a year."

Maureen laughed in spite of herself. She installed the program, which took ten agonizing minutes. She nervously looked over the tool bar, her eyes stopping on "Open File."

"Cross your fingers."

The file opened. It was indeed a spreadsheet. She recognized the businesses but was confused by the dollar amounts and initials. The picture became clearer as she scrolled down the page, however.

4/13/00	Sneed Plumbing	$2500	
4/16/00	WITHDRAWAL	$2500	FC
4/14/00	Walker Brothers	$10,000	
4/18/00	WITHDRAWAL	$10,000	AD
4/18/00	Henderson Electric	$15,000	
4/22/00	WITHDRAWAL	$15,000	SH
4/20/00	Davis & Sons	$1000	
4/27/00	WITHDRAWAL	$1000	FC
4/25/00	A&D Foundation Repair	$5000	
4/29/00	WITHDRAWAL	$5000	AD

There was a summary at the bottom of the sheet.

THROUGH 6/21/00
AD $86,500
SH $64,500
FC $71,500

"Oh, my God!" Maureen said, printing the two pages. "Everything Lisa said was true! Money comes in, and a couple of days later it's taken out and given to Frank, Ashleigh and Sonny! Lisa told me there wasn't a dime in the account!"

"How much would they get over a whole year?" Tom said,

eyeing the collection totals.

"Depends on how much came in. But if the last ten months were like the first two, well over a million dollars. Divide that by three."

"Put the next disk in," Jeff said.

It was named CONSUMER2.XLS. It was also a spreadsheet.

4/13/00	*Sneed Plumbing*	*$125*
4/14/00	*Walker Brothers*	*$600*
4/18/00	*Henderson Electric*	*$350*
4/20/00	*Davis & Sons*	*$100*
4/25/00	*A&D Foundation Repair*	*$250*

Maureen frowned at the dollar amounts. Her eyes widened when she glanced at the bottom of the sheet.

YTD COLLECTIONS THROUGH 6/21/00 . . .$12,500

"What the hell is this? We hit Walker Brothers for five figures! None of it is right!"

A smile spread across Jeff's face. "That's the copy they want the State Auditor to see, I bet. To make it look like hardly anything was coming in."

"They're crazy," Maureen said, removing the single sheet from the printer. "This was right after the bill passed! The Audit department would have to know more was coming in, because Frank was telling the press how much latitude we now had to enforce the laws! I remember the Walker Brothers fine like it was yesterday. The big cheese offered to write a check on the spot for one hundred dollars. When I laughed and said it was ten-thousand, he threatened to go right to Frank."

"But he backed you on that one."

"Damn right he did. 'You have my blessing, Maureen.'" She scrolled through the figures. "Look at this Henderson Electric fine. Three-fifty? Like hell! We hit them for fifteen," she said, grabbing the first sheet for confirmation. "They were talking about going to the Justice Department."

"And the N.A.A.C.P. I remember Sherry predicting they would play the race card the second you talked to them. But Frank stood firm on that one, too. Now I know why."

"Who's Davis and Sons?" Tom said from over her shoulder.

"A side-of-the-road vendor. They were selling bird feeders without registering with us. Nice country folks. That was as little as I could hit them for and still send a message." She rubbed her temples. "I just don't understand, though. They all make a quarter-mil, maybe as much as three-hundred grand each over an entire year. That's chump change for Eleanor and Ashleigh. Hollins, too. I've heard he's worth millions."

"It's not the money. It's control and power," Tom said. "Think about it. If Ashleigh talked Frank into bed way back when, she's had him under her thumb since, especially if Eleanor and Sonny are involved and both plotting against him. Maybe she's been waiting all these years for the iron to get hot."

"But he's the Attorney General, for crying out loud!" Jeff said in disbelief, turning to Maureen. "Can these people just push him around like that?"

"Jeff, maybe Craig is right. Maybe Ashleigh, Eleanor and Sonny have all gotten their jollies over the years squeezing this ambitious politician who had his eye on Washington. And if he's knee-deep in something like this, maybe he's into things we don't have a clue about. Craig mentioned he's heard rumors about gambling."

"Craig has a role in this somewhere. I know he does."

She tented her fingers. "I'm not so sure. I think all he wanted was Washington. He made a big deal about Frank being scared of Ashleigh, but I think he is, too. He sold his house, found a new job and girlfriend and won't say squat to anyone about his future."

"Maybe he wants to make a quick getaway while her sights are set on you," Tom said.

Maureen nodded. "I'm wondering the same thing. Anyway, hand me that last diskette. I can't wait to see what's on it."

WordPerfect documents appeared when she opened the directory. She glanced at Jeff in surprise, then exited Microsoft Excel. A moment later the first file was open. Her jaw nearly hit the floor.

"Is that a memo?" Jeff said.

"It's from me!" Maureen said, gasping. "It's to Lisa, asking for withdrawal authority to the Consumer Account!" She printed, then opened the next file. "Great—here I am asking for $2500 on April 16. I never asked for any money! Hand me the first spreadsheet. I'll bet everything I own one of them got $2500 that day."

"Frank did," Jeff said.

"Oh, dear," Maureen said after opening several more files. "Lisa was right! Ashleigh has me making off with every bit of this! Does she think I'd really be that stupid?"

"This was a back-up plan, remember? They'd only trot this out if someone noticed the money was gone."

Maureen drummed her fingers on the desktop. "You said there were copies of my memos on the hard drive. We have to show how much money was really coming into Consumer. And we can do that right now, I hope."

She opened the C: drive and searched the back-up directory. "Bingo."

Lisa—Sneed Plumbing paid $2500 on 4/13/00. Please deposit entire check in Consumer account. This covers their entire penalty—no payment plan will be necessary.

Maureen

"Jeff, you were right! This proves everything." She turned to

Tom. "I always stapled a note like this to each check and sent it to Lisa."

"I do the same thing," Jeff said. "Know who suggested I do it that way?" Maureen and Tom turned to him. "The Attorney General himself, when he made me Interim Consumer Director."

Maureen laughed hollowly. "Son of a bitch. So he is out to get me."

"I doubt it, Maureen. Tom is probably right—and Craig, much as I hate to admit it. Pressure may have been on him to do this, and Ashleigh may have turned up the heat when things began falling apart. Maybe that's why Frank went to the press about her. She screwed herself by going so far out of her way to get you. But maybe that's how she operates. Sounds like she's been watching Frank all these years, waiting to strike."

There were nearly fifty files on the third diskette. Forty-five minutes later all were printed. Jeff handed the last two diskettes to Maureen. "Before we forget, let's pop these in."

She inserted the first and frowned. "Here we go with this XLS nonsense again."

She switched back to Microsoft Excel. A moment later her face fell.

"What is it?" Jeff said, quickly over her shoulder.

"Public Integrity! Look! The same kind of spreadsheet—the same initials, deposits and withdrawals. Money in, money out, all to Frank, Sonny and Ashleigh. And this has been going on a lot longer than April."

She printed the file, then inserted the second disk.

"They're doing the exact same thing, Jeff! There's no way in hell Public Integrity has collected only $6800 this year!"

"They may be doing it in every department."

"This should be enough to sink them," she said, printing the final spreadsheet. "When I wake up—if I go to sleep at all—I'll call Haynes. May just drop by there."

"I almost hate to ask—do you trust him?"

"Jeff, if the U.S. Attorney is dirty, too, we're all in trouble. He's given me every indication that he and the F.B.I. are ready to jump if I have evidence of a crime." She stood and retrieved the diskettes and spreadsheets. "I'll call you tomorrow. Make that later today."

SEVENTY EIGHT

It took three glasses of wine to calm her down. She and Tom made love, then fell asleep shortly before the sun rose. She sent Tom to work two hours later and prepared herself. She guzzled coffee and styled her hair carefully. She donned her nicest suit, rehearsed what she wanted to say and entered the U.S. Attorney's Office at precisely nine o'clock.

"Mr. Haynes should be here any minute," the receptionist said, eyeing Maureen quizzically. "Do you have an appointment?"

"No, I don't. I just need a few minutes of his time."

The receptionist frowned. "I know he's booked all morning. He might be able to squeeze you in late this afternoon."

Maureen forced a smile and nodded. She leafed through a magazine, then jumped to her feet when Haynes appeared ten minutes later.

"Hello, Maureen," he said. Curiosity was on his face. "I don't remember you calling."

The receptionist stood territorially, but Maureen stepped forward. "Jimmy, ten minutes, and get her to hold your calls. This is more important than anything you'll do today. Maybe this month."

A smile spread across Haynes' face. He nodded at the receptionist and showed her to the conference room.

"Mr. McNulty was here the other day," he said, pouring coffee. "He thinks you're hiding something."

Maureen scowled. "I was hiding the fact that his wife was having a sexual relationship with another woman. I didn't think that should come from me."

Haynes nodded sadly. "I told him you were the last person who would try to cover something up."

"Reason I'm here: Last night, acting as a private citizen, I got my hands on the missing diskettes Lisa was going to tell you about. They were at Eleanor Dunn's house. Ashleigh's mother."

"Do they know you have them?"

Her poker face. "I'm not sure. They're out of town."

Haynes grinned. He nodded for her to continue.

"We went to the A.G.'s Office and printed them out. Just like Lisa said, the Consumer money is being divided between Ashleigh, Frank and Sonny. They had all the money routed to me on a second diskette to cover themselves. There's a third diskette with phony memos to make it look like I was withdrawing money myself. What saves me are the memos I wrote when I was Consumer Director. They were still on my computer. They'll match up exactly to what the businesses actually paid."

"But there's evidence Cash is involved? And the others?"

"Yes, sir. Four people are listed by initials: F.C., S.H., A.D., and L.M."

"Cash, Hollins, Ms. Dunn, and who?"

"Lisa. She was paid ten thousand dollars in the beginning. Everything else, just like she said, went to them."

Haynes frowned. He crunched numbers on a legal pad. "Million-two over twelve months, in round numbers. And Cash gets a third?"

"That's the way it looks."

"Why the hell would that kind of money be so important to him when he has such a bright future? Everybody knows his eye is on Washington."

Maureen shrugged. "I've asked myself that a thousand times."

"This may be just the tip of the iceberg. Maybe he's into some things in the Legislature." Haynes said rhetorically. "I've also heard rumors about gambling. But I'm shocked he would take part in something this risky for these figures."

"We found the same scheme in Public Integrity. There's even more money involved there. I have the diskettes to prove it. But I'm a little concerned about their admissibility in court."

"Don't worry about that right now. I have enough to start a federal investigation." He hit the speaker phone and dialed. F.B.I. Special Agent Bob Dent, the man Maureen met the morning Lisa didn't show, was on the line a moment later. Haynes explained the situation. Dent asked if Maureen could come straight over.

"I'll be right there."

*   *   *

The federal building was several blocks away. Dent was a short, dark-haired, well-built man in a suit, perhaps fifty. Maureen accepted another cup of coffee, made herself comfortable in his small office and told her story. An hour later she was confident she had covered everything.

"This will take a while," Dent said, tenting his fingers. "We'll contact the businesses you dealt with and ask for invoices and canceled checks. We'll also subpoena bank records to see when the withdrawals were made and by whom. Could be several months, maybe longer. But it'll confirm everything you brought to us."

Maureen nodded.

"What I can't believe is Cash in the middle of this. I talked to Jimmy again right before you got here. He's not stupid—he knows what busting this up will look like on his resume. So you can expect him to come after these people with everything he's got and then some."

"What do you think they're looking at, besides the embezzling? What federal charges?"

"It's a little early to tell. Depends on what we dig up. Racketeering, perhaps. But I can promise you we'll put Cash through the wringer."

"One other thing: I told you about the relationship Ms. McNulty was having. The woman's name is Jennifer Green," she said, handing Jennifer's business card across the desk. "She was here temporarily and left to go back to Dallas a couple of days ago. Her next-door neighbor is a woman named Hillary Bankston. Hillary works at the A.G.'s Office and is big buddies with Ashleigh. I haven't talked to her, but my hunch is that she saw Lisa and Jennifer together and told Ashleigh. Lisa immediately agreed to oversee the embezzling when Ashleigh said she knew who Jennifer was and threatened to go to her husband."

"Interesting. We'll certainly talk to them. Maybe we can add extortion," Dent said, getting to his feet. "Nice meeting you, Maureen. You're a tough lady. It takes a lot of courage to do what you've done. What's ahead for you?"

"Not sure yet. I know I won't be working for Frank Cash."

* * *

She emerged from the federal building and glanced at downtown Jackson. She wiped her brow on what promised to be a hot, humid day. Just four short months ago, on a cold, blustery February morning, she had trotted up the steps of the Capitol to watch as the House passed the Consumer Protection Act. It seemed like a lifetime ago.

She drove home and called Jeff. Then Janine, Tom and Erica, who went into hysterics when she revealed the break-in. A call to Bay St. Louis was last.

"Hi, Dad. It's your darling daughter," she said cheerfully. Graham was decidedly neutral.

"Can we agree we were both wrong about what happened? I'd sure like for us to be on speaking terms again."

"I suppose so," he said after a moment.

"I love you, Dad."

"I love you, too, Mo. I don't like being mad at you. In fact, I can't stand it." A long pause. "I apologize for interfering. As long as you find something that makes you happy, I'm all for it. I don't ever want you to think my motivations are any different."

"Thank you. How 'bout I come down with Tom and visit? Fact, I'll bring Erica and her boyfriend."

"When might this be?"

"Today."

"Today? Let me check with your mother," he said, doing his best to hide his excitement.

"Hello, dear," June said quickly. "Graham says you and Tom and Erica and Keith are coming!"

Maureen smiled at how quickly she was on her mother's good side again. "We'd love some étouffée. And tell Dad we have a lot to talk about. The F.B.I. is getting involved."

"In what?"

"I'll explain."

Ten months later

ATTORNEY GENERAL INDICTED
By Janine May, Jackson Times Staff Writer

A shocking development in Mississippi politics at the federal courthouse yesterday. Attorney General Frank Cash, Capital City Motors President Sonny Hollins and former Special Assistant Attorney General Ashleigh Dunn were indicted on charges of felony racketeering, conspiracy and extortion by a federal Grand Jury. A former state Senator, an employee with the State Department of Audit and a Division Chief at the Attorney General's Office were also indicted.

"Critical information was brought to us last June by a former employee of the Attorney General's Office," said Southern District U.S. Attorney Andrew Haynes. "It took months to complete our investigation because of the complexities of the crimes and the web of people involved. The federal charges center around an elaborate scheme to embezzle money from the Consumer Protection Division of the office.

It was clearly the intent of those involved to siphon money from that department and frame the employee who came forward if suspicions were aroused."

If found guilty of the crimes, Cash, Hollins and Dunn face up to thirty years in prison and fines of up to $500,000. Haynes stunned the gathering at his press conference when he revealed further charges against Cash.

"Our investigation also revealed a variety of scams within the Attorney General's Office," Haynes said. "Over a million dollars has been laundered through the Public Integrity and Medicaid Fraud divisions. Attorney General Cash, Ms. Dunn and Mr. Hollins were dividing this money between themselves, just as they did with money embezzled from the Consumer Protection fund.

"We're indicting Jerry Eckland, who oversaw the computer network within the office and conspired with the Attorney General and the others to make these schemes work, on conspiracy charges. We're also indicting (former state Senator) Hamilton Dunn and Buddy McGilberry with the State Auditor's Office on conspiracy charges.

"We are confident our investigation has stopped what might be the biggest web of corruption in our state's history dead in its tracks."

Cash, who barely edged little-known Brandon Buckhalter in November of last year to win a fourth term as Attorney General, proclaims his innocence and vows to fight the charges.

"I beg the people of our state not to rush to judgment. These allegations are false. I will fight them and be vindicated, just as I will continue to fight for the people of Mississippi.

"I will not resign from this office, because the people of this state have made it clear that they want me to stay."

Attorneys for Hollins and Dunn had no comment, except that they would fight all charges in court. Hollins remains

hospitalized after major injuries suffered in a March
automobile accident. On a related note, Capital City Motors
spokesman Irv White announced that the dealership has set-
tled a wrongful-termination lawsuit with former mechanic
Ronnie Landrum. Terms of the settlement were not disclosed,
although anonymous sources estimate a six-figure amount.

"The day Attorney General Cash's name first came up in
connection to this stuff, I had a sneaking suspicion it was
true," Governor Bobby Greene said.

"Out of professional courtesy I've kept my mouth shut,
but it's high time all of us demand the man's resignation. I
hope Mr. Cash will look the people of our state in the eye,
admit what he and his friends did, and quickly and quietly be
on his way. Our state deserves a lot better from its top cop."

"You know the worst thing about this?" Buckhalter said
via telephone. "Our state has a history of hatred, mistrust and
corruption, most of which was brought on by a bunch of good
old boys making back room deals forty and fifty years ago.
People all over the country are going to hear about this and
decide that things haven't changed a bit down here, even
though we've entered a new millennium.

"And that's a shame."

Maureen read the article on her parents' porch swing as she
sipped coffee, her cell phone alongside. It was a chilly April
morning with bright sunshine and clear blue skies. Tourist sea-
son and the stifling humidity which made summers so difficult
was still weeks away. The cell rang as she put the paper down.

"Didn't wake you, did I?" Janine said.

"No. Waiting for you to call, actually. Out here listening to
the surf. Got half an hour before I need to get ready for school."

"Off the record: Cash is resigning, either today or tomorrow.
You'll love the way they'll spin it: The right wing and the scan-
dal-happy media are out to get him. He'll make a big deal about

going out the honorable way, rather than being scraped out with a spatula."

Maureen was laughing. "Which I thought they were gonna have to do. It amazes me that after everything that's happened, he can still talk directly to a camera and talk about leading the state forward."

"Also off the record: Divorce proceedings between he and Joyce are getting uglier by the minute. He's apparently gambled away a ton of money the last several years."

"He's taking a long fall, isn't he?"

"What's interesting is Eckland. His name hasn't surfaced until recently. Rumor is that he's Frank's gambling buddy."

"He just might be. I was thinking back to that night Aaron and I printed the e-mails. I'm convinced that burrhead security guard called Tom West because a black man was up there and looked at him the wrong way."

"I have no doubt."

"And I'm convinced West is clean. He probably called Eckland out of legitimate security concern. But now it makes sense why Eckland went ballistic. He thought Aaron was on to him and everyone else. What else?"

"Everybody's tight-lipped about Hollins and the intimidation of the car dealers, so I don't know what's new on that. But I had drinks with Ashleigh's lawyer last night, and he probably said a little more than he should have." A pause. "She's about to cut a deal, hon'. A big one."

Maureen's heart froze. Cold sweat popped out on her forehead. "Don't tell me she's gonna walk."

"She just might. She apparently has all kinds of stuff on Cash, going back a long way. He basically gave her Consumer to run while he was stealing from the office to feed his gambling habit. She'll be portrayed as a sweet, naive girl caught up in a web of corruption engineered by a big-time politician. We can expect her to pour on the sugary-sweet, poor-me persona."

Maureen glanced at the house. "You know, Janine, part of me is still waiting for the phone to ring here, or an e-mail from an address I don't recognize. She walks, I wouldn't put it past her to make trouble. Even with me living on the coast. Might be the first thing she does."

"I wouldn't sweat it, hon'. Out of sight, out of mind. I get the impression talking to her attorney that she spends every waking minute working on ways to destroy Frank further. She probably hasn't thought about you in months. By the way, the lawyer said Ashleigh finally agreed to give custody of the baby to Warren."

"How old is that child now? Year and a half?"

"Something like that. And this is just a rumor, but I'm hearing she's pregnant again. The lawyer is supposedly the father. I did not get that from him," she said, chuckling. "But think about it, Maureen—the idea of Ashleigh walking away from all of this might hinge on whether Eleanor would sell out Sonny. The ultimate irony would be mother and daughter fighting over it. They gang up on him, and he probably spends the rest of his life in prison. Of course, that may not be very long."

"Was he drunk? I've meant to ask you that each time we've talked for the last month."

"He wasn't, but Nathan McMichael couldn't walk a straight line. Hollins was sober, but he shouldn't have been driving on icy roads. He likely won't walk again, and McMichael, of course, walked away with a scratch." A pause. "Speaking of health, how's your father?"

Maureen sighed. "Not well. He was diagnosed with Alzheimer's last week."

"Oh, dear. I'm so sorry."

"We are, too. But this heart attack a few weeks ago may have been a blessing, actually. The cardiologist doesn't give him much longer. Our hope is that he'll go before the Alzheimer's gets real bad. His, too, actually. I'm very proud of him," she said, tears welling in her eyes. "He's a lot braver than I realized."

"Wow. How's your mother?"

"Up and down. Scared. Bitter. Terrified of being alone. Furious at my brother for not being here. I just do a lot of listening."

Janine sighed. "I'll be praying for him. You, too, kiddo. It takes a special person to do what you're doing."

"Thank you, Janine." She got to her feet. "And thanks for the scoop. I really would live in a little vacuum down here if it weren't for you."

"Glad to do it. Tell your folks hello, and give Tom a hug for me. I miss you guys."

"We miss you, too. I'll talk to you soon."

EIGHTY

A month later Maureen was perusing an aisle of a North Jackson grocery store when a familiar voice brought a smile to her face.

"Fancy meeting you here. We play our cards right, maybe we can get into the store computer."

Aaron Penn, distinguished as usual in his designer frames and preppy clothes, gave her a big smile. She hugged him, then glanced around. "How's my favorite co-conspirator?"

"Just great. What are you doing here? I thought you moved home."

"Spending a few days with my best friend and her husband. She's pregnant and sick as a dog, so I'm running errands for her. How are things at the office?"

"Funny you should ask. Put in my two weeks this morning. I'm about to start teaching at Jackson State. Couple of classes this summer to get my feet wet, then a full load this fall."

"I'm doing that, too, believe it or not—eighth grade history. The kids just finished exams, so I thought I'd take a few days."

He smiled, pretending to inspect the items in Maureen's basket. "Maybe we can e-mail. MLewis at aol.com, right?"

It took a second, but her smile faded. "It was you, wasn't it? How'd you know my e-mail?"

He glanced around, then signaled for her to follow. He didn't speak until they were in the small dining area of the store, safely tucked away in a booth. The lone diner was an old woman nibbling at a carry out plate twenty feet away.

"I was in your office one day long ago, and you were giving your e-mail to someone on the phone. I just barely heard it. I have a good memory, and it just stuck—I don't know why. My wife's niece started in Administration two falls ago. Name is Alicia. Lisa hired her, was a mentor and sort of a second mother. Great person to work for. But Lisa became impossible to be around almost overnight. Alicia was bewildered, especially when the blow-up about that memo took place."

"The one Alicia didn't see."

Penn nodded. "She said it was obvious something was going on. Frank in and out of there every day, Ashleigh Dunn popping in all the time."

"Did Alicia send the e-mails?"

"Too scared. She finally talked to us. When your name came up, I demanded we bring you into it. She agreed to let me send you the clues," Penn said, shaking his head. "It was all I could to do get her to commit to that. When you wrote back and said you needed more, she refused to say anything else. My wife and I talked to that girl all night before she told everything she knew. That's why there were delays in getting the information to you, because we were having to reassure her every two minutes that her identity wouldn't be revealed. We e-mailed from my house."

"Tell her how much I appreciate what she did. You, too,

Aaron. If I can ever help you . . ."

"Maureen, you helped me more than you know. Lots of folks talk a good game, but I don't know anybody else who would have risked their job for mine."

A laugh. "I nearly cost you your job."

"A job I realized wasn't going to take me anywhere." He sipped his coffee. "So what's your take on all this stuff?"

"They got what they deserved." She glanced around, then gazed at him. "Confidentially, Aaron, Ashleigh is trying to cut a deal and avoid prison altogether."

Penn's face fell.

"It's too bad from a historical perspective, because Mississippi is the state everybody loves to hate. But that's not my problem, I guess. Like my mother says, you can turn every negative into a positive. I think there was a teacher inside me who struggled to get out all these years, and I'm enjoying the kids a hell of a lot more than I enjoyed Consumer. I was offered a job at the U.S. Attorney's office last month and turned it down flat. Didn't even drive up and interview."

Penn raised an eyebrow. "Thought that's what you always wanted to do."

A sigh. "My father and I have had some pretty serious problems. Unfortunately, he doesn't have much time left. But his illness has brought us a lot closer and made my issues seem pretty meaningless. I think a lot of why I went into law was to please him. Funny how things turn out. If Sonny Hollins hadn't put him to it, Tom Chapman never would have called me in the first place."

"What do you mean?"

"Long story. But it's the truth."

Penn stared, then shrugged. "How's he doing? He the one who put that pretty ring on your finger?"

Maureen smiled. "Next spring. We'll send you an invitation. He's fine. Selling ads for a TV station in Gulfport." She got to her feet. "Before I forget, Mother and I ran into Craig Grantham a few weeks ago. Care to guess what he's doing now?"

"We heard he went to a private firm in New Orleans."

"The firm was either a smokescreen or something that didn't work out. He's in New Orleans, but he's in Seminary. He plans on starting his own church, Aaron."

Penn nearly spilled his coffee. Maureen laughed. "I had the same reaction. I told Mother I fully expect him to become one of those worthless televangelists who cheats old people out of their life savings."

"We'll visit him in prison together," Penn said, roaring with laughter.

"It's a date. Stay in touch." Her eyes twinkled. "And if you e-mail, sign your name."